ON THE LINE'S

NAOMI LOUD

ADVANCE READER COPY

This is an advanced copy of On the Line. Please excuse any minor typos as this copy is still going through its final proof-read. Thank you for reading!

CONTENT WARNING

Although this is *technically* a contemporary romance, it's still written by yours truly. It deals with heavy subject matter and may contain triggering situations such as parental neglect, emotional abuse, SA while drugged/asleep (not on page), cheating (not between the two main characters), maiming, somnophillia, CNC, degradation, alcohol abuse, recreational drug use, financial abuse, exhibitionism, parental & minor incarceration, intimate partner violence (sexual, on page, not by MMC), parentification of eldest child, food play, panic attacks, family in hospital, undermining SA credibility, and gaslighting.

To my husband Aldo (my real life Ozzy):
no love story can ever compare to ours.

Here's to the rest of our lives, baby.

And for those who once believed they were unloveable, I wish you all to be loved by someone like Ozzy McKenna …

Good food does lead to sex. As it should.

— ANTHONY BOURDAIN

PROLOGUE
JAMES

"So you're basically disowning me?" My bottom lip trembles as I spring up from my seat. Tears stream down my face while I do nothing to wipe them away, petulantly hoping mascara tracks down my cheeks.

Behind his precious oak wood desk, my father scoffs, leaning back into his leather chair. His gray suit impeccably pressed, dirty blond hair slicked carefully to the side. "Good lord, James. I simply said that I was no longer paying for your education. Why do you always need to be so dramatic?"

"That's the *same* thing," I hiss, my eyes still swimming in tears. I sniff. "I might as well drop out. How do you think I'll be able to afford any of it?" I pause, hoping my father will suddenly change his mind but only silence follows. "Don't do this to me, Daddy ... *Please*."

His icy blue gaze holds no empathy. Manicured hands folded over a slim waist, he assesses me from behind the desk as if I'm just another one of his summer associates at his firm whom he's judged and found wanting.

"You should have thought of that before switching majors behind my back," he replies with a snide curl of his lip. "You really thought there wouldn't be any consequences—"

"But—" I try to interject.

He raises his hand. Years of discipline have me biting my tongue.

"I'm not paying for something as *useless* as a 'fine arts degree'." He air-quotes the last three words, enunciating them with such arrogance and disgust that I wonder if that's how he thinks of his only daughter as well. "You should know better," he adds.

I'm shaking with anger.

I've always hated that I cry when I'm angry. But the tears fall, nonetheless.

"*Fine*," I say after a loaded beat of silence, straightening my shoulders and clearing my throat. "Then I'm moving out."

My father lets out a long sigh, pinching the bridge of his nose before saying, "James stop acting like a child. I never said you needed to move out."

I throw him a bewildered look. "How do you expect me to live under the same roof as you, after … after *this*?" I swipe the tears off my cheeks, peeved that I'm still crying this much.

"Your mother will certainly have something to say about your decision," he says casually, his attention now on the pile of papers he's shuffling from the side of his desk.

I roll my eyes. "My mother is too busy doing a *ridiculous* pilgrimage in France, I doubt she even cares," I spit out with as much ire as I can muster, before storming out of my father's study and down the long hall into my bedroom. I slam the door closed and throw myself onto my bed, sobbing into my silk pillows.

A distant, rational, part of myself is slightly horrified that I'm acting this way—like a spoiled brat, screaming at my father as if I was still a teenager and not almost twenty-three. But I can't stop. Not when all of it feels like a savage betrayal.

I consider packing a bag and storming out right this second but resist the urge.

I need a better concocted plan.

Instead, I sit up. While I continue to sniffle, the tears still miserably leaking out my eyes, I pat my bed trying to locate my phone. I find it hiding under a sketchbook. Scrolling to my best friend's name in my favorites, I hit the video call. It's only when Connie answers and I see she's in a pitch-black room that I remember Los Angeles is three hours behind Marsford Bay, Massachusetts. She moved just a few months ago to pursue a career in acting—her parents supported her decision. Must be nice.

"Hello?" she croaks, red hair sleep-mussed while one of her hazel eyes is still shut trying to hide from the glare of her phone.

"Oh god, I'm sorry," I mumble trying to hide the angst from my voice. "I didn't mean to wake you."

I guess I didn't do a good enough job because Connie lifts herself up on her elbows, turning on the light beside her bed.

"What's wrong?" she murmurs, her tone now laced with worry, then adds, "What did Zachary do this time?" Her latter question has a lot more bite. I also don't miss the exaggerated eye roll that follows it.

Connie has been my boyfriend's number-one hater since we met in our first year at Damhurst, three years ago.

She claims he's made me cry far more than he's ever made me smile.

I sometimes wonder if she's been right all along.

"Nothing." I let out a small sob, feeling sorry for myself. "It's not him. It's my father …"

"Great," she snips. "What now?"

Not a fan of his either.

"He somehow found out I switched majors." I hiccup. "Told me if I didn't switch back to economics before next fall, he'd cut me off."

"What?" Connie says surprised, rubbing her eyes. "How the hell did he find out?"

"I don't know," I whine, letting the last word trail into another small sob. "But you know him, he has eyes everywhere." I fall back into my pillows wanting to die. "I should have known I couldn't keep it a secret for long."

Connie falls silent, seemingly mulling everything over. After a few seconds, she asks gently, "So what are you going to do?"

Rolling over, I prop my phone on the nightstand and hug the pillow under me before answering. "I told him I was moving out …" I say a little meekly. "Then stormed in here and called you."

She lets out a dry laugh. "So you're fucked."

My bottom lip starts to tremble, the tears once again flowing freely.

"What am I going to do?" I say softly.

"Well, are you *actually* moving out?" she asks as delicately as possible.

I chew on my words before answering.

I've never been on my own before.

The thought nearly knocks the breath out of me. It scares me. But if I let my mind grow quiet, behind all the tears and the comforting melodramatics, I can almost hear a small voice inside chanting: *Do it, do it, do it.*

"I think so ..." I whisper, my voice still shaky.

I watch Connie stand up through the screen, suddenly in planning mode.

"Okay, great, so here's what we're going to do. I'm going to call my cousin Steve, my mom told me he was looking for a roommate last week. While I do that, you're going to start packing okay? The *essentials* Jamie, you hear me? This isn't the time to be sentimental."

"But—"

"The essentials, Jamie. I swear to god."

"Fine. Okay. I heard you," I say with a huff.

"Great. Love you," she says. "Everything is going to be fine, trust me."

I nod distractedly, but she's already hung up.

For a while, I can't move. The screen on my phone has since turned black while I stare at my puffy-eyed reflection, too busy having a silent existential crisis to lift myself off of the bed. Everything in me wants to just continue to wallow and wither into nothing.

Eventually, after questioning everything ten times over, I find the courage to move and pull my Louis Vuitton suit-cases out from my walk-in closet. Putting on some music, I start packing, the essentials being mostly clothes and my art supplies.

I'm not surprised that my father never comes knocking to tell me to stay.

The little voice inside tells me I should have left years ago.

"IF YOU'RE GOING to spend the entire time complaining, then you can just leave, you know," I say through gritted teeth. "I can manage the rest myself."

I'm halfway up the third flight of stairs, annoyed, tired, and out of breath. Zachary is trailing behind me, carelessly dragging one of my suitcases up the creaky steps.

His brown eyes narrow. "Is this neighborhood even safe, Jamie? Did you do *any* research before agreeing to this half-baked plan?" Zachary grunts out, his Burberry winter coat open and falling off one shoulder, blonde strands sticking to his sweaty forehead.

Connie was right, her cousin Steve did need a room-mate. I jumped on the opportunity immediately. I threw everything in my Audi and left within the hour, not even bothering to tell my father that I was leaving.

All I know about my new roommate is that he's Connie's cousin, twenty-six, and works in sales.

That was good enough for me.

Zachary, on the other hand, has not stopped pestering me with questions since he first showed up to help me move. He nearly had a fit in the parking lot when he learned that my new roommate was a guy. I placated him as best I could, unwilling to have another one of our classic public fights when *this* was much more important.

This, as in: Uprooting my entire life in the span of an early winter morning.

Whatever I told Zachary earlier to stop his interrogation has seemed to work ... for now. It hasn't stopped him from bad-mouthing everything about this place in the meantime. Luckily, Steve isn't here. He came during his lunch break to let me in, handed me a set of keys, and left shortly thereafter.

It was quite unceremonial for something that feels so monumental.

Pushing the front door open, I walk into my new apartment. Zachary follows right behind me, dropping my suitcase on the floor while he lets out a curse.

"Jesus fucking Christ, Jamie. You can't be serious." Pushing his hair back from his face, his eyes dart around the room with what looks like disgust, lips pressed into a thin line.

To my left is a small half-open kitchen, the brown vinyl cupboards looking like they've never been renovated since the inception of this apartment complex.

"It's ... quaint," I mutter with an assured shrug as I try to ignore how cramped the living room looks, a threadbare couch facing a decade-old TV, surrounded by yellowing white walls with an old poster of Arnold Schwarzenegger as decoration.

I keep a resolute expression on my face but inside my stomach sinks.

Never have I lived in a place so bleak.

But I would rather *die* than admit those thoughts to Zachary. I huff an errant strand of light pink hair away from my clammy cheek before looking over at him. His nose is still turned up, a sour expression marring his round face while he takes it all in.

"Can you just ... not, for once?" I ask gruffly.

His eyes slowly slide to mine. "Jamie." He says my name with such a condescending lilt that it practically makes my skin crawl. "No one we know would be caught *dead* living in a place like this. You can't be serious." He sweeps a hand toward the living room as if to further prove his point. Then lowers his voice before saying, "This is embarrassing."

Ire slices through my chest, a thousand insults on the tip of my tongue but I swallow all of them back down. I know better by now than to believe I could ever speak that way to him without any dire repercussions. I shoot him a murderous look instead and head for the hallway next to the living room.

I find my bedroom empty. A few dust balls trailing lazily across the crooked floor welcome me to my new life. Scanning the room, I notice a dirty window on the opposite wall. It faces the parking lot, letting in a trickle of light, the rays illuminating the dust hanging in the air.

I spot Zachary's incredulous expression from the corner of my eye. "This place doesn't come furnished?"

I stifle an eye roll. "I'll get an air mattress," I say, crossing my arms. "Anyway, don't you have lacrosse practice to get to?"

The small empty room falls silent. "Yeah, I guess I should leave," he grumbles from behind me. Turning around, I kiss him on the cheek out of habit. I regret my decision immediately when the smell of his cologne hits my nostrils, immediately making me nauseous.

I take a step back, cloudy memories choking me even more than the scent itself.

"Did you change your cologne?"

Zachary's eyebrows dip. "Ran out. Borrowed Spencer's, why?"

Just the name of his best friend makes my stomach churn but I casually play it off in front of my boyfriend. "No reason." I turn away, reaching for one of my suitcases. "Thanks for the help."

I don't mean it. But there's a lot I tell Zachary that I don't truly mean just to pacify him. This time it's just to get him out of here.

"I'll call you later," he says with a quick tap of his fingers on the doorframe and finally leaves—taking his rank attitude with him.

I listen to his steps through the apartment, then the sound of the front door closing before I let out a relieved sigh. I don't even know why I asked for his help in the first place.

Walking back into the kitchen, I drag the rest of my belongings into the bedroom. I stand in the middle of the space and take a deep breath, letting the silence settle all around me.

Then I burst out into sobs.

I'm not even sure what I'm crying about, it could be a multitude of things at this point. All I know is that it feels necessary to cry and the resulting catharsis allows me to think straight.

Slumping my body onto the floor, I sit and stare off into space.

I stay motionless for what feels like forever.

Long enough for the tears to eventually slow down until I stop crying entirely.

What did I just do?

Will choosing my passion over financial stability even be worth it?

Spring semester just started, and luckily it's already paid for. But now I have rent to worry about, on top of all my classes and extracurriculars. Not to mention I now need to apply for school loans for my next, and final, year at Damhurst.

I still have money left from my trust fund's annual distribution that my father gave me at the start of the school year, but eventually that too will run out. My access is dependent on doing what he wants—in this case on me graduating with a BA in economics.

Come summer, I'll definitely need to find a job.

The tears threaten to fall again, but I blink them back down, finally finding the strength to stand up from the dusty floor. Needing to make myself feel at least a little better, I unzip one of my suitcases, carefully and deliberately lining up all my art supplies against one of the grimy walls.

A little reminder of why I'm here in the first place. I take a step back and spend the next few minutes just staring at them, unsure what to do next.

I feel stripped bare.

Tender and vulnerable.

But again, that small distant voice inside seems to keep trying to catch my attention.

It echoes far into my chest, a small tenor of faith.

This is just the beginning, it says.

My life will never be the same again, I reply back.

I close my eyes, trying to feel my feet firmly planted on the floor beneath me.

I can do this.

You can do this, it repeats.

1

JAMES

Four months later

Dipping my paintbrush into the now-murky water, I follow it with a swirl into the small travel-size watercolor palette that's laid out beside me on the blanket. The birds are quietly chirping, the wind sleepily rustling the leaves in the tree above me, and my mind feels as quiet as this beautiful early summer morning. Focusing on the watercolor pad I brought with me, I continue adding different hues of red, pink, and blue. At first, I wasn't sure what I was creating until an abstract-looking bouquet of flowers appeared.

I'm not surprised. It's always been my favorite thing to draw even as a child. I even have a bouquet of larkspur tattooed on my upper left thigh. Hidden, of course, my mother would have never allowed it.

I spent hours sitting in our lush yet neatly manicured gardens when I was younger, drawing flower after flower, never tiring of their beauty. My nanny would constantly find me tucked away somewhere under the tree's canopy lost between the sketchbook and nature around me. A small twinge plucks at my heart at the thought, followed by a heavy wave of nostalgia.

Pausing, I take a deep breath, letting the emotion roll through me. I try to remind myself not to get lost in those feelings. Romanticizing the past has always been one of my favorite activities. It's a dangerous game of letting the rose-colored glasses recall a time that didn't actually exist. Even the bad parts can easily be cloaked in nostalgia.

Because the harsh reality was that my parents were never around. They were simply absent. Too busy working, or traveling together, leaving me alone with my nanny for days, sometimes weeks.

Still, I can't help remembering those moments in the gardens with fondness. For now, I allow myself the grace to do so. Maybe it's needed when I'm still trying to find my footing four months after the biggest upheaval of my life.

I've managed. But nothing feels easy. Zachary isn't much help, Connie is far away in LA, and so yet again I find myself alone. But this time, I can't lose myself in comforting daydreams—even if I desperately want to.

Time once spent daydreaming is now spent on job-hunting—with not much luck. Although it broke my heart, I sold my car a month ago, needing all the money I could to get by. Looking back now, with a more realistic outlook on how expensive it is to live, I shouldn't have splurged on brand-new furniture for my bedroom. But the harm is done. Besides, it's the only place that feels remotely like home. Or at least like *a* home.

I learned fast after those first few weeks that my spending habits needed to change if I wanted to sustain this new lifestyle. Thankfully, I managed to secure a private loan for next year's tuition. But I need to face the hard truth: I need a job.

Especially now that summer has begun.

Lost in a swirl of anxious thoughts, I realize I've stopped painting, the brush hovering over the watercolor palette. I puff out a heavy sigh and close my eyes. Trying to recenter, I focus on the quiet sounds of the small neighborhood park I found close to my apartment, adjacent to a communal garden. The sun's rays peak through the leaves, warming my cheeks, the sunlight red against my closed eyelids. Gradually, my mind wanders back into a state of mindfulness. Until my phone jars me back to reality. I pat the blanket beside me, reaching for it.

It's a text from Zachary.

Before heading to the park, I'd messaged him, asking him how his day was going.

Now staring at his one-word answer to my question, my stomach sinks.

Because I know what one-word answers mean.

He's in a bad mood.

I don't know what caused it but one thing I know for sure is that it's somehow my fault. My mind suddenly flies into high alert, quickly trying to decipher what previous actions could be to blame.

Did I post something too provocative on social media?

Did I say something in the wrong tone?

Whatever it is, it leaves a hard rock of anxious anticipation in the pit of my stomach.

What's wrong? I message back. Immediately on fix-it mode. Hurriedly gathering my things, I walk back home and wait for Zachary to text me back.

Or maybe he'll ignore me all day.

I never know how he'll react.

I simply brace for the worst.

.

I'VE BEEN WALKING all afternoon.

I didn't wear the right shoes for this. The balls of my feet are aching, and my thighs are chafing under my button-front skirt. Inside my tote, I only have one resume left inside the blue legal folder. I had to go print it out at FedEx since I don't own a printer anymore.

I've never been so humbled than when my employment history was staring back at me on a white sheet of paper ... It screamed *rich kid who barely worked a day in her life.*

Swim coach at the Royal Bay Yacht Club.

Internship at La Porte Rouge Gallery.

Babysitter.

I deleted the last one out of sheer embarrassment and added a few carefully constructed lies instead. And then added a few well-known restaurants to solidify the fib.

Luckily, I did waitress one summer at a crab shack in the small town near our summer home. Zachary called it cosplaying at being poor. I didn't need the money, it was just another one of my whimsies, a glamorized scenario where the reality was much more boring.

I didn't last a month.

At least now it helps me embellish my resume.

I feel like a fake but I'm desperate.

I'm standing on the corner of 23rd and Miller, in the busy Central Business District, deliberating my next move, when my gaze lands on an unassuming sign.

Orso.

Black block letters. No frills. The name of a restaurant as far as I can tell.

I chew on my bottom lip while I deliberate further. I can't peel my eyes away from the front door. I'm not sure why. Only that I feel called to it. A gust of wind pushes at my back as if coaxing me forward. I take it as a sign from the universe and cross the street. Trying not to let my nerves get the best of me, I force myself not to second guess it. I reach for the door. The metal handle is warm from the afternoon sun under my palm.

I pull.

It opens.

I walk in.

The place is quiet. With a quick look around, I estimate that the dining room holds around twenty tables. The place is decorated in muted greens and black, with an eclectic collection of frames lining the dark walls. The restaurant feels intimate. It's somehow unassuming but impressive.

There's not a customer in sight, but it's still early, they must have just opened.

I almost double back and run out.

"Can I help you?" a voice says from the shadows of the bar to my left.

Startled, I look over. I find a woman in her late twenties, dressed all in black, with a high ponytail pulling her blonde hair tight against her scalp. She's polishing a wine glass and staring straight at me.

I take a few steps toward her, then abruptly stop. "Oh, uh, sorry." I push my hair out of my face. Move my weight from one foot to the other. "I just wanted to drop off my resume. I'm not sure if you're hiring but I thought I'd just … I don't even know if this is how it works—" I laugh nervously, letting my words trail off.

I suddenly feel pinned by her stare as she continues to slowly polish the glass. Her gaze is meticulous as she sizes me up. I start to question my outfit—*Is it too casual? Maybe I should have worn a blazer. Did I even pack my blazer?*— followed by an existential deep dive into why I'm here in the first place before she speaks again.

"Have you ever worked in this kind of restaurant before?" Her voice is cool but not frosty.

"This kind?" I can't help but repeat.

"This isn't an Olive Garden."

I'm not quite sure what that means but I pick up on the implications: This place is superior.

I decide not to lie. "No, but I'm a hard worker and I learn fast." I stick on an assured smile while her face stays impassive. She makes a low non-committal hum in response while curling her finger to wave me toward the bar.

As I quickly skitter over, she puts down the wine glass and white rag before taking my resume out of my shaky grasp.

While she studies my utter lack of experience, an employee appears from the back, clipboard in hand. Based on the chef jacket and blue apron, I'm assuming he's coming from the kitchen. His light brown curls are kept off his face by a folded blue bandana over his forehead.

As he gets closer, I make out that he's slightly taller than me with a slim build, although it's hard to tell with the bulky uniform he's wearing. His blue-green eyes travel to mine, lingering before looking away when he reaches the bar.

"Here's the list you asked for, Elle," he says, pushing a few crumbled pieces of paper her way then shoving a Sharpie into his apron pocket.

"Thank you," Elle says distractedly.

When his gaze skates back to mine, he flashes me a

quick grin, followed by a wink before disappearing into the back.

I jump, surprised that something so simple made me startle.

Elle's eyes finally lift back to mine. Her nude-painted lips pressed together. "Can you start tomorrow? One of our servers quit on me last night," she says with the smallest of eye rolls as if even speaking about whoever she's referring to is beneath her.

My heart slams into my throat but I'm quick to answer. "Yes of course. I can definitely start right away. Absolutely. No problem." *Shut up.* I clear my throat and smile.

My resume flutters down to the bar. "Right then. Dress code is all black. Pants or skirt, whichever is fine. Minimal cleavage, minimal makeup, and always have your hair up." She disappears under the bar before popping back up. "Menu. Study it, know it by heart. We open every day at five, except Mondays when we're closed. Be here at least an hour before opening. Understood?"

I make a quick mental note of everything she just enumerated and nod enthusiastically, reaching for the menu and sliding it into my tote bag.

"Thank you so much. You won't regret it. I can't wait," I gush, cringing at my almost teary tone.

She gives me a thin closed-lip smile. "Welcome to Orso."

She starts back on her polishing, effectively dismissing me.

Not wanting to overstay my welcome, I chirp, "See you tomorrow." And turn on my heels.

Outside, I feel slightly turned around. The sun is almost glaringly bright. My interaction with Elle is already replaying in loops while I squint up at the blue sky. Still, I walk back home with a permanent smile on my face, unbothered by my previous aches and chafes, knowing I'll be officially employed starting tomorrow.

I CLOSE my bedroom door behind me, freshly showered and smiling from this afternoon's small win. Even with the furniture I bought, my room still looks bare—empty white walls, and a popcorn ceiling. Sad and uninviting, like a wilted balloon clinging onto the memories of joy and laughter.

I also *pleasantly* discovered that the window was completely painted shut. I wasted a whole afternoon and ruined a perfectly good palette knife trying to crack the paint. Now that I know how fast money can just … disappear, it hurt to even buy a fan for this place.

It felt frivolous somehow.

My roommate Steve and I barely talk. Which is perfectly fine by me. He keeps to himself and I keep to mine.

The one tangible thing I miss from still living at home is the clawfoot bath in my ensuite, which I had imported from Italy.

Here, the only thing I dare to take are showers, and that's only if I don't look down and avoid making eye contact with the grime on the tiles. Even cleaning a bathroom myself was a learning curve. But, at least between these four walls, the decisions I make are my own.

The mistakes too.

While sitting on my bed, my wet hair dripping onto my shoulders, towel wrapped loosely around my body, my phone rings.

"Hey, I was just about to call you," I say a little hesitantly, not sure if Zachary has warmed up since this morning.

I had been right about his sour mood. We fought for over an hour when I got home from the park, with him accusing me of flirting with his friend Yannick while at a frat party over the weekend. His accusations were completely unfounded as usual, still, I had to plead my case as if they were.

It's a bizarre feeling having to constantly defend myself for things I haven't even done.

It would be a lot simpler to just cheat instead. I'm still being accused of it whether it's true or not.

"Were you?" Zachary snaps. "This is my third time calling in a row. Where the hell have you been?"

My heart drops, guilt making me chew on my bottom lip.

I hadn't realized I had missed any calls.

"Sorry I was in the showe—"

"Probably fucking that roommate of yours," he sniffs indignantly.

"Zachary, how many times do I have to tell you that nothing is going on between me and Steve?" I reply with exasperation.

"I hate that you live in that shithole."

"Yeah, you've said that already." Rolling my eyes in exasperation.

He huffs. "Whatever."

My fist tightens around my towel, a bottomless well of frustration bubbling inside of me.

"Were you really calling just to keep tabs on me?" My voice is hard, it's a gamble, I might just be making everything worse for myself.

He stays silent for a beat then answers, "I'm going up north to Gran's cottage tomorrow for the weekend. You're coming with me."

"Can't. I found a job. My first shift is tomorrow," I reply, partly relieved that I can avoid spending time with his family, especially his hyper-conservative grandmother.

"I already told the whole family you're coming, you're trying to make me look bad, Jamie."

"I'm not *trying* anything, Zachary." My tone noticeably softer. "I need this job."

A few loaded seconds pass before he speaks again. "So you found a job," he scoffs. "Where?"

"Just this restaurant downtown."

"And you weren't going to tell me?"

"It just happened," I answer, trying to keep my cool.

He makes an annoyed grunt and I say nothing more, waiting for him to speak.

"What are you going to do there?" he finally asks.

"Server."

The silence that follows is pointed and I already brace for what he'll say next. His words are often like acid, they sizzle and burn on my skin and soul, yet I know he's just being protective.

"So you're just going to spend your days flirting with random strangers for money? Absolutely fucking not Jamie, I won't allow it."

I know I shouldn't, it will only exacerbate his already piss-poor mood but the words fly out of my mouth. "Well, good thing I don't need your permission then." I sigh loudly. "Look, I don't feel like fighting right now. I don't have a choice, Zachary, okay? I need the money."

He lets out another one of his disdainful scoffs. "This is

beneath you … *serving* people at a restaurant? You're a Ferdinand for god's sake."

"That name isn't doing me any good now, is it?" I say with resignation. I push myself off the bed and drop the towel, sticking my cell phone into the crook of my shoulder. Before he can reply I cut him off. "Anyway, I've got to go. Have fun this weekend, say hi to your mom for me. Text me when you get there." I hang up before he has a chance to throw another accusation my way. Tossing my phone back onto the bed, I breathe out a heavy sigh.

No matter how short, our conversations always manage to deplete all of my energy. I don't even know why we're still together anymore, other than that our families approve and are hoping marriage and babies will follow quickly after our impending graduation.

I used to value my parents' approval more than anything … until I realized living for their approval meant sacrificing parts of myself.

Funny how much things can change in just a few short months.

Things with Zachary seemed so perfect when we first started dating. Those first six months were blissful. He was so attentive back then. Made me feel so adored. Spoiled. Safe.

Things eventually just became … harder between us. He turned jealous. Controlling. His temper on a shorter and shorter fuse.

Yet, I stay.

Because deep down, I still believe he's a good guy.

I *need* to believe he's a good person.

The memories of Zachary at the very beginning are holding me hostage, as comforting as a gun to the temple while I hope that one day he'll revert back to how it once was. My habitual tendency to romanticize the past playing accomplice to my unnervingly confusing feelings.

I change into a matching set of sage green sweats and tie my hair into a bun. Fishing out the Orso menu from my bag, I settle into bed. The musty bedroom air sticks to my comforter but I pretend I can't smell it. I read through each item diligently, finding a mix of French and Italian dishes. Just looking at the prices makes me feel poor.

"Well, I won't be eating foie gras any time soon," I say mockingly under my breath.

Anxiety suddenly claws up my throat.

What if I can't do this?

What if Elle realizes I don't know what I'm doing and fires me on the spot?

What if I'm a failure just like my father predicted?

Groaning out loud, I try to shake off the intrusive thoughts and the tears I can feel prickling my nose. Now suddenly dreading tomorrow and the new job I was so happy to get, I reach for my sketchbook and put on one of my comfort shows.

I spend the rest of the night drawing, trying to keep my mind as quiet as possible.

2

JAMES

I t's eight p.m. on a Friday, and Orso is slammed. I've been shadowing Michelle—the server training me—trying to keep up with her, but the busier it gets the more she seems to speak in codes.

Everyone is.

Jargon that sounds simple but leaves me feeling stupid, like a castaway washed up on a foreign island called Orso.

Front-of-house, four-top, eighty-six, in the weeds.

The words slip so easily from their lips as if it were their mother tongue.

I can't do this.

I try to keep a permanent smile on my face but inside I'm a nervous wreck.

It's not as if I've never stepped foot in a restaurant before. But it's as if the staff and guests exist in two different realities while still sharing the same space. The restaurant employees operate within a world invisible to the paying guests. Omniscient entities who understand the guest's needs before the words are even uttered.

The staff answer prayers. They make the patrons feel chosen.

What I still can't wrap my head around is how Michelle manages to carry so many plates at the same time, like an acrobat gracefully wowing the crowd.

The kitchen sits at the far end of the restaurant. It's a closed kitchen, but the pass—the area where the servers and food runners pick up the orders—takes up most of the wall, creating a large empty space where guests can peek through and see the cooks preparing their dishes.

It's almost voyeuristic. A pleasurable glimpse into a world they're not supposed to see.

It's a world filled with direct commands and shouted directives that are meant to be followed and followed fast, paired with a curt ding of the call bell.

Order up! Pick up! Hands!

By the time the kitchen closes at eleven, and the last table has received their orders, I've been on my feet for almost eight hours with no break. I'm exhausted, my back hurts, and my brain feels overheated like a low-grade computer on its last legs.

But … I also feel strangely exhilarated.

I feel accomplished, like I've spent my whole shift climbing a steep mountain and now I can finally sit down and enjoy the view.

After closing out our last table, Michelle and I tuck ourselves into a corner of the dining room. Taking her dark brown hair out of her hair clip, she shakes it free, fingers on her scalp while letting out a small pleased hum. I watch her intently as if studying her every move will give me key insights on how to fit in. The littlest of things could be what makes or breaks my admittance to this secret club I now desperately want to be part of.

My hands inconspicuously find my high bun and let my hair down too. Then she shows me how to roll up cutlery into white cloth napkins. Her fingers work fast, adept and nimble, while mine fumble through the steps barely managing one to her five.

"So?" Michelle says, her gaze on her task at hand. "What do you do?"

I pause, not sure what she's asking. Her brown eyes slowly lift to meet mine.

"You must do something other than work here. Most of us do." She quirks a smile, her eyes falling back to the table.

"Oh. Uh … I'm a student at Damhurst."

"Cool, my brother goes there. What's your major?"

"Used to be an econ major. I switched last year." Her perfectly tweezed eyebrow quirks and I realize I haven't answered her question—hiding the truth like a dirty little secret. "Fine arts," I quickly add, "I sketch and paint, mostly. You?"

"Ballerina," she states while finishing another rolled cutlery. "I study at the Plyscovski Conservatory."

Noticing my slightly surprised expression, she laughs. "Yeah, you'll find that a lot of creatives end up here. Flexible hours and the money is half decent too." She gives me a small shrug, then points her chin toward another server. "For example, Gustavo plays drums in a rockabilly band, and Quinn over there," referring to the bartender busy cleaning the bar, "They're an actor. Been in a few local commercials even."

I nod while surveying the room, yet again another layer of existence peeled back for me to observe. During service, everyone seemed so serious, their personalities somehow enmeshed with the restaurant's, their own urges and desires wiped clean in order to please and serve. But now that the last of the guests are trickling out, most of their masks are slipping. Smiles and grins seem more genuine. Like a weight has been lifted from the staff's shoulders. Jokes are flung freely across the dining room. Collars are being unbuttoned, sleeves pushed up to the elbows.

My gaze lands on one of the cooks coming out of the kitchen, drinking out of a clear container that seems to be filled with ice water. It's the same guy I saw yesterday when I dropped off my resume.

His gait is relaxed while he strides to the side of the bar. Leaning his forearms against the top, he crosses one foot over the other. His white chef jacket is half-unbuttoned, the same rolled bandana tied around his forehead keeping his brown curly hair off his face. He exchanges a few words with Quinn, who then pushes a shot toward him. He grins, his cheek dimpling, and shoots it back.

"What about him, what does he do?" I find myself asking.

Michelle looks over, then chuckles. "Who, Ozzy?" she asks while shaking her head. "Pretty sure Orso is his entire life."

I realize I've been staring when Ozzy's crystalline eyes find mine, lips curling into a half-smirk. A small jolt runs down my spine and I quickly look away, busying myself with the never-ending task of rolling cutlery. By the time I drudge up the nerve to sneak another glance, he's gone.

Before I clock out, Elle tells me I did good and that she'll see me tomorrow. My heart flutters like I've won a prize for *best new server*. I reiterate how excited I am to work here and she gives me another thin-lipped smile.

Finally back home, I leave my shoes by the door, feeling like I'm walking on pins and needles as I head for the bathroom. While I wash off the restaurant smells still sticking to my hair, I can't help but smile, a strange sense of accomplishment blooming inside my chest—it almost feels like the beginning of a new chapter. It's a tentative kind of hope, one I barely acknowledge in fear that it startles and disappears.

It's close to one a.m. by the time I crawl into bed. I'm tired but still wired and when I finally manage to fall asleep my dreams are filled with anxiety-ridden scenarios of overbooked tables and spilled drinks.

3

OZZY

"Chef, fire two tartare for 54, one for 23, niçoise salad for 10," Itzel—the chef of Orso—barks across the busy kitchen, handing me a copy of the bills with the orders.

"Yes, chef!" I holler back, stashing the papers above my garde-manger station along with sixteen other tickets I need to either hold or fire. Garde-manger is responsible for all the cold dishes on the Orso menu.

Although only Itzel holds the real title of chef, we all call each other *chef* in the kitchen, no matter the status. Whether it's the dishwasher, saucier, or the garde-manger like me, it's a sign of respect. When in the kitchen—we're in this shit together, we are all equal.

It's a muggy Saturday night outside, and the heat from the ovens and burners is making the kitchen feel like it's reached tropical temperatures. Sweat pours down my back under my chef jacket and I'm starting to believe that I won't experience a fresh breeze ever again.

It's a full house and we're in the throes of the second

wave of service. All around me, cooks are shouting, calling out, and communicating their demands the only way they know how: Loudly.

Behind! Corner! Sharp!

I focus on my station, opening the small fridge under it to grab three already-portioned servings of tartare. Crouching down to peer in, I only find two.

Shit.

I was sure I had prepped enough for tonight. But we got slammed and now this oversight is going to set me back. My mind is already on high alert, thinking about ten things at once. Keeping track of everything while executing all the necessary steps in the right sequence is like a well-honed choreography. The steps are quick and efficient—until someone fucks up.

Quickly, I mentally rearrange everything I need to do to make time to prep more tartare on the fly. I curse under my breath, but keep my head down, trying to drown out the noise around me. Wiping my sweaty hands on my apron, I grab the beef, then my knife and start working against the clock.

I'd kill for a cigarette right now.

Like an angelic godsend I hear Alec, my roommate and best friend, behind me, "Chef, here's your water bottle."

I turn my head and see the smirk behind his mustache, the bottle pointed toward me.

I snatch it from his grasp. "My hero," I answer with a wink. His laugh is conspiratorial as he returns to the pasta station, his own water bottle in hand.

Twisting the cap, I take a large gulp. Even though I was expecting it, the burn of straight vodka is still harsh down my throat. I conceal a cough, stashing the bottle in the fridge under my station as a little treat for after I'm done prepping this fucking bullshit tartare.

Here's the thing about cooks: We're all adrenaline junkies. Feral workaholics. And most of us are incapable of the nine-to-five grind. It takes a special kind of crazy to work in the kitchen. We incessantly complain about the hours, the waitstaff, the guests, and even the debilitating stress.

But given an option or way out, we'd be hard-pressed to find something better suited to our non-conformist person-alities—if the lifestyle doesn't kill us first. Our bodies are in constant pain, and burnouts are just the way of life. And if having a secret water bottle full of vodka tucked away somewhere helps us get through service then fuck, that's just how it is.

THREE HOURS LATER, and after a much-needed cigarette break near the dumpsters, final service is finally over. The kitchen is closing and I'm cleaning my station when I spot the new girl through the pass. Her light pink hair is tied up in a ponytail, swishing back and forth as she walks across the dining room, her black skirt hugging her curvy hips and deliciously thick thighs.

"Hey Alec," I say while keeping my eyes on her.

"Yeah?" he responds half-distracted while he mops the floor, brown wavy hair falling into his eyes.

"Have you seen the new girl greet the kitchen since she started yesterday?" I say with a small curve of the lip.

Most cooks worth a damn share a long list of pet peeves. The waitstaff not greeting the kitchen when they start their shift is at the top of it—as if the back-of-house is somehow beneath them, simply there to answer their beck and call. Servants instead of peers.

"Nope," he says with a small bite.

I hum in response, still watching through the pass. When she gets closer, I let out a short whistle through my teeth to get her attention and she jumps like a startled deer. Our eyes lock and I smile dryly.

"Hey new girl, come in here for a sec." I flick my chin up, indicating the kitchen.

She looks around as if trying to figure out if I'm actually addressing her but finally she walks to the swivel doors and pushes through, slowly stepping into the kitchen.

"Uh hi ... what's up?" she says with a shy smile.

"What's your name, princess?"

"James," she mutters, her blue eyes wide and worried as if I'm a monster she found hiding in her closet—which makes fucking with her maybe a little *too* satisfying.

I let out a small chuckle, my face falling to the side, then back at her. "Cute. Well, *Jimbo* ... Do I look like a fridge to you?"

She stays silent for a beat. "A what?" she mumbles, looking confused but also slightly miffed.

Must be the nickname.

"An appliance? A kitchen tool? A *stationary* object," I volley back, leaning my palm on the station to my side. "'Cause it's either you think we're inanimate objects or you're just too good to greet the kitchen staff. I don't know ..." I say while scratching my head. "Could be both."

I hear Alec chuckle somewhere in the back of the kitchen, and I swallow back my grin, much too amused with seeing the new girl flustered.

"Oh! Oh my god ... I didn't mean to—I just didn't know ... well I was just ..." she says, her eyes growing even wider, and … *shit*. Are they getting watery? "I'm sorry," she says sheepishly, her gaze falling to the floor, her fingers toying together nervously in front of her.

I suddenly regret this little game we're playing.

"No worries," I respond quickly, pushing off the counter. "Now you know." I give her a quick once over while she looks like she's trying to shake herself out of whatever overcame her. "So what do you do next time you clock in?" I ask, trying to sound teasing and less of a jerk.

Her face brightens, a shy smile returning. "I greet the kitchen," she says with a small nod.

"Quick learner," I mutter, taking the cigarette from behind my ear.

"Anyway …" she says tentatively. "I've got to go … See you tomorrow?"

I smile, the unlit cigarette between my lips. "Yeah, see you tomorrow, Jimbo."

Her eyebrows pinch together but she doesn't say anything further. I keep my gaze glued to her bouncy ass as she walks out of the kitchen.

She won't last the week.

4

JAMES

Staring out the window, I watch as Zachary adjusts his collar before opening the car door for me and I climb out. Taking my hand, he leads me inside Harvest, a renowned Michelin-star restaurant famous for only using local ingredients.

"What's the occasion?" I ask again since he evaded the question earlier when he picked me up.

"Why do I need a reason to spoil my girl?" he says with a grin, smoothing his salmon-colored button-down shirt. My flowery dress matches the white in his trousers, cinched at the waist and revealing just enough cleavage to make it sexy yet classy. I wanted to wear my favorite wedge sandals but chose a shorter heel since I know how much Zachary hates it when I'm taller than him.

"I guess you don't," I answer with a quiet giggle. To my ear, it feels a little forced.

That small inner voice again …

Hinting to me that he's acting squirrelly. Something

about his demeanor makes me nervous and I can't seem to shake it.

Walking up to the maître d', he doesn't greet the employee but simply says, "Reservation for two under *Garret.*" He enunciates his family name as if expecting some kind of recognition for his ancestors' achievements in founding Marsford Bay. I roll my eyes behind his back. The maître d' simply raises an eyebrow and shows us to our table.

The restaurant is industrial, with open ceilings that reveal uncovered beams and pipes, giving off an impersonal atmosphere. If I had to guess, it's on purpose—one of those places where the food served is the only thing that needs any flair.

Sitting down, Zachary reaches over the table and wraps his hand around mine, his thumb gently making circles on the back of my hand. "You look stunning, honeybun." I smile coyly, squeezing his hand as a thank you. Pausing, he seems to study me, then adds, "I do miss the blonde though."

I drop the smile and take my hand back, my fingers grazing my hair, now slightly self-conscious. Picking up the menu, I try to hide my reaction to his comment behind the pretense of perusing the wine list. "I like the pink," I mumble, mostly to myself.

Zachary doesn't say anything else, but I've been with him for long enough to know he'd prefer I listen to his heavy-handed suggestion about my appearance. After a loaded silence, I decide I need some wine to relax—ridiculously expensive now that I notice these things.

Eventually, the cold shift thaws and I warm up to Zachary again. His good mood is infectious, reminding me of the playful charmer I first met. These moments feel rare when we're simply enjoying each other's company. I take full advantage, trying to enjoy every second—it proves harder than expected when I tend to always feel on high alert around him, constantly monitoring his mood for the potential downward shift. Even though I'm used to it, it's exhausting.

Trying to keep the more negative thoughts at bay, I distract myself by observing the waitstaff. I notice things around the restaurant I never would've before working at Orso—even if it's only been a little over two weeks.

It's in the way the staff communicates with each other, and how they flow around the dining room in an effortless waltz; water glasses are always filled, never a crumb left on the table. I have the reflex of helping the server clear our table when we're done eating, but clasp my hands on my lap instead, letting her do her job and thanking her profusely for every little thing.

I hate guests like Zachary, I now realize. His rude attitude toward the staff is grating, and at times embarrassing. I wonder how it took me this long to realize it. I bite my tongue every time he snaps his fingers, or demands something instead of politely asking, not wanting to ruin the mood.

But the way he speaks to our server as if she's beneath him …

Makes me wonder if that's how he sees me now.

By the time the dessert comes, I'm ready to leave. Zachary doesn't seem to have noticed my pointed silence, regaling me with one of his lacrosse stories as we share a buttermilk and strawberry panna cotta. I've become painfully self-aware, my gut feeling telling me that the waitstaff is counting the seconds before we leave.

I let out a small sigh when the bill finally comes, but it's short-lived as I watch in horror while Zachary signs the receipt, barely leaving a five percent tip. Internally, I feel like I'm slowly withering away in embarrassment but keep my expression placid as we stand up from the table.

Putting my hand on Zachary's shoulder, I say, "Actually, I just need to pop into the restroom before we go." I give a little nod towards the exit. "I'll just meet you at the valet."

Still in a lively mood, he gives me a quick peck on the cheek. "Sure thing, honeybun." Then gives me a quick smack on the ass. "Be quick."

My laugh is dry but he doesn't notice, turning on his heels and heading for the door. I pretend to walk toward the restroom but immediately circle back to our table as soon as Zachary disappears outside. Luckily, the check presenter is still at our table and I hurriedly stuff two twenties in it. I give a shy wave to the waitstaff on my way out and join Zachary outside, none the wiser.

5

JAMES

"Some of us are going to Stanley's, it's just around the corner if you want to come?" Michelle asks. "It's a shitty dive bar but the drinks are cheap and they let us stay after hours," she continues with a shrug while she changes beside me in the staff room.

It's after midnight on a Friday, my back hurts and the soles of my feet have been throbbing for the past five hours but I perk up at the invite, and jump at the opportunity Michelle is offering me.

It's my third weekend working at Orso, and I still painfully feel like the new girl. It seems like everyone has known each other for years, and I'm the odd one out. "Sure," I say, smiling. "Let me just freshen up first, I'll be quick."

"Great," she answers with her own smile. "I'll wait for you out back."

I'm stepping into some bike shorts when Greta, the hostess, storms in, looking flushed and angry.

"Ugh!" she practically shrieks, slamming her locker

door open, huffing and puffing as she pulls her personal belongings off the shelf.

Pulling my baby doll dress over my head, blush pink to match my hair, I eye her wearily. I wonder if I should ask her what's wrong or let her pretend she's alone in here.

Greta decides for the both of us.

Swiveling around to face me, she says, almost haughtily, "Word of advice." She sniffs as if holding in a sob. "Don't fuck the kitchen staff. You'll just end up regretting it." Slamming the locker door closed, she adds, "Especially, that fucking *slut* Ozzy." Her voice cracking on his name.

She doesn't give me the time to speak before storming out, leaving me slightly stunned but also kind of amused. I quirk a smile while I finish buttoning up my dress.

I was told by Michelle that no matter what restaurant you end up working at—drama between coworkers always follows. Especially between the kitchen and waitstaff. My little interaction with Greta makes me feel like I've finally been let into the secret life of Orso.

Although, I know firsthand that it's only amusing when the drama is not your own.

I don't know much about Ozzy, except that he's continued to call me Jimbo ever since that first week and *god* do I hate it. But receiving this valuable piece of information about him intrigues me, simply because it humanizes him. And admittedly, he kind of intimidates me.

We've only had a few interactions here and there, mostly me greeting the kitchen staff before clocking in or slinking up to the pass to ask for a side of salad dressing. Nothing past words exchanged between coworkers during a busy service.

But I still can't quite gauge his personality. At times, he's cracking jokes, aquamarine eyes bright with humor while serving us that day's staff meal, but then turns militantly serious during the dinner rush, barking orders at the servers when he deems us too slow with pick up.

He's hot and cold, and it leaves me slightly unnerved. But come to think of it, most of the back-of-house acts similarly to Ozzy. As if service is to be taken seriously and with the utmost respect.

Maybe it's a kitchen thing.

After applying a fresh coat of peach-flavored lip gloss, I leave the staff room and cross the dark kitchen heading toward the backdoor.

"Careful there, new girl, you might slip." Ozzy's cocky voice seems to come out of nowhere.

I nearly jump out of my skin, letting out a small yelp.

"*Jesus*, Ozzy you scared me," I say breathlessly, hand over my racing heart.

He grins, a dimple appearing while he leans his hip on a counter, still in his chef jacket, brown curly hair looking disheveled. "The floors have just been mopped," he drawls, gesturing to the white tiles with a lazy sweep of the hand. "Wanted to warn you."

He takes a bite from a chocolate bar, drawing my eyes to his mouth. They catch on a small scar on his bottom lip, my gaze lingering a few seconds too long before my eyes lift back up.

I find him staring, ocean eyes sparkling and my stomach somersaults. Clearing my throat, I laugh to break the tension and point behind me. "I think the yellow *wet floor* sign was warning enough," I say teasingly.

He huffs out a small chuckle. "Fair enough." While pushing himself off the counter, he asks, "Heading home, Jimbo?"

I cross my arms, followed by an exaggerated eye roll. "Can you *please* stop calling me that?"

He scoffs. "Stop? When I know it annoys you this much?" Another chuckle bounces off his lips as he flashes me a side grin. "Not a chance, sweetheart."

I drop my smile. The pet name feels too intimate, and guilt hits me like a freight train.

Zachary would lose his shit if he heard Ozzy calling me that.

"Hey, you okay?" Ozzy says, taking a step closer, he lifts a hand as if to touch me but then drops it. Instead, his head dips down and sideways as if trying to catch my gaze.

My eyes snap back to his face, realizing I must have been staring into space. I force a smile and a laugh. "Sorry," I say quickly, shaking my head slightly. "Not sure where I went there."

"You looked like you saw a ghost," he says, his eyes narrowing as if studying me while tossing the candy wrapper in the trash.

"Yeah, maybe," I answer uselessly. "Anyway …" I need to leave this conversation as fast as possible. I point my thumb behind me. "I've got to go, Michelle is waiting for me outside."

He nods, his expression still looking slightly quizzical, sending me off with a lazy salute. "See you around, Jimbo."

The nickname feels a little less grating this time around, as if he deliberately used it as a way to lighten the mood. I give him a genuine smile over my shoulder before heading out.

I find Michelle smoking near the dumpster. When she sees me, she throws the half-smoked cigarette on the ground nearby and grinds it into the pavement. "Don't tell my ballet teacher," she says with a giggle, linking arms with me while we leave the parking lot. "My body is a temple and all that."

I answer with my own snicker, pleased to be making a new friend. "My lips are sealed."

STANLEY'S IS EXACTLY as I expected. A dark and smoky bar, that smells like stale beer, with a broken jukebox and a few pool tables off to the side.

I'm on my second gin and tonic when I see the door of the bar open, a few of the kitchen staff walking in, Ozzy included. My stomach does a small flip as if excited to see him. It's immediately followed by the same guilt I experienced earlier. I can never seem to evade it. Like an unwarranted fear of getting caught—somehow a baseline daily emotion when being Zachary's girlfriend. I never know what will set him off, so I constantly walk on eggshells. Even when he's not around.

I shift in my bar seat, feeling uncomfortable. Or maybe it's just the deep-seated paranoia taking too much space around me. Michelle and Quinn are talking to my right, but I'm distracted watching Ozzy lazily stroll toward the bar, greeting everyone he passes.

It's the first time I've seen him out of his kitchen clothes, and I'm left a little dazed.

The black Johnny Thunders t-shirt he's wearing is cut off short at the waist, leaving a sliver of skin uncovered just above his faded blue jeans. A chain clipped to a front loop disappears into his back pocket. His arms and hands are peppered with patchwork tattoos, most of them looking like he got them for free in his friend's basement. But somehow they suit him perfectly. He looks skinnier without the bulk of a chef jacket, like he hasn't had a hearty meal in months. Which is ironic all things considered.

When his blue-green gaze finds mine, my stomach shoots into my throat. Quickly, I dip my chin down, breaking eye contact, trying to focus back on the conversation happening beside me. Seeing Ozzy in street clothes rattles me and I don't know why.

It takes me longer than expected to shake the feeling.

Half an hour later, I excuse myself, dipping into the bathroom to take the opportunity to freshen up. I ignore the shameful twinge the quick dab of blush on my cheeks creates. It's as if I'm trying to convince my guilty conscience that the touch-up is for no one but myself—and not because I need to walk past Ozzy to get back to my seat.

Heading back into the main bar area, my path is immediately blocked by a pool cue as soon as I near the pool table. I look up to find Ozzy smirking at me.

"Have you ever played pool, princess?"

I place my hands on my hips and glare at him. Still, a small grin peaks through my hard expression. "At this rate, I'm starting to think you don't actually remember my name."

Laughing, he moves the cue out of my way. "Oh James," he says slowly while rubbing chalk on the tip of the cue. "How could I ever forget?" he says with mock sincerity.

Hearing my real name out of his mouth feels strangely sexual and I regret it instantly.

It dawns on me that no one at Orso knows about Zachary.

Ozzy certainly doesn't.

I should tell him. But now doesn't feel like the right moment.

Grabbing a cue from the wall, I change the subject. "To answer your question: Yes, I *do* know how to play pool." I straighten my shoulders. "Actually, I'm great at it, salad boy."

Perking up, his eyes sparkle while he rounds the corner of the pool table. "Say that again, I liked it."

I laugh nervously, even though warmth spikes in my stomach. "Oh, shut up."

He chuckles darkly, challenging me with his gaze while racking the balls. "So princess is good at pool?"

I scoff, annoyed by the small dig but reply light-heartedly. "You barely know my name, what makes you think you know anything about me?"

His lips curl up, giving me a long once-over as he nonchalantly leans on his cue. "There's just an air to you, it's how you carry yourself—I can practically smell the trust fund on you."

My throat tightens, feeling like I've been caught in a lie. Something about people at Orso knowing I come from money—not that I have any now—makes me uneasy. I keep my expression amused. "I don't know what to tell you." I give him a little unassuming shrug. "You done stalling?" I say, nodding to the pool table.

He stays silent as if studying me, then finally says, "Care to make it a little more interesting?"

I raise one eyebrow. "Like a bet?"

His laugh is goading. "Exactly like a bet, Jimbo."

Hand on hip, I give him a cocksure look. "What kind of bet?"

"Why? Afraid you're going to lose?" His smile is wide

and toothy, and I can tell he's playing with me but something about him doesn't make it feel mocking.

"I said I was great, didn't I?"

"Well then, it shouldn't matter." He winks. "But I promise it'll be fun."

Feeling like I've entered a dangerous landmine, I push the uneasy feeling down and steel my spine. I'm allowed to have a bit of fun for once.

"Sure," I say, flashing a confident smile. "You can break."

He chuckles. "That confident, huh?"

I shrug a shoulder, leaning onto my pool cue and crossing one foot over the other but say nothing. He smirks, looking me up and down, his tongue running over his teeth while he leans over the pool table.

My cheeks heat with the weight of his look. Suddenly paranoid, as if I'm doing something wrong and sinful, I look around half-expecting to find one of Zachary's friends staring back at me. Or god forbid, Zachary himself. Although, knowing his taste, he wouldn't be caught dead here. Hell, I would've thought the same about myself only a few months ago.

After Ozzy breaks, he misses. I stifle a laugh, our expressions full of competitive levity as I walk around him to get my ball. I manage to sink two before the third ricochets. When it's Ozzy's turn to play again, his attention seems more on me than the actual game. I play dumb, continuing to treat this as a friendly game when deep down I know there's nothing *friendly* about it.

Getting into the rhythm, we take turns shooting, throwing lighthearted threats at each other hoping the other one misses. We both only have a couple of balls left when Ozzy pauses the game for a smoke break.

"Coming?" he mumbles around his unlit cigarette.

"I'll wait here," I respond, smiling.

He gives me a quick wink and a nod, disappearing outside.

With a smile still tugging at my lips, I fish out my phone and realize, far too late, that I have multiple missed calls from Zachary and a slew of angry texts demanding to know where I am.

"Fuck," I mutter, suddenly feeling sick.

Knowing that Ozzy is somewhere near the front door, I grab my purse and find another exit, unable to make up a flimsy excuse for why I'm leaving while I'm this anxious.

It's only after hailing a taxi, that I realize I didn't say goodbye to Michelle or Quinn.

Whatever.

My coworkers' feelings are the least of my worries right now—not when my hands are shaking and my breath is shallow. I dial Zachary's phone number and brace for the worst.

6

JAMES

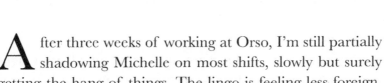

After three weeks of working at Orso, I'm still partially shadowing Michelle on most shifts, slowly but surely getting the hang of things. The lingo is feeling less foreign. The point-of-sale system, the software we use to punch in orders, is starting to make more sense. And the need to pull out the small cheat sheet I keep tucked inside my check presenter is diminishing with every shift.

I observe and study my peers, picking up on subtle tips and tricks. Where to hide and hoard dry rags, which are a rare commodity on busy nights, is one. Or how to effortlessly open a bottle of wine while chit-chatting with the guests. And at this point, the burning pain of a hot plate resting on the sensitive skin of my arm is something I've just learned to endure.

But the most important thing I've learned is that the best place to cry is the walk-in fridge.

I discovered that valuable piece of information this past Saturday.

Zachary had been particularly ruthless when I'd showed

up at his house after Stanley's Friday night. I was already apologizing when he'd opened the door, flinching when he threw a beer bottle against the living room wall, shattering it into pieces. I simply stood there, making myself as small as possible, repeating over and over that I was sorry. That it wouldn't ever happen again.

That *what* would never happen again?

I wasn't even sure. All I knew for certain was I needed to calm him down by any means necessary. I needed to remind him how much I loved him. How good we are together. But he'd been drinking before I showed up, so nothing seemed to help. He kept me up till dawn.

Fighting.

Always fighting.

I was emotionally raw when I got to Orso for my shift the next day.

I ended up standing beside a case of broccoli, sniffling back tears more than once that night. I had no clue what I was even crying for. But the tears kept coming. Luckily, it was so busy that it was easy to avoid Ozzy's gaze all night. I didn't have to justify why I had basically ghosted him the night before.

Thankfully, I had the next two days off, but tonight?

I can't ignore Ozzy, even if I wanted to.

He's not in his usual spot in the kitchen tonight, instead, he's shucking oysters behind the bar with Quinn. Which means he's in full view from my section in the dining room. I can't help it, whenever idle my gaze unconsciously finds his. Then I immediately chastise myself for it.

Around nine p.m., I get cut. Although I'm happy to be done early, I'm not rushing to get out of here. Zachary thinks I'll be working late, I don't plan on telling him otherwise.

In the staff room, I change into a breezy skirt and a simple white top. My movements are deliberately slow as if I'm trying to delay what I'm about to do next.

Maybe if I don't name it out loud, I won't feel so guilty.

Straightening my shoulders, I slip my cross-body purse over my head and let out a long exhale.

You're not doing anything wrong. This is nothing.

I swing the door open, walking through the small corridor that heads into the dining room. Reaching the bar, I sit down at the very end, near the front door which also happens to be directly in front of the oyster bar—with Ozzy standing right behind it.

"Done early, Jimbo?" he says as a welcome.

Hanging my purse on the hooks under the bartop, I roll my eyes and give him a saccharine smile. "Thought I'd make use of that free drink per shift we get before heading home."

"Good call," he answers with a smirk, before focusing back on the order of oysters he's shucking.

Turning my attention to Quinn, who's come up to take my order, I take full advantage and ask for a Beaujolais— one that's now way above my means. When they come back with my wine, I take my first indulgent sip while my gaze naturally lands back on Ozzy.

I try my hardest not to overthink why I can never seem to keep my eyes off of him for long when he's around. I chew my inner lip distractedly, toying with the stem of the wine glass while I study him.

The sleeves of his chef jacket are pushed up his forearms, his muscles corded with the skilled movements of his hands. I get lost in the repetition of his actions, shucking one oyster after another, then plating them on a bed of crushed ice.

"So where did you disappear to last Friday?" he asks all too innocently.

"What?" I say out of reflex, snapping my eyes up to his. My cheeks heat hoping he didn't notice me ogling his hands just now. It takes a few seconds for his question to load. "Oh, uh—" I laugh nervously, playing with my hair. "Yeah, sorry about that ... something came up, I didn't have time to find you."

I've had a few days to come up with a legitimate excuse but I still manage to serve him the vaguest answer to ever exist on planet Earth. I try not to visibly cringe.

He studies me for a beat, and I consider running out the front door.

Instead, he changes the subject.

"Ever had an oyster, new girl?"

I let out a small relieved laugh and shake my head. "No actually ... which is a little surprising considering the circles I grew up in."

"And which circles are those?" he asks distractedly, head down while shucking another oyster.

I immediately regret divulging that detail, hoping Ozzy doesn't pick up on the context clues. I evade the question as best I can. "I just mean, I've been around oysters before. Never had one though."

"Would you like to?"

"Not really, no," I answer quickly with a dry chuckle and a shake of the head.

His lip curls upwards, ocean eyes looking up to find mine. "Where's your sense of adventure, sweetheart?"

I sigh dramatically. "I *am* adventurous." His gaze darkens as it lingers on me, seemingly turning what I just said into an innuendo. I ignore the small shift in tone, take a sip of my wine, and shrug. "They just don't look appetizing, that's all."

"Well." Throwing a dry rag over his shoulder, he leans his fists onto the bar, gaze full of mirth. "It's because you've never had me make one for you."

"Oh?" I say amused, "And what makes *your oysters* so special?" The comment is meant as a joke but my smile drops, suddenly worried he'll take it the wrong way. I watch his facial expression carefully, expecting his mood to turn sour, but instead he barks a laugh and my body inadvertently relaxes at the sound.

"You're about to find out." He shoots me a wink, perching one of his closed fists on his hip while still leaning toward me. "Trust me."

His tone is smooth and reassuring, and my chest blooms with warmth.

I stay silent for a beat, studying him, not sure what to say. I don't know how to tell him that I usually stick to familiar foods. That meals I've eaten a thousand times before feel the safest and the most comforting, especially when I'm overwhelmed. How I can't eat food with certain textures without completely losing my appetite. It's not that I don't like to be adventurous, it's just that when it comes to food … I'd rather stick to what I know.

But something about Ozzy's gentle expression makes me want to say yes, even if it feels irrationally scary.

I nod slowly, hesitantly. "Okay."

He perks up, clapping his hands and rubbing them together. Reaching for an oyster, he places it on the counter and grips a rag over top of it. The small shucking knife disappears into the shell, pushing and then twisting with his wrist.

His movements are a little slower this time, his actions

more deliberate. Brows furrowed, forehead slightly creased behind his blue bandana. Watching someone shuck an oyster shouldn't be this tantalizing. But as usual, when it comes to Ozzy, I can't look away.

After cracking the oyster, he carefully garnishes it. I recognize the essentials: Mignonette—made from red shallots, pepper, and red wine vinegar—a pinch of fresh horseradish, and a squeeze of lemon.

I'm surprised to find my mouth watering at the sight. I convince myself it's just the promise of an oyster and has nothing to do with the skilled hands holding it.

"Now," he says, looking slightly reproachful as if I need to listen to his instructions *very* carefully. "A perfectly shucked oyster will slide effortlessly into your mouth. Then, I want you to chew once or twice before swallowing. Got it?"

"Got it," I repeat a little too studiously, before reaching over to grab the oyster.

Ozzy moves my hand away, lets out a small tsk and holds up a finger. "Let me."

Realizing he intends to feed it to me, I drop my hand onto the bar, slightly stunned. My body heats up, having no control over any of its reactions. Good or bad.

Telling him that I have a boyfriend is on the tip of my tongue, but that would mean admitting that I see us as something more than *just* coworkers. I press my lips inward instead, thinking about my next move.

To hell with it. This doesn't mean anything. It's just an oyster.

We have a silent stand-off, him holding the innocuous oyster, a small smirk fixed on his face while I'm busy questioning my morals. I finally cave, and give him the green light with the smallest of nods.

His grin grows mischievous as he leans his waist over

the bar, while I meet him halfway. Our eyes are glued to each other, his face turning serious when the rough shell touches my lip. His fingers are so close to my opened mouth, that I can almost feel the heat of them on my skin. I watch his eyes darken as if he's having similar thoughts to mine.

My heart is beating wildly, everything about this feels forbidden.

Still, I'm starving for more.

Carefully tilting the shell, he slides the oyster into my mouth. He mimics me, subconsciously, his mouth falling open ever so slightly, the thin scar on his bottom lip more defined now that I see it up close. I fight the urge to squirm in my seat when the flavors explode on my tongue seconds later. It tastes like the sea. Briny, and salty, the acidity of the red wine vinegar and lemon brightening the taste.

I lean back into my seat, chewing once, then twice, before swallowing the oyster like he carefully instructed. My eyes are still fixed on him, while his dip down to my lips when I give them a small lick. When he looks back up, his open smile is back, blue-green eyes twinkling.

"So?" he says, almost prideful.

"That was …" My smile grows as wide as his. "*Amazing.*"

Hours later, I'm still at Orso when Ozzy walks back into the dining room, shrugging a battered jean vest full of patches over his black faded t-shirt. "Coming?"

I almost blurt out *where* but I know what he's asking. Michelle's sitting beside me, having also finished her shift. She smiles wide and nods, coaxing me into saying yes.

Quinn is busy counting their cash behind the bar, blonde hair still carefully slicked back with gel, even after such a long shift. "Y'all go, I'll meet you there," they say, eyes still on the bills they're counting. Leo, the busboy, who's mopping the bar floor echoes Quinn's response.

Ozzy looks at me expectantly, while I just sit there internally deliberating.

I should just go home.

I should just text Zachary and tell him I'll meet him wherever he is.

Instead, I agree to one drink at Stanley's and follow Michelle and Ozzy out the backdoor.

It's a weekday, so the bar is less crowded than last time, mostly concentrated near the bar, but we still manage to find some free stools and sit.

I'm about to order a gin and tonic from the blue-haired bartender when I see Zachary walk out from the bathrooms. My stomach lurches into my throat and there are a few harrowing seconds where the cognitive dissonance is so intense that I convince myself I'm seeing things.

What the fuck is he doing here.

My first instinct is to hide, but somehow I end up on my feet instead. He spots me immediately. His steps stutter as if startled, his eyes darting to the left, looking past my shoulder for half a second before landing back on me. I brace for the worst, but shockingly Zachary smiles and heads my way.

"Zachary … I, uh—what are you doing here?"

The words coming out of my mouth feel strangely distant while I try to predict his reaction but he confuses me even further, by playfully kissing me.

"I came to meet you, of course," he says, swiping his hand through his hair.

"How did you know I'd be here?"

Skirting my question, he steps around me and turns his attention to Michelle instead. "Hi, I'm Zachary Benjamin," he says while offering his hand. He always introduces himself with his two first names, a small quirk I secretly hate. "Jamie's boyfriend."

Shit. Shit. Shit. Shit.

"Boyfriend ..." Michelle says, and I quietly swivel around, trying to catch her eye. Fear and anxiety about what she'll say next make my throat close up as I try to gulp in air. Somehow she deciphers my alarmed expression and quickly changes her tone. Her smile is wide and bright when she continues, "Right! I've heard *so* much about you. I'm Michelle, so nice to finally meet you."

I'm not sure if it's relief I feel when I notice Ozzy missing from his seat.

I don't even have the wherewithal to wonder where he's gone.

My emotions are a muddled mess, especially with Zachary acting so unusually charming. If I wasn't so messed up with simply finding him here, maybe I'd be questioning a lot more than what I am at the moment. But for now, I ease back into my seat, Zachary taking Ozzy's place at the bar.

For the next hour I feel foggy, as if I had slammed my head against the wall and suffered a concussion. Luckily Zachary carries the brunt of the conversation, mostly talking about himself. Michelle deserves an Oscar for the performance she's giving, not even mentioning Ozzy's sudden absence in front of Zachary, as if effortlessly picking up on everything that I've left unsaid.

Eventually, Quinn and Leo join us. I use the distraction to hide in a bathroom stall for a few minutes, desperately trying to regulate my erratic emotions. After a quick breathing exercise and a small splash of water to my nape, I walk out and spot Ozzy.

He's tucked in a corner facing me, talking to an alt-looking girl who has her back to me.

His gaze is pinned to mine.

His smirk is slow when he raises his pint to his lips, missing its usual levity. Putting down his beer on the table next to him, he reaches up and gently strokes her hair. Ozzy's eyes drop to hers, then swiftly back to mine. His fingers trail her naked shoulder, and I shiver, swallowing hard.

What the hell is happening.

Breaking eye contact, he lowers himself to whisper something into her ear. And then catches her earlobe with his teeth. His gaze skates briefly to mine before grabbing her face with both hands, kissing her. It's rough, and heated, and … and … and I'm rooted to the spot, a swirl of contradicting feelings threatening to pull me under. But I keep watching.

My breath hitches when his eyes lift back to mine, his mouth still on hers.

His gaze is hot, yet it doesn't burn.

Suddenly, the brunette feels like a proxy.

As if I'm the one he's actually kissing.

As if it's my body he's groping.

I can almost feel the dig of his fingers into my hips.

The warmth of his lips on mine.

The guilt is sudden and visceral, consuming me as I remember Zachary is just a few steps away, sitting at the bar waiting for me.

I rip my gaze away, smoothing my skirt with my hands as I try to collect myself. I won't survive the night if I spend another minute in this place. I walk back to the bar, effectively ignoring Ozzy. I tell the gang I'm feeling sick, faking nausea, and Zachary seems as eager as I am to get out of here. We quickly say our goodbyes, leaving in a cab a few minutes later.

We head straight to bed when we get to Zachary's, and relief washes over me when he doesn't try to initiate sex, simply turning off the light and going to sleep.

7

JAMES

"Jamie, what the hell!"

I wake up with my arms flying, shoving Zachary away as if I'm being physically attacked. I push myself into a sitting position and look wildly around the room, catching my breath.

I'm in Zachary's bed, having slept over after Stanley's. It's still dark, early morning based on the quiet chirps of birds outside.

"What *was* that?" Zachary says.

His tone is slightly worried, but I instantly pick up on the accusation in his voice.

My heart is beating hard against my chest as I lick my dry lips, still unsure of what just happened. I'm left with a lingering feeling of fear, shame, and unease. I can sense myself slipping back into a memory from six months ago. Of when I woke up one morning with similar forebodings … although there was a strong tint of anguish last time that took me weeks to recover from.

Or maybe I never did.

"What happened?" I croak.

Zachary, shirtless and wearing gray boxers, shifts in bed. He averts his gaze for a second, looking away and then back. His subtle evasiveness makes my heart sink. "You started fighting me like you didn't want it," he mutters, dragging a hand in his messy hair. "Like you didn't know who I was."

It takes me a few seconds for his words to properly load. But when they finally do, they feel more like a virus rotting my body from the inside out.

His words echo. Shatter.

As if I didn't want it?

The sinking feeling morphs into something harsher, sharper … into something I'd rather not name out loud.

Looking down, I realize my sleep shorts are pushed halfway down my hips. I stare at my uncovered thighs numbly, before finding Zachary's gaze again.

"I was asleep …" I say limply.

His eyes narrow into something hard, his face darkened by the early morning shadows. It's quick, he blinks and it's gone, his face softening into a roguish smile. "Oh come on, honeybun," he says with a sickly sweet tone. Reaching over, he strokes my arm before giving it a squeeze. "You never seemed to care before."

My reaction is visceral. But quiet. I collapse into myself, like a star swallowed up by a black hole. Zachary doesn't seem to notice. He slides closer, and this time I do nothing to push him away. Dragging his nose up my neck, the cold tip makes me shiver, he whispers, "I just can't help myself." He squeezes my thigh. "I mean, look at you."

He gently pushes me down and I let him.

I can feel myself shutting down and I don't know how to make it stop.

Make it stop, make it stop, make it stop.
I watch myself from somewhere above me.
Zachary pushes my shorts all the way off.
I let it happen.
He spits in his hand.
Deep down, I know I don't want this.
He thrusts, grunting in my ear.
This is what good girlfriends do.
I mechanically wrap my arms around his neck.
I love him.
I pretend I like it.
I love him.
I pretend.
I love him.

8

JAMES

I 've been waiting twenty minutes for my table's order when I realize I forgot to even punch it in. Dumbfounded, I stare at my notepad and then up at the screen as if somehow this will magically make my mistake disappear. The wave of defeat and anxiety, knowing I'll have to ask the kitchen to rush that order when they're already slammed, is damn near suffocating.

The sounds of the busy restaurant rush into me all at once like a crushing wave. It overwhelms me, especially when I'm trying to think and I can feel tears prick my eyes.

When I left Zachary's place this morning, I thought I had it all in control. I thought I could just push it all down and I'd be fine. But somewhere between then and now, the numbness thawed and I'm left with bone-deep sadness.

Maybe this morning was a catalyst but this sadness doesn't seem to have a middle, beginning, or end. It's as if I've been wading in this feeling my whole life and only now have woken up to it.

"*Shit*," I mutter hopelessly under my breath. I take a

slow inhale, looking upwards to try and swallow the feeling back down. There's no time for tears. I'm in the weeds and I can hear the bell on the pass ding. Quickly punching my forgotten order into the POS system, I scurry over to the kitchen.

"Chef?" I say to no one in particular, my voice is meek but loud enough for the whole back-of-house to hear. "I fucked up, I'm sorry but I forgot to punch in two niçoise for table 5, can I have it on the fly?"

The kitchen answers *no* in unison. Some rather creative curses follow the outrage.

I know they're fucking with me but I still feel like crawling in a hole and dying.

I force myself to stand there and wait.

"I'm on it, princess," Ozzy barks through the noise and my gaze snaps to his station. His eyes are serious but there's a barely-there smirk that manages to ease my inner turmoil a little. "But you better go apologize to your table, you aren't pinning your mistake on the kitchen."

"Yes, chef," I say sharply, nodding diligently and Ozzy's smirk widens.

I don't wait around, turning on my heels to pick up drinks waiting for me at the bar.

An hour later, the moment I've been waiting for my whole shift arrives. The rush has finally ended, and I speed-walk through the kitchen, heading for the walk-in fridge. Luckily a lot of the cooks are outside smoking near the dumpsters, so I can evade any snarky remarks. The oddly comforting smell of *cold* wraps around me, and I hurriedly close the door.

But I need more than just cold air.

At the back of the fridge, there's another door, which leads to the freezer.

When I can finally see my own breath and goosebumps prickle my skin, I take a deep inhale. Closing my eyes for half a second, I finally let the tears flow freely. They feel hot on my cold skin, the sensation somehow soothing, and a wave of relief finally settles over me. I bite back a sob, trying to keep as much decorum as I can, but it feels impossible. I know I only have a few blissful minutes and I'm afraid if I really let go, I won't ever stop crying.

I'm dabbing some tears with the sleeve of my black button-down shirt when the door opens and Ozzy walks in. *Shit.* I'm so embarrassed I feel like I might start crying all over again. My knee-jerk reaction is to whip around to try to hide my face but I realize just as fast that there's no place to hide. I sheepishly turn back around to face him, while holding back a few sniffles.

Ozzy's hand is still on the door handle while he looks me up and down. And I fight back more embarrassment.

He whistles. "Uh oh, penguin mode ..." he drawls casually. "Rough night?"

I give him a small dejected laugh while trying to pat the bottom of my eyes dry. "Yeah," I answer with a long exhale. "Something like that."

"The walk-in fridge is overrated anyway," he says with a shrug, finally closing the door behind him. "If you ask me, the freezer is superior when you need a good cry."

"Is that so?" I ask, letting out a small humorless chuckle, followed by a small sniff. I force out a half-grin. "Talking from experience?"

He shoots me a mischievous look. "These walls have seen my blood, sweat, *and* tears, Jimbo." Reaching over, he grabs a Snickers bar from the shelf and shoves it into his chef jacket. Seeing me watch him, he adds, "Personal stash, help yourself."

I laugh a little bit more genuinely this time. Finally starting to feel the freezing cold seeping beneath my skin, I cross my arms. "That's all you came in for?"

He flashes me a bright smile, dimple appearing and disappearing. "A little something sweet for later."

I let out a half-hearted huff as we both fall silent, his joyful expression slowly fading while he studies me. I can feel the emotions swell up as he carefully watches me, my vision blurring with tears.

Shit.

If only I could control my emotions for once.

Ozzy notices immediately and steps forward. "Ah come on, Jimbo, don't cry," he coos, reaching over as if to comfort me. Seeming to think better of it, he stops in his tracks and lets his hand fall.

"It's nothing, I'm fine," I reassure him, fanning my hands near my eyes while looking up, trying to dry up yet another emotional outburst. "I just need this shift to end." I laugh sheepishly, hoping to cut the tension.

He pulls the bandana off his head and runs his hand through his curly hair. Looking down and then up he says, "Just not a big fan of seeing you like this."

I smile weakly. "Thanks, that's … sweet," I murmur softly.

Silence settles between us, the buzz of the freezer now loud in my ears as we continue staring at each other.

My heart rate spikes, the air around us thickening.

Until his phone rings, and I jump.

Ozzy's serious gaze lingers until he finally clears his throat, fishing his phone out of his pocket. I can't help noticing the name Sophia before he flips his screen over. An unwarranted zing pinches my chest. Must be the same girl I saw him with last night.

"I need to get this," he says distractedly.

"Yeah, no worries," I mutter.

He goes to walk out but pauses, saying over his shoulder, "Are you going to be okay?"

I try to keep my tone light. "Of course." I smile meekly. "I just needed a moment."

He returns my smile and nods. I watch him close the door behind him, while I stay standing in the middle of the walk-in freezer alone … wondering what the hell I'm doing with my life.

9

OZZY

"Everything okay?" I ask, the phone pressed to my ear while I exit the walk-in fridge.

There's silence through the receiver until my sister sighs loudly and says, "*Well …*"

I spot Alec heading for the fridge. "Hold on, Soph." I grab Alec's shoulder while addressing him, "New girl's in the walk-in, give her a sec."

He gives me a loaded look but says nothing, simply giving me a small salute and walking away. I tuck my phone between my ear and shoulder while patting my chef jacket for my pack of smokes, my kitchen clogs squeaking on the freshly mopped floor. "Okay I'm back," I mumble around the unlit cigarette now between my lips, pushing the back-door open. "What's going on?"

She lets out another sigh before saying, "It's Dad." My heart squeezes painfully, knowing whatever she says next won't be good. "He hasn't been home since Monday morning."

"*Shit,*" I curse under my breath while taking a long drag.

I rub the back of my thumb on my forehead, doing a quick calculation. "Soph, that was *three days* ago, why didn't you call me sooner?" I can feel all the muscles in my body seizing up with rage.

Fucking deadbeat piece of shit.

"I didn't want to bother you ... I know how busy you are."

"Sophia." I try to keep my voice calm. "I'm never too busy for you. We've talked about this." My hand is shaking when I bring the cigarette up to my lips. She's only fourteen, she shouldn't have to take care of herself like this. "Where's Hux?"

"I don't know ..." she says dejectedly. "He hasn't really been around either."

"Fuck!" I bite out, kicking the dumpster wondering where my teenage brother has disappeared to. Being seventeen, I depend on him being there when I can't be.

"Don't freak out," she mumbles.

"So you've been taking care of Charlie by yourself this whole time?"

"Yeah," she states.

She makes it sound so normal. As if growing up in such a dysfunctional family makes having our dad disappear on a three-day bender just a typical weekday for her.

I hate myself for leaving her there. I moved out when I was sixteen. Now I carry an insidious kind of survivor's guilt that sinks deeper and deeper into my skin the longer I leave my siblings back home with our piss-poor excuse for a dad.

I blame myself for how Hux is turning out, constantly worried he'll end up following in our mother's footsteps and land himself in prison. She was convicted five years ago for drug possession with intent to sell. We don't bother visiting her much. Just like she didn't bother with us much when she was out.

My vision is blurring, my chest tightening, the anger burning a hole in my stomach. But there's also debilitating fear attached to the rage—the panic of knowing Sophia has been alone with our eight-year-old brother Charlie for this long.

I hold back the urge to punch the dumpster, reminding myself that I need my hands to work. Crushing the butt of my cigarette under my heel, I tell Sophia I'll be right there. I text Alec from the parking lot, asking him to cover for me before I jump into my car and get the hell out of there.

THE NEXT MORNING, I wake up on my dad's couch with a crick in my neck and a sore back. That couch was old and busted even when I was a kid, and it's not much better now. Can't be surprised it was never replaced, since my dad prefers to spend the family's money on himself.

I'm busy making breakfast burritos with whatever I was able to scrounge up in the fridge—making a mental note to buy groceries before I leave—when Charlie bounds into the kitchen.

His brown curls are sticking up in wild angles from sleep, wearing his faithful but too-small Spider-Man PJs. He's a carbon copy of me when I was young, except he has a splatter of freckles across his nose and cheeks.

"Ozzy!" he squeals, running into me, his face squishing into my ribs while he hugs me tightly. He was already sleeping when I arrived last night and I didn't want to wake him.

"Hey buddy," I say, ruffling his hair before he lets me go. "Staying out of trouble?"

He lets out an amused laugh, sitting up on the counter next to the dirty sink. "If you don't count when the cops drove me home last week," he says with no remorse.

I give him a pointed look, flipping one of the burritos over in the pan. "What did you do this time?"

"Set a garbage can on fire," he deadpans.

"For fuck sake, Charlie." His laugh is infectious and I can't help but smile, turning my back to him so as to hide it. "What did I tell you about that shit?"

"He's going to burn this shithole to the ground one day," Sophia mutters while walking to the kitchen table, rubbing her eye. Sophia takes after our mother, dirty blonde hair and green eyes.

"Breakfast's ready," I tell them.

Charlie jumps down from the counter, following behind as I carry their plates to the table. Sophia pushes a pile of letters and loose flyers to the side before grabbing her burrito.

"Thanks, Ozzy." She smiles, taking a large bite. She surveys the table and with a mouthful of food she looks up to where I'm standing and asks, "Where's yours?"

"Not hungry," I reply before turning around to clean up the kitchen. There wasn't enough food for three, but I don't bother telling them that.

"I got hold of Hux, by the way," I say from over my shoulder. "He'll be here later this morning."

Sophia hums in acknowledgment while she continues to eat. I omit the part where I had to bribe him a hundred bucks for it. A part of me understands his complete disinterest in being home. I was even younger when I left.

But *fuck*, I can't always be around.

Pushing myself up on the kitchen counter, I idly sit and watch the kids eat. If I didn't notice everything wrong with this house, from the cracks in the leaky ceiling to the dirty walls, the image of them eating breakfast at the kitchen table could almost be wholesome. I wonder if their easy smiles and laughs have anything to do with me being here this morning, which only exacerbates the guilt of leaving them here alone with my dad.

I try to remind myself that I'm doing my best.

Even though my *best* is not nearly good enough.

SWINGING THE DOOR OPEN, I march into O'Toole's, one of the many places I know to look for my father when he's disappeared for this long. It's only a few blocks from the house and known to be open before noon. This shithole is dark and dank, but I spot a lone figure sitting at the end of the empty bar.

I see fucking red.

Most likely already wasted, he doesn't notice me when I stomp up to him. I grab my father by the collar of his shirt and pull him out of his seat.

"Woah! Hey, get off me!" he slurs, trying to tear himself out of my grasp but goes limp when he realizes who's slamming him against the wall. "Ozzy," he mutters.

"Miss me?" I spit between my clenched teeth. I tighten my grip and give him another hard shove. "I sure hope it's not *my* fucking money you're drinking away this time."

"It's not like that," he says uselessly, his breath reeking of stale beer.

I'm so disgusted that I let him go and take a step back.

He stumbles, barely regaining his footing, grabbing onto the back of a chair.

I stare at him, wanting nothing more than to beat the living sense into him. But I know it's useless. There's barely anyone there. He looks so old … his body frail, thinning white hair, and eyes that look more bloodshot than green. He's swimming in his stained jeans as if all these years of abusing his body with alcohol have finally caught up with him.

Stepping away, I point a finger in his face. "If you're not back home by tonight, I'm cutting you off. You hear me?"

"Don't be like that," he mumbles almost incomprehensibly. "We're family."

Hearing him call us family makes me nauseous.

"That doesn't mean fuck all coming from you," I answer with disdain. Turning to leave, I grit out from over my shoulder, "Get your shit together, Richard. You're an embarrassment."

I storm out before I do something rash like spit in my own father's face.

THE SOUND of the printer behind me sends me into a sudden rage. It's a quiet kind of rage, but inside I'm fuming. It's 10:59 p.m. The kitchen closes at eleven. This has been the longest twenty-four hours of my fucking life.

"Piece of shit customers," I mutter under my breath, clanging some tongs onto the cutting board. "Entitled fucking assholes."

I've been ready to close for an hour. My run-in with my father has kept me in a tight coil all day. The last thing I wanted was for the final order to come in *one* minute before close. I let out a long exhale. I can't catch a break today.

From the corner of my eye, I see James run up to the pass. Her hair is done up into a high bun, leaving her neck exposed. I pretend not to notice her.

But she's impossible to ignore.

Especially after she let me feed her an oyster the other day. I've already replayed that perfect moment in my head too many times to count.

"Oh my god I'm so sorry, Ozzy," she says, a little out of breath. "I really tried to have them order from the bar menu, but they just weren't having it. Said they came here specifically for the beef carpaccio."

Great.

I keep my expression flat while I stare at her. She trails off, her throat bobbing when she swallows, her gaze fixed on mine.

An idea forms in my mind and I suddenly couldn't care less if these late-arriving customers have to wait for their precious carpaccio.

"Come over here," I tell James with a quick jerk of the head.

"What, why?" she says, while already walking towards the swinging doors. She reappears a few seconds later, and I snatch her wrist.

"What are you doing?" she says in a small hushed shriek but she doesn't struggle, doesn't even make any attempt to pull her wrist out from my grasp. Instead, she follows me all the way into the dry storage.

Closing the door behind us, I turn back around to face her.

She has her arms crossed, staring at me with suspicion. "Why did you bring me in here?"

The rational voice inside my head tries to warn me to stay away. I shouldn't play with fire when she so clearly has a boyfriend.

The disappointment I'd felt, deep in the pit of my stomach, when I saw her with him was startling, to say the least. I'm usually not the one to care, but it was jealousy that had me kissing that girl while James watched. And it was complete disinterest for anyone else but the pink-haired princess that drove me to walk away from the other girl seconds after James left the bar with her boyfriend.

I decide to disregard any rational thought for now. Especially today, when everything is pissing me the fuck off, and toying with James is the perfect way to assuage my shit mood.

"Time to pay up," I say conspiratorially with a small curl of my lips.

Her eyebrows rise and then narrow, arms tightening over her chest. "What are you even on about?" she answers suspiciously.

"You lost, sweetheart. You owe me," I chide while closing in on her. She takes a few steps back to keep the distance between us. I can tell she still isn't catching on so I spell it out for her. "Our game of pool? A bet is a bet."

Her mouth falls open, and *fuck*, all I want to do is catch her plump lip between my teeth. "We never finished the game," she utters slowly as if suddenly weary of how to navigate the situation I've put her in.

"You forfeited the second you disappeared." I take a step towards her, staring her down. A dark grin pulling up my lip. "I win, princess."

She looks like she wants to say multiple things at once but ends up closing her mouth, chewing on her bottom lip before finally saying, "You never told me what I'd have to do if I lost."

A small chuckle rolls out of my mouth, positively fucking *bemused* by the turn of events. Quickly, I try to scrounge up the most outlandish idea I can come up with. Having her execute the bet isn't exactly what's giving me such a thrill, it's seeing her squirm that entices me the most. The soft shade of pink her cheeks turn when I've pushed her just a little too far. It's the first fun thing that's happened to me in the last twenty-four hours.

I take out the Snickers bar from my pocket, still cold from the freezer, and push it into her palm.

"What's that for?" she huffs, trying to sound casual.

"You know," I say while I slowly trap her between my body and the shelves. Her back hits them and she startles but does nothing to push me off. "I'd love for you to prove me wrong. Show me you can be bad …" I rasp, looking her up and down. "Why don't you do something a little depraved? Can you do that, sweetheart?"

Her eyes are wide, swiftly searching my face. The primal urge to pin her hips with mine is almost unbearable but I don't move, waiting to see if she'll object.

Finally, she holds up the chocolate bar, looking at me questioningly, before she whispers, "What does this have to do with anything?"

Slowly, I grin. I'm salivating. The anticipation of her reaction already tastes so sweet on my tongue.

"You're going to go in the back, unwrap this." I tap a finger on the Snickers bar. "And slide it up your pretty cunt." Her breath hitches, and my cock swells against my boxers. "Then bring it back to me." I crowd her just a little bit more. "I want to taste you on it."

The silence that follows is electric, her eyes still wide

and fixed on me. The air is practically crackling around us, and for one perfect second, I think she might actually do it. Until she shoves me off and throws the chocolate bar on the floor.

"You're out of your fucking mind, salad boy," she says heatedly, storming out of the storage room.

I regain my footing while I watch her march off. A sick thrill still racing through my veins.

That was even more entertaining than expected.

10

JAMES

My table is hemming and hawing over the menu, I keep my smile prim and proper while I wait for them to make a decision. In an effort not to *tap, tap, tap* my pen on my paper pad, I let my gaze drift.

Like a compass always pointing north, my eyes land on the kitchen. I can't see Ozzy from where I'm standing, but it doesn't stop me from staring at the pass like I'll eventually conjure him up from force of will alone.

I've been avoiding him since he cornered me in the storage room a week ago. I knew he could be crude—all the line cooks are—but hearing him say the word cunt, especially referring to *mine*, unraveled me in ways I wasn't expecting.

I ran out of there, terrified of what I would do next. But it's left me craving to hear every single, filthy thing that could come out of his lewd mouth.

And that's why I need to stay away.

I've avoided Zachary for almost as long. Luckily, he was

busy with lacrosse practice all weekend so he didn't have much free time to question my absence.

I've never even considered cheating on Zachary before. Although with all the illicit daydreams I've been having, it almost feels like I already am.

Maybe … I should've broken up with him a long time ago.

But it's just not that simple … I can easily convince myself that I love everything about him—except the way he makes me feel. I've grown numb to the pain, not to mention that he's somehow convinced me I'd be miserable without him.

The irony is painful to admit.

Anytime I try to imagine a life without Zachary, his words snake into my hypothetical freedom and tarnish it.

No one will ever love you like I do.

I'm the best you'll ever have.

You'd be nothing without me.

"Miss?"

My eyes snap back to my table.

Shit.

I hope I wasn't staring off into space for too long. I widen my smile. "Ready?"

After taking their order, I head back to the computer near the bar. I'm listening to Ji-min, the bartender, complain about a customer stiffing him when Zachary strolls in. It takes me a few seconds for the sight of him standing inside my place of work to fully solidify.

He's never come to eat at Orso before.

When I realize that it *is* him, I leave Ji-min mid-conversation, walking swiftly up to my boyfriend.

"Hey honeybun," he drawls.

I might be paranoid, but something about his smile feels condescending.

"Zachary, what a surprise ..." I say, still a little taken aback. "What are you doing here?" I hope my tone sounds like I'm happy to see him and not accusatory.

He leans over for a kiss and I move my head out of the way, narrowly avoiding his lips.

"I'm at work," I say just low enough for him to hear me, trying to justify my reaction.

His eyes harden, and between the span of a few blinks he wordlessly promises me that I'll pay for my little move later.

His cocky grin returns. "Well since you *refused* to take your birthday off, I thought I'd come to you."

I swallow back down the need to tell him that I simply couldn't afford to take time off. He wouldn't understand anyway.

I force a smile. "That's so sweet. Thank you, I can put you in my ..." My words trail off when Spencer, Zachary's best friend, walks into the restaurant. My reaction is immediate. I feel light-headed, revulsion spearing my stomach as bile burns up my throat. I'm usually good at avoiding him, but today, I feel cornered.

He was with Zachary when ... when they ... when it happened.

I don't know how I'll manage to serve him all night.

I lean close to Zachary. "You brought Spencer?" I whisper.

"Of course, I wasn't going to come dine by myself was I?"

"Happy birthday, Jamie," Spencer says casually as he walks up to us.

"Thanks," I mutter, avoiding eye contact.

Swiftly turning around, I lead them into my section and settle them at a four-top near the corner—pointedly ignoring the kitchen pass.

"Why don't you sit with us? I'm sure you can take a break," Zachary says while I hand him a menu.

I struggle not to snap when I answer him. "That's not how it works, Zachary."

His nose crinkles with annoyance, rolling his eyes.

"Fine, I'll have an old-fashioned," he says abruptly. "Spence?"

"Same thing," his friend replies with a smile and I feel sick.

My vision tunnels as I walk back to the bar, ignoring everything around me, including my tables.

"Are you okay?" Ji-min says as he slowly approaches me, his brown eyes looking worried. "You look a little pale ..."

"I—uh ... I think I just need some air," I blurt out, feeling my hands turning clammy. "Can you cover for me?"

Thankfully, it's not busy tonight, so as soon as he nods, I dart into the back and run outside. The moment the back-door closes behind me, I double over, leaning my hands on my thighs, and gulp in lungfuls of air trying to get my heart rate down.

"Jimbo?"

I let out a startled yelp, swiveling around to find Ozzy leaning against the wall, one foot up. "Oh my god, I didn't see you there," I say breathlessly, hand over my heart.

He pushes himself off the wall, flicking his cigarette into the parking lot. "Everything okay? You seem a little ..." He makes a vague gesture trying to convey my current emotional state.

My laugh is wry but somewhat genuine as if I'm trying

to make Ozzy feel at ease. Why is it that he seems to always find me in a state of emotional disarray lately?

"I'm fine," I say distractedly. "It's just." Looking over to the door, I half-expect Zachary to burst outside and catch me talking to Ozzy. I meet his gaze. "It's my birthday today, and my boyfriend decided to show up and I——" *I don't want him here.* "I don't know ... I just wasn't expecting him is all." I finish my sad little explanation with a wobbly smile, waiting for Ozzy to roast me for my overreaction.

"It's your birthday?" he says with a wistful grin, taking a step closer. "Why didn't you tell anyone?"

Ozzy skirting around the elephant in the room somehow alleviates a bit of the tension. I latch on to it. "Yeah," I answer with a timid smirk. "And ... um," I add with a shrug, "I just didn't think it was worth mentioning."

"You like keeping secrets, don't you?" he says amused, his aqua eyes sparkling as he casually crosses his arms.

"No," I blurt out a bit too seriously.

Ozzy chuckles. "Well, happy birthday, Jimbo." Walking up to the door, he opens it before looking back at me, his lips tugging into a cocky smirk. His eyes narrow in mischief. "I'll make sure to send out something *extra special* to your boyfriend's table."

Hearing Ozzy acknowledge Zachary leaves me uneasy. It makes me want to scream as loud as I can just so I can try to let out some of the pressure behind my chest.

I feel like I'm spinning out of control.

And I can't make it stop.

———

AN HOUR LATER, Gustavo lets me know that Ozzy wants to see me in the kitchen and I jump on the opportunity to avoid my section—boyfriend included. Both Zachary and Spencer are getting more and more intoxicated as the night progresses and I'm terrified they'll do something to embarrass me. I already had to tell Zachary to stop snapping his fingers at the busser.

"Yes, chef?" I say, entering the kitchen.

Ozzy's busy cutting onions, but he points to a plate of nachos beside him with his knife.

"What's this?" I ask innocently. "We don't even sell nachos."

"Thought you might be hungry. You weren't at staff meal today," he says, his gaze down while he continues chopping. "I made them with Doritos."

I stare at the nachos, slightly stunned. The image of him running to a corner store to buy a bag of Doritos just to make me nachos has me feeling a whirl of conflicting emotions.

But my heart squeezes in gratitude nonetheless.

I blink up at him. "I love Doritos," I mutter.

His eyes meet mine, his lips curling into a loaded grin. "I know." Reaching up on the shelf above him, he grabs a small birthday candle, sticks it into the melted cheese, and uses a small torch to light up the tip. "Happy birthday, princess."

"Thank you ..." I say softly, my heart beginning to race as I stand beside his station, my hand toying with my skirt.

His smile makes his blue-green eyes crinkle and I can't stop staring. I have a sneaking suspicion my feelings are written clear across my face—a mixture of joy and affection —but I make zero attempt to hide it from him. The moment feels ever-expanding like I could spend my whole life inside this bubble of time and not regret one second of it. Ozzy juts his chin as if wordlessly telling me to blow out the candle, a smile still on his lips.

"Behind!" Alec yells out as he passes us, effectively snapping us out of whatever *that* was.

"Anyway," I say hurriedly, blowing out the candle while Ozzy resumes his task. "I'll take it to the server station. Thanks again. It looks delicious."

"Enjoy," he says.

His gaze returns to his work before I walk out of the kitchen.

LEANING AGAINST THE BAR, I repeatedly tap my check presenter on my thigh. I'm pretending to wait for my drink order but in reality, I'm watching Zachary and Spencer from across the bar. They barely notice me, having migrated to the bar half an hour ago when the kitchen closed. They're damn near belligerent now.

I give Ji-min a sorrowful look, trying to wordlessly apologize while he serves Zachary a scotch with a side of water. My shift isn't over for another hour but I can't stomach another minute of this quiet embarrassment, so I let out a long sigh and head over to their seats.

Pretending to be nothing but smiles, I offer to meet them at a bar nearby, telling them I won't be done for a while.

Zachary loudly objects, "We're fine right here, honeybun!"

"What?" Spencer says, leaning his elbow on the bar to get closer to me. "Are we not good company?" His smile cuts like a sharp knife. Slowly—or drunkenly, I can't really tell—he slides his gaze to Zachary and then back to me. His

81

Cheshire cat smile only grows wider. "Actually, as a little birthday gift," he continues, giving my arm a small tap with his finger. "We thought maybe we could celebrate, all together." His voice dips low. "Revisit some fun times we've had together if you know what I mean."

My skin turns ice cold. My eyes dart to Zachary. I wait for him to intervene, to come to my defense, *something*, but he says nothing and simply snickers.

"Are you fucking serious?" I say incredulously, not even sure who I'm addressing.

"Oh come on," Zachary mumbles, he leans closer, the smell of alcohol on his breath burning up my nose. "Don't be such a prude."

I swallow hard and take a step back as if physically pushed.

"Don't be such a ..." I repeat slowly.

In the span of one harried heartbeat, I snap.

Turning on my heels, I storm through the dining room, ignoring Zachary's loud protest. I fling the kitchen doors open and snub the curious looks as I rush toward the walk-in fridge.

"Prude," I mutter heatedly, opening the door. "I'll show you who's a fucking prude."

Inside the freezer, I feel crazed, looking for Ozzy's stash of Snickers bars. I know I'm fighting fire with fire, that every single thing I'm doing right now is leading up to one monumentally irrational decision. But I don't *fucking* care. Some desperate part of me needs to take back control and this is what my mind has latched onto.

Who am I to deny myself this small sliver of control?

With the chocolate bar in hand, I storm back out and head for the staff bathroom. Locking the door, I spin around and catch my reflection in the mirror. There's a wild look in my eyes, but it doesn't give me pause, it simply spurs me further.

Hiking up my skirt, I pull my thong all the way off and bring a knee up to lean on the sink. Unwrapping the Snickers bar, I barely have a moment of indecision before I bring it between my legs.

Feeling a little less crazed, I slow down and think about what I'm doing.

But I have no plans to stop.

The bar is still frozen, icy against my sensitive skin as I delicately slide it into my pussy. It meets friction, obviously, since I'm not at all turned on. But then the image of Ozzy standing there, a small smirk on his lips as he watches me do such a deviant thing has me letting out a soft gasp.

A small shiver of pleasure skitters up my spine, and it becomes a little easier to push it all the way in, until finally, I pull it all the way back out. A little dazed from the fantasy of Ozzy I'm creating, I let my hand move on its own accord, the frozen tip of the bar circling my clit, then pushing it back into my pussy a second time.

Oh my god.

Heat curls low in my stomach at the sensation, but I manage to snap myself out of it. I bite my bottom lip, trying to calm down my burnt-up senses while I slide the Snickers bar out and place it back into the wrapper.

My breathing is still erratic as I slip my thong back on and fix my skirt. I give myself one last, good long, look in the mirror, before washing my hands and leaving the bathroom. Heading back into the kitchen, my gaze sweeps the area, looking for Ozzy.

He's about to exit into the dining room.

"Hey, salad boy!" My voice travels loudly across the kitchen.

He spins around at the sound of my voice.

"Here," I say, taking his hand and forcefully placing the bar in his palm. "All paid up."

His eyebrows disappear under his blue bandana, shock written clear on his face. I don't even let him respond before stepping out into the dining room, still buzzing with adrenaline.

Walking up to Zachary, I say forcefully. "You need to leave." Both he and Spencer start to laugh, but Zachary's smile drops when he realizes I'm being serious.

"Don't embarrass me," he slowly mouths in warning.

Usually that threat would scare me.

But not tonight.

"I said—*out,*" I hiss, pointing my finger to the door.

"You heard her," I hear Ozzy drawl from behind, coming to stand next to me. He takes a casual bite of the chocolate bar, and for a beat, my mind blanks.

I watch his Adam's apple bob on a swallow.

I can't deny my skin heating up at the very sight.

Ozzy motions the Snickers bar toward the door. "She told you to leave, buddy."

"Who the fuck are *you?*" Zachary says in disdain as he stands up from his seat as if trying to intimidate him even though they're both of similar builds, Zachary only having a few inches over Ozzy.

Ozzy doesn't move an inch. Quietly, he takes another bite of chocolate.

"I work here. You don't, so skedaddle," he finally answers, giving his hand a small flick. He takes a step toward Spencer who is now standing next to Zachary. "Wouldn't want to cause a scene now."

It takes a few seconds for Zachary to finally move, his

eyes darting to mine. "You'll regret this, Jamie," he warns before turning for the door.

After years of these types of threats, I know that it's not an empty one, but tonight I've lost the ability to care.

Spencer gives us one last dirty look before following his friend out. I cross my arms and say nothing as I watch them half stumble out of Orso.

There's a long beat of silence.

And then.

"You taste better than I could've ever dreamed," Ozzy whispers near my ear, his hot breath tickling my skin. "I'll make sure you lose to me more often."

11

JAMES

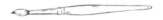

"James Elizabeth Ferdinand, you better wake up right this second."

My head pops up from being buried face-first into the pillow. My eyelids pitifully peel open, dry from drinking till the early morning hours with Michelle and Quinn at Stanley's.

It takes me a few lagging moments to realize whose voice just woke me up.

Until she speaks again.

"James, did you hear me?"

My heart sinks and speeds up in the span of a strangled gasp. I roll over and scamper off the mattress. "Mom? What are you doing here?!" I shriek.

My first reaction is to half-heartedly try to flatten the wrinkles on the silk top I slept in as if that would lessen the curl of disdain on my mother's lip, while she studies my bedroom. She looks painfully out of place here, holding her Givenchy sunglasses limply in her flawlessly manicured hand. Her white palazzo pants and top probably cost more than everything in my bedroom combined.

Last I heard, she was still vacationing in France.

"The strange man you're living with let me in," she answers with a small sneer, still looking around the room. "Why don't you have a bed frame?" she adds appalled.

Although I've been actively complaining about the same thing myself, I struggle not to get defensive.

"Yeah … well," I say as I cross my arms. "Whose fault is that?"

Her green eyes snap back, blonde hair swishing over her shoulders as she shoots me a searing glare.

I hide a small wince.

"We gave you *everything*, James," she whispers heatedly, waving her hand around the room. "And you chose *this*?"

I give her a deliberate eye-roll. "That's a little melodramatic, even for you."

"Funny," she quips, taking a small step back, laughing dryly. Readjusting her Birkin in the crook of her elbow, she pinches her lips, ignoring my slight dig, and says, "Get dressed, we need to get you an outfit for tonight."

My eyebrows dip. "Tonight?"

"It's your birthday isn't it?" she says as if *I'm* the one being ridiculous.

"It was on Thursday, Mom … *three* days ago. You didn't even call me," I say incredulously.

She waves me off. "I was busy planning your party," she responds flatly as if this justifies her complete lack of motherly instincts.

I hold her gaze, narrowing my eyes. "You really expect me to come to that?" I grit. "I haven't even been to the house since I moved out five months ago."

"James, you will not embarrass me in front of our

friends and family. You *will* attend tonight, and that's final. Understood?"

We're at an impasse and we both know it. I chew on my lip while I deliberate, until finally, I let my mother get her way and huff out a *fine* under my breath.

At least I'll be getting a new designer dress out of it.

"Good," she sniffs. Perching her black sunglasses on her nose, she turns for the door. "I'll wait in the car."

———

I ADD one last touch of peach lip gloss to my lips and take a step back to give myself a final check in the full-length mirror. Spending the day shopping with my mother was a special kind of torture but I can't deny that the lavender dress I picked out is gorgeous, hugging my lush hips to perfection, my soft stomach supported by the material yet not hidden. The low neckline could have been a little too risqué for a family event but paired with the ethereal-looking open sleeves, it balances out. Plus, the long leg slit up my right thigh shows off the Valentino chunky heels my mother insisted I get.

I didn't put up much of a fight.

Although, two parts of me now war against each other: The one who's relieved to be back in designer clothes. And the other, who wants to sell the dress and shoes after the party for some extra cash.

I genuinely don't know who will win.

Being back in my old bedroom is another form of torment. It's as if I've become unaccustomed to such decadence. My four-poster bed near the large arched windows feels goading, the pristine walls delightfully decorated in soft pastels have somehow become judgmental.

Everything feels askew, like I shifted dimensions when I moved out. If I squint my eyes, I can almost see the ghost of my past self still haunting these walls. I barely recognize who I used to be. My priorities have drastically changed. What I thought was important—the picture-perfect image I tried so hard to uphold—now feels inconsequential.

Especially as Zachary Benjamin's girlfriend, and future wife, the sole heir of the Garret empire. The social status alone was worth turning a blind eye to his abusive behavior.

Not anymore.

Now, he feels like a rotting corpse I've desperately been trying to pretend isn't putrefied, poisoning everything it touches the longer I try to drag it around my new life.

The thought of being single terrifies me, though. I've always measured my self-worth by everyone else but me. First, I was my parent's daughter. Then, I became Zachary's girlfriend. Who am I without those labels? Who am I when all that's left is me?

But the thought of staying with him is equally terrifying. I know that breaking up with him will lead to an explosive reaction on his part, which leaves my skin clammy and my breath short at the thought—but I know what needs to happen.

I need to end it.

It's hard to explain why my birthday was the breaking point. What was so different from all the other times Zachary has treated me like shit? I just don't believe these types of decisions call for rational thought.

It's about this sense of *knowing*, and finally having the strength to act on it.

Except …

Zachary's been MIA since I told him to leave Orso three days ago.

It's not that unusual for him to ghost me after one of our fights, but the anticipation is killing me. I want out. I have a suspicion he might be here today, for appearance's sake, but I hope that he won't be.

It wouldn't be the right time for the conversation we need to have anyhow.

I can hear the classical music from the live band gently rise up to my second-floor window, accompanied by soft and polite laughter. The party is taking place on the garden grounds, and I'm sure it's a charming and delightful affair if my mother is behind it.

I sigh, knowing I can't avoid the inevitable. Fixing a few flyaways back into my braided updo, I grab my clutch, throw my lipgloss inside, and finally leave the bedroom.

"JAMES, DEAR, THERE YOU ARE," my mother coos, clearly putting on a show for appearance's sake. "You remember the Lanchesters? They were at your cousin Nicky's wedding."

So was every other upper-crust family in this stupid city.

I keep my bitterness to myself and smile sweetly.

"Of course," I answer. "A pleasure to see you again."

The conversation drones on and I keep my smile casually fixed while I pretend to listen. It comes naturally, I've had a lifetime of these events to practice.

Eventually, I find the perfect lull in the conversation to excuse myself, now in dire need of champagne. Walking deeper into the gardens, I take one of the small hedged paths, decorated with low-hanging string lights for the event. It leads to another clearing and I freeze when the first group of people I see is Zachary's parents.

Shit.

His mother, a petite redhead with her statement pearls dripping from her neck and wrists, notices me first. Her face brightens as she waves me over. My blood turns to ice when I realize who has their back turned to me.

The golden boy himself.

"Jamie sweetie, happy birthday," Zachary's mother sing-songs when I approach her, giving me a kiss on each cheek, although her lips never actually come close to my face. "You look gorgeous, is the pink new?"

I flash her a bright smile, pointedly ignoring her son standing beside me. "Thank you, Mrs. Garret—no I've had this color for a while now …" I trail off, my mind reeling from the effort to act so casually, when inside my body has flung itself into fight or flight mode.

"Oh well," she replies with a small wave of the hand, laughing warmly. "It looks great, very … *edgy*." Looking over to her son, his perfectly coiffed blonde hair brushed off his face, she adds, "Don't you agree, Zachary darling?"

"Jamie is a vision as usual, Mother," he drawls, and I finally look over to him. His smirk makes my skin crawl. He wraps his arm around my waist, and tugs me a little too forcefully into his side as he kisses me on the cheek. I freeze up but don't resist it, too well-trained to show any cracks in my mask in front of his parents.

"Anyway, we'll leave you two lovebirds to it. Henry here is hungry," she says with a laugh as if that's the most outlandish thing her husband has ever told her. He huffs out a small grunt but says nothing, clearly used to having his wife do all the chit-chatting.

"Let's talk more later," I say, although I'd rather throw myself into traffic than spend more time with them.

"Of course, of course. You two be good now," she replies while she and Henry walk away.

Waiting for them to be out of earshot, I rip myself out of Zachary's embrace.

"What the hell are you doing here?" I hiss.

"It's my girlfriend's birthday party," he says flatly, looking anywhere but at me while he slides his hands into the pockets of his beige trousers, pompous as ever. "You should have known I'd be here."

Inside, I'm fuming but I keep my voice low. "You've been ignoring my calls for three days."

He slides his unimpressed gaze my way. "So?"

I didn't know I had more anger left to spill. "So?!" I whisper-yell.

Telling him that we're through right then and there is on the tip of my tongue. But Zachary is a loose cannon and the small possibility of him making a scene makes me chew on my words and swallow hard. "I don't have time for you right now."

I try to storm off but Zachary catches the end of my gauzy sleeve and I hear a rip. Surprised by the sound, I look down at my arm. It's a small rip, barely noticeable but it dawns on me then that the old James would have cared about the dress.

But this James doesn't.

All I care about is getting away from Zachary. My gaze slams into his, but I say nothing, pulling myself away from him. I guess there's enough defiance in my eyes that when I turn around and leave, he lets me go without any more of a fight.

I stomp further into the gardens, not really looking

where I'm going until I finally stop near a marble statue of Venus, catching my breath and trying to slow my heartbeat down.

I freeze when I hear someone laugh behind me.

I know that laugh.

"Looks like the princess *does* like keeping secrets after all."

12

OZZY

I'd be laughing a lot more at James' bewildered expression if I wasn't so dumbfounded by the vision of her in that lavender dress. Her soft curves are on full display, and seeing her perfectly manicured feet in those heels makes me want to fall to my knees and crawl.

I crave to do a lot more than gape.

"Ozzy?" Her tone is frazzled as she looks around before taking a small step forward. "What are you doing here?"

Smirking, I wave my hand over the meat carving station in front of me. "Working." She gives me a searing glare, and I snicker. "I pick up catering shifts here and there when I know the money will be good." Now it's my turn to narrow my eyes at her. "Question is: What are *you* doing here, Jimbo?"

Her expression shutters, arms crossing over her chest, pushing her plump tits upwards. After a beat, she reluctantly answers. "This is my party … my family's house."

Holy. Fucking. Shit.

"You're a Ferdinand?" I say slowly, pointing a finger at her almost in accusation.

Her nose wrinkles as if peeved. "How would you even know that?"

"I cater to the rich, remember? Gerald Ferdinand isn't exactly a nobody in this world, princess."

Her arm tightens around herself. "Stop calling me that," she mutters while looking across the gardens. "Anyway, I really don't have time for your shit right now, salad boy."

I follow her gaze until I find the source of her agitation. And *fuck* … I should have guessed. Suddenly, I'm walking away from my station—I'll deal with the repercussions later. I grab James by the arm, dragging her in between two tall hedges nearby.

I crowd her but keep a distance between our bodies when I lean close to her face.

"I thought you would have dumped him by now?" I try to keep the venom for the guy out of my tone but it's hardly working.

Maybe I'm presumptuous but the clues have been there; from her crying in the walk-freezer to the fucking blow-out on her birthday. The dude is total scum and if she needs someone to tell her that, I'll gladly volunteer as tribute.

Her cheeks pinken, a multitude of emotions traveling across her irises until she lands on irritation. Her face hardens. "First of all, that's none of your business," she spits, giving me a hard shove in the chest. I stumble back, but can't help but get a small thrill at her brazenness.

Her face softens a little, her brows knitting, looking down. "And … I will … I just—"

I'm not interested in hearing the rest. Zachary can fucking die for all I care, I won't spend another second talking about that loser when I finally have James alone again.

Like a dog with a bone, I crowd her once again. "Enough about him," I tell her, my hand smoothing over her hip. Her blue eyes snap to mine in surprise. "You know …" I whisper, my mouth now dangerously close to hers, "I still remember how you tasted. I can't stop thinking about it."

Her breath hitches. "Ozzy, we can't——" she mutters in protest.

But I don't let her finish that sentence, tilting my head into the crook of her neck, my hand now trailing down her ass. "I'd crawl on my hands and knees …" Leaning closer, I caress her cheek with the back side of my hand and whisper in her ear, "To have you on my tongue again."

I pull her against me, her hips pressed against my own. Her eyes widen, darting back and forth but this time she doesn't protest. Silence pulses between us—the tension rising, rising, rising … until I crack, catching her lips with mine.

James locks up for only a second before her body lets go and I press her even harder into me. After a few soft quiet moans and a taste of her peach lip gloss, the kiss quickly turns desperate. "We shouldn't be doing this," James whispers feverishly, while her lips still crash into mine, her tongue in my mouth.

I push her a few steps back, slamming her against one of those god-awful statues placed all around the gardens, hopefully far enough from the party so we don't get interrupted. Although, they could all be watching and I'd still do what I'm aching to do. The clinking of glasses and the muted conversations in the air only heighten the thrill of this moment.

I find the slit in her dress with my hand while the other digs into her nape. "Tell me to stop, princess," I say raggedly, my movements becoming more heated and demanding while I hurriedly push her dress up higher. "Tell me you don't want this." Sliding my palm over the fabric of her panties, I add, "Tell me you don't want my fingers inside your cunt, while your piece of shit boyfriend is within earshot."

I give her half a second to respond, but in reality, I don't need it—her answer is in the hitch of her hips. Circling her clit over the fabric with my thumb, I wait for her to speak, her eyes hooded as her hands slide around my neck, pulling me into another kiss while murmuring *don't stop* over and over against my lips.

I tug her thong to the side, finding the wet warmth of her pussy with my fingers and I let out a long groan, catching her bottom lip and biting down roughly. She whimpers while I pin her against the statue. I'm so fucking hard I don't know what to do with myself. "If I could swallow you whole I fucking would, consume all of you just for another taste."

I don't even know what I'm fucking saying, I'm just babbling, my mind feverish and focused solely on hearing James' perfect little mewls.

I push a finger inside her pussy, then another. I pump in and out with aching hunger as she arches her back and moans loudly. Covering her mouth with my hand, I bring my body as close as I can get to hers, my lips to her ear. "Careful princess, you wouldn't want mommy and daddy to find out that their perfect little girl is getting finger fucked by the help."

Feeling her get wetter around my fingers, I smirk, digging my cock into her hip while I lick the column of her throat before nipping at her earlobe. "You like when I talk to you like that, huh James?" I taunt darkly. "You want to be called a filthy little princess, don't you?"

Grinding her clit into the heel of my palm, her body's reaction is answer enough. But then, through my clasped fingers still around her face, she desperately moans, *"Yes, chef."*

My body flares at the sound.

"Don't stop what you're doing," she pleads, her eyes falling closed, her eyebrows pinching in concentration. "Just like that, oh my god, just like that."

Fuck, fuck, fuck.

The things I'd do to feel her tighten around my cock.

Rocking her hips once, and then again, I feel her body shudder against me, muscles tightening, her cunt *squeezing* my fingers. She seems to lose herself to her orgasm and I barely feel deserving enough to witness it.

When she finally relaxes around me, I carefully uncurl my hand from around her mouth. Her lips are still kiss-swollen from earlier, her chest heaving as she watches me with an expression of delightful shock in her darkened gaze.

With my gaze burning into her, I bring my fingers up between our two faces, wordlessly showing her how much of her arousal is still on my fingers before bringing them into my mouth, eager to savor her once again.

The taste of her blooms on my tongue. "Even better than I remembered," I rasp.

Pulling her in for one last kiss, I then step back and flash her a quick grin. "You better go freshen up before rejoining the party, sweetheart. You wouldn't want your boyfriend to see you freshly fucked."

I might not know much, but I *do* know her asshole boyfriend never made her feel like I just did.

13

JAMES

Ozzy has been gone for several minutes but I'm still standing here, against the statue, feeling like I've been living my whole life without my five senses. And having Ozzy touch me like he just did suddenly restored them. He might have gifted me with a sixth sense with how hard he just made me come. Zachary never made me feel like that—*ever*.

What the fuck *was* that?

Was it the sneaking around that made it so hot? The lingering shame attached to the whole exchange fueling my climax like gas to an already burning flame?

Or was it simply Ozzy? Tapping into a debased part of myself I didn't know even existed. That linked with the unspoken knowledge that if I wanted him to stop, he would have stopped.

I held the power. And that makes me feel ... invincible.

Like I could take on anything and come out the victor.

There's only one thing I want to do while this sentiment lasts.

Finally shaking myself out of my stupor, I pick up my clutch from where I let it fall to the ground and take my phone out. Opening my camera in selfie mode, I quickly fix my makeup and hair before putting on a fresh coat of lip gloss. When I deem myself acceptable enough to rejoin the party, I walk out from inside the little recess Ozzy pushed us in.

Needing to pass his station to get to Zachary, I keep my shoulders straight, my gait assured while I saunter across his path. My eyes can't help but slide his way, and I find him already staring back, a cocky grin fixed on his face while busy serving a party-goer.

I'll be honest. I don't hate how his gaze makes me feel. Not at all. But he's also not the reason I'm breaking up with Zachary. Maybe our little tryst was a needed catalyst for me to gather enough courage to finally do it. But one thing I learned after moving out and living on my own was this: I'm done with the world where the decisions are made for me.

Zachary is the last tether I need to cut to free myself from this world. I need to end it before it's too late. Although that rusty link to my former self feels embedded in my skin, I tell myself I can do this. No matter how much it'll hurt, the relief will be tenfold.

I spot Zachary near the stage, the band now crooning some smooth jazz. When his smug gaze flicks to mine, his lips purse and I can barely stand looking at him.

How I ever found him charismatic is beyond me.

I pull him by the crook of his arm, but he doesn't budge. A searing blade of white-hot rage impales itself through my chest and it takes heroic effort not to snap at him in front of everyone here.

"We need to talk," I growl low. "And I don't think you want to hear what I've got to say in such a *public* setting."

Zachary's eyes turn hard. I know he's not above making a scene. But here, with both our parents witnessing it—well, that's another matter entirely. He has an image to maintain after all. I'm the only one *lucky* enough to experience the real him. The only one who could paint an accurate picture of who he really is with the years' worth of emotional wounds I've been forced to carry since we started dating.

Finally, his lips twist into a sarcastic smile, tugging his arm away from my hand while his stare turns vicious. "Lead the way, *honey.*"

For a moment, I can't move. Years of insidious abuse has me rooted to the spot, questioning if I can do this when I can already feel his violent words tearing my skin open.

I'd crawl on my hands and knees to have you on my tongue again.

Ozzy's heated declaration floats back to me, reminding me that words can act like a healing balm. That words don't need to hurt. They can glide over my skin, making me shudder with pleasure instead.

With that small flash of reinforcement bursting in my chest, I lead Zachary into the house and up to my bedroom. Carefully closing the door behind us, I swiftly turn around, finding him standing in the middle of the room like a raging bull ready to charge.

"We're done," I declare calmly, even though I can feel my heart slamming against my chest.

Zachary laughs dryly, looking up at the ceiling, then back at me. "What? You start working at that little restaurant of yours and you suddenly grow a backbone? Are you so desperate to fit in with your new working-class friends that you want to break up with your rich boyfriend now? Is that it?"

I'm unsure how to respond to his bizarre accusation. Already too exhausted to justify what he just said with a retort, I decide to just agree with him.

"Something like that."

His face falls. There's a beat of silence so loaded I can feel it pulsing against me.

Zachary moves so fast I barely have time to process what he's done until the entire content of my vanity crashes to the floor.

The silence returns.

I stare at the floor. I don't react to his sudden flare of anger. His behavior usually scares me.

Not today.

No.

Today his actions feel childish.

My eyes are locked on the remnant shards of my Baccarat Rouge bottle. The perfume lingers between us, smelling like loss, instead of tea and jasmine.

"That bottle cost four hundred dollars," I mutter as if any of it matters.

Hearing his footsteps, I snap my gaze back up. My mind is screaming for my limbs to move but they don't. I stay planted near the door while Zachary rushes up to me. His face is inches away from mine.

"Do you really think I *care* if we break up?" Spittle lands on my cheek but I don't move a muscle. "You're worthless without me. *I'm* the one who still has money, family connections, a *proper* education." His eyes turn even harder, and I start to shake. "And what do you have? Huh? Your fucking *paints*? Your silly job at the restaurant?" His mouth stretches into a leery smile. I suddenly feel nauseous, my heart pumping noxious adrenaline into my veins. "The only reason I was still with you was for your family connections.

If I wanted to sleep with the help, I'd already have that covered since I've been fucking Marguerite for months now."

My eyebrows furrow. "Marguerite?"

"That blue-haired bartender from Stanley's, you *stupid* bitch."

My blinks are slow while I let his confession sink in. It shouldn't hurt this much but my insides bleed nonetheless.

"What?" I whisper. "When did it—how did you even …" I can't finish my sentence. Every question feels suddenly trivial to the overarching fact that he's been cheating on me. And as if reading my mind he answers the question I was too scared to ask.

Taking a few steps back, he tugs on his sleeves, and straightens his tie before saying, "She was hardly the first."

At that, I regain my voice, boiling ire splitting me in half. I grasp at the first thing I know will hurt him. I'm like a dying animal trying to maim before receiving the fatal blow.

Trying to send him an equally disturbing smile, I straighten my spine. "Well, I guess that makes the two of us then. Although … my indiscretion was a little bit more recent than yours, I'd say …" I look at my wrist as if I have a watch. "Half an hour ago? And at least with him, I didn't have to fake it."

I'm shaking, a part of me is still terrified of him, but I carefully keep my expression bored while I wait for his reaction.

His face twists in disgust, nostrils flaring. "I always knew you were a fucking slut," he says slowly but savagely. "You letting Spencer fuck you at Carson's toga party should have been evidence enough."

I take a step back as if struck, hitting the door behind

me. My mind grows hazy like I'm slipping into an abysmal spiral full of jagged edges and broken shards.

Did he just …

"Let?" Angry tears well up in my eyes as my voice grows higher and higher as I speak. "I didn't *let* Spencer do anything. I was *passed out*, you fucking monster."

It's my turn to charge him, shoving him hard in the chest. The tears spill but I continue, suddenly desperate for the words to exist outside of me, instead of rotting, festering inside of my body. "I was fucking passed out!" I scream. "And you just watched as your best friend *raped* me." I shove him again. "You did fucking nothing to stop him!"

He's laughing. He's fucking laughing, and I feel like I'm dying.

"If you say so, Jamie," he spits, pushing me hard enough for me to fall backward, landing on the floor close to the bed. "That may be true but no one would believe you."

I watch him storm out of the bedroom, slamming the door behind him.

The silence hurts and I feel the sharp claws of hysteria start to dig their way into my brain.

The sobs that eventually follow wreak havoc through my body, painful and distressing. Picking myself up, I lock my door, and undress in a fit of rage, practically ripping my dress off, and end up on the shower floor weeping for the next hour.

The pain flowing out of me is ever-expanding, I never seem to reach the end, even after I've calmed down into a state of emotional stupor. It just throbs under my skin, every beat of my heart reminding me how much it hurts to be alive.

14

JAMES

It's after midnight. I can hear the party winding down from my bedroom window, people still linger in handfuls around the garden, wine-drunk and mouths full of gossip.

As expected, even if this was technically my party, no one came to look for me.

But this time I'm grateful for the lack of interest.

My thoughts are slow. They feel like they're caught in a giant vat of petroleum jelly, everything sticks and drags, sticks and drags. I'm tapped out, emotionally eviscerated. My sobs turned into sniffles about an hour ago, I've been staring at the mess Zachary made on the floor ever since.

I should clean that up.

The only place I've ever seen a broom in this house is the utility closet near the kitchen. I roll my eyes, and huff. That's downstairs. I have a fleeting thought that Zachary might still be somewhere around, but knowing him he most likely left after our fight.

It takes me another minute to get myself to stand up from the edge of my bed.

I walk out of my bedroom in a sage green sweatsuit set, my hair pulled into a bun and no makeup. Maybe old James would bother to still look put together for strangers in her own home, but I no longer care. I also don't give two shits if it would embarrass my mother.

What's she going to do? Kick me out?

I've already left.

The marble tiles are cool under my bare feet as I walk through the wide hallway connecting the foyer to the kitchen. My steps stutter to a stop when I notice someone leaning over the double sinks, their back to me. My eyes roam over their shoulders, their arms with the sleeves rolled up to their elbows, and a shock of curly hair.

"What are you doing here?" I blurt out while I simultaneously consider pulling a one-eighty and leaving before he notices me. I guess my mouth made the decision for me.

Ozzy's head tilts to the side, turning off the tap before swinging around.

His chef jacket is half-unbuttoned, his trusty navy blue bandana keeping his curly hair out of his eyes, and I've never seen a man be so effortlessly hot. His smirk dimples his left cheek while he grabs his rag from over his shoulder to dry off his hands, but it fades quickly from his lips.

Eyebrows dipping low, worry carves a divot between them. "Are you okay, Jimbo?"

Hearing the playful nickname, which originally sounded grating, now soothes something inside of me and the irrational urge to burst out crying battles with my need to save face.

My first reflex is to lie.

I'm fine. Everything is fine.

But watching Ozzy's ocean eyes convey such genuine concern towards me makes a wall crumble somewhere inside of me, and I shake my head, bottom lip shaking.

I lift my eyes up to the ceiling and take a large breath in and then out, refusing to let one single tear drop past my eyelashes. When I've managed to collect myself—minimally—my gaze falls back to where he's standing.

"Do you want to talk about it?" he asks carefully.

Heading for one of the cushioned bar stools placed around the kitchen island, I sit down and sink my chin into my open palm. "Not really no."

His face softens and a small smile returns. "Okay well …" he says while scratching his head as if thinking. "Are you hungry? I can make you something."

I've been starving for hours. I just couldn't bring myself to leave my room. I don't tell him that, instead I repeat, "Ozzy, what are you doing in my kitchen?"

He chuckles, leaning against the sink behind him, crossing his arms in a casual stance. "I'm working this shindig, remember? The rest of the guys are packing up the van, I'm just cleaning up the kitchen."

I guess it makes sense. I nod, head still perched in my hand, but don't bother answering.

He tilts his head, one brow raised. "So, princess?"

"What," I mumble.

"Are you hungry?"

"You don't need to do that," I answer flatly.

"Do what?"

"Feed me."

His tongue swipes over the small scar on his bottom lip, then he pushes that same tongue into his cheek. "What if that's exactly what I *want* to do?"

I'm suddenly, and all-consumingly, reminded that I

know first-hand how his tongue feels trailing up the side of my neck. I clear my throat, shifting in my seat and the cocky glint in his eyes tells me he knows exactly where my mind just went.

"I just meant it's not your job to cater to me."

Ozzy bursts out laughing as if what I just said was pure nonsense. "You think I offer to cook for any random girl, minutes before the end of my shift?" His gaze dances over my face. "Just answer the goddamn question, James." Then his voice drops. "Are. You. Hungry."

Straightening in my seat, I let my hand drop from where it was cradling my chin. A beat passes while he continues to stare at me. His expression is now soft but serious.

Finally, I slowly nod. "I'm starving, actually."

Looking relieved, he heads for the fridge. "I hope you're giving me permission to go through your fridge 'cause that's technically against the rules," he says playfully.

I laugh. "Yeah, of course. Knock yourself out."

With both hands placed on the open double doors, he turns to look at me and gives me a quick wink. Then, his face falls studious while he takes in the contents of the fridge.

"Quesadilla?" he asks, his head disappearing behind the doors.

My stomach growls at the thought. "Sure."

"I'll make them nice and good for you," he says with a wide grin, eyes sparkling as if genuinely excited to be cooking for me.

I smile back, ignoring the resulting thrill tickling low in my stomach at the sight of him looking like that.

Bringing the ingredients over to the island, he stands facing me.

With his head down, busy grating the cheese, he makes conversation. "So what's your story outside of Orso, sweetheart?" His eyes flit up to mine. "Why so squirrelly about coming from money?"

I want to lie, to pretend I wasn't hiding my past just to fit in, but it all feels just too exhausting so I lead with the truth.

"I just didn't think it mattered anymore." I shrug. "My father found out I switched majors last year." I roll my eyes. "Said he would only continue to pay for my tuition if I switched back to economics."

"I'm guessing you didn't?" Ozzy asks from over his shoulder while adding butter to the hot pan on the stove.

"I didn't," I answer with a small victorious smile. "Moved out the same day … that was five months ago."

Turning back to face me, he watches me with an expression I can't quite place. "Good for you," he says, smiling. Sprinkling some shredded cheese directly onto the pan, he then folds the tortillas in half, and places them into the now sizzling pan.

"Thank you." Picking at my nails, I add, "It's been … hard."

He laughs but it's not quite teasing. "I'm sure." Flattening the quesadillas with a spatula, he asks, "So what was the major worth giving all of this up for?"

Swiveling around, he leans on the counter beside the stove, waiting for my answer.

"Fine arts. I'm a painter."

His eyebrows jump up but he quickly schools his expression.

I burst out laughing. "Was that … shock, salad boy?"

He snickers as if caught, rubbing his hand over his chin. "I just wasn't expecting that, I guess."

While he flips the tortillas over, I tease him some more. "Isn't that a tale as old as time? Spoiled rich kid gives up everything to follow their artistic passion?"

"Touché," he responds with mirth. "You see that?" he says, referring to the quesadillas, "See how the shredded cheese is now the perfect crunchy crust? You're gonna love it."

"That sounds amazing," I answer genuinely, perking up. I'm salivating at the thought … but there's also something quite touching about watching him put so much care into such a simple thing as feeding me a late-night snack. But it's not just that. The conversation itself feels like a balm. It's effortless and easy-going, and Ozzy seems genuinely interested in what I have to say.

Those small, innocent moments are not lost on someone like me.

Someone so used to words like *hard* and *complicated*.

When the cheese is properly melted, he slides the plate of quesadillas across the island, handing me a fork and knife.

"Thank you …" I stare down at the food before catching his eye. "This was really nice of you."

He gives me a small nod, his gaze warm. "Careful not to burn your tongue, princess," he says while wiping his hands on the rag still over his shoulder. Then, his cocksure smile widens. "I'm pretty fond of it."

I snort a laugh, followed shortly by a hum of delight, my mouth now full of melted cheese, which only makes his smile even brighter. Looking at the time on his phone, his gaze glides back to where I'm sitting and he gives me an apologetic press of his lips. "Anyway, I need to go find the guys, the van is leaving soon."

"Okay, no worries," I answer quickly, a twinge of disappointment squeezing my heart. "I'll uh—I'll see you at work."

He pauses. "Where's your phone?"

"Upstairs."

He shoots me a quick eye roll as if I'm inconveniencing him. Then pushes his phone over to me, his screen open to his contacts but doesn't say anything.

I let out a small teasing laugh. "Is this your way of asking for my phone number?"

"Something like that," he answers with a shrug, trying to look casual but his eyes glimmer roguishly.

Trying not to overthink it, I add my number to his phone and give it back. He pockets it with a smile. Turning serious, he asks, "You sure you'll be okay tonight?"

I give him an assured nod and wave him off.

He mirrors my nod and sends me a quick salute. "See you soon, sweetheart."

15

OZZY

It's Monday, which means it's my only day off—simply because Orso is closed on Mondays. I should still be sleeping but I'm awake at the ass crack of dawn sitting on my balcony sipping a cup of coffee and smoking a cigarette.

It overlooks the parking lot of the fried chicken joint downstairs. At first, I'd liked the idea of living on top of a restaurant, until I realized my entire apartment would smell like fried chicken all the time.

Not a fan of it anymore.

I plan on driving over to the house to see Sophia and Charlie. I usually don't bother checking up on them this early in the morning but after my dad's most recent bender, I've been keeping a closer eye on their general welfare.

Huxley, as per usual, continues to disappear on me. I haven't seen him since I paid him to stay with the kids for a few days. As soon as our dad was back and, somewhat, on top of things, he was gone again.

I toy with my phone in my lap, taking a long drag. My fingers itch to pull up James' phone number and text her. It hasn't even been twelve hours since I left her alone in her parent's kitchen. By the distraught expression that she kept trying to hide from me I'm selfishly, and hopefully, assuming she dumped her piece of shit boyfriend.

She wouldn't have given me her number if she hadn't.

But she wasn't exactly single when we hooked up earlier that night either.

Fuck. Maybe I should have pried more.

But as I sip my now tepid coffee, and recall the way her body felt against mine, how her pussy drenched my fingers —and well … maybe I don't necessarily care either way, as long as she lets me touch her like that again.

Fuck it.

Caving, I snap a quick picture of my coffee and cigarette and type out a quick text.

> **Good morning, sweetheart.**

Sweetheart? No, maybe just princess.

No. That doesn't feel right either.

Jesus fucking Christ, Oz, get it together, you dipshit.

I settle for something safer.

> **Morning, Jimbo.**

I promptly send the text along with the picture before the need to throw my phone over the balcony overtakes me.

"Ozzy!"

Charlie is jumping on the ratty couch still in his faded pjs when I walk in. Morning cartoons blare on the TV as he flashes me a toothy grin but doesn't stop what he's doing.

"Hey, buddy," I say, turning the volume down. "You sleep okay?"

His smile fades, abruptly stopping his jumps mid-air, landing on an askew cushion with a pout. I guess the ear-piercing volume of the TV was an important factor in whatever he was up to. "Yeah," he says with a shrug, jumping off the couch, seemingly already moving on to something else.

When he scampers down the hallway, I yell, "Great talk!"

A muffled laugh from somewhere in the house is answer enough. In the kitchen, I start unloading the bag of groceries I brought with me into the fridge.

"You're doing it again," I hear Sophia say behind me.

"Doing what, miss Soph?" My tone is innocent but I already know what she's about to say as I put the last of the food in before facing her.

"Hovering," she says with a yawn, grabbing a glass from the cupboard. "You're like the big brother version of a heli-copter mom."

I scoff. "Thanks." Giving her a small shove to the shoulder.

She laughs, pouring orange juice into her glass before sitting down at the table.

"Dad's been better, I swear. He even managed to get his job back at the factory."

"Good for him," I mutter, swallowing the insults trying to fly out of my mouth. Instead, I ask, "Where is he now?"

"Sleeping." She takes another sip of juice. "Nightshift."

My phone buzzes in my pocket, and my stomach flips

but I keep my face neutral, resisting the urge to whip it out immediately.

It's probably just Alec or something. Chill the fuck out.

"Anyway, I'll make you and Charlie a breakfast sandwich. You still going through your anti-tomatoes in sandwiches phase?" I ask.

She wrinkles her nose and nods.

I snicker. "Alright, they'll be ready in fifteen."

My thumb taps against the steering wheel to the beat of the music while still parked outside of the house. My eyes dart down to the middle console. I take my phone out from the cupholder as casually as possible, as if I wasn't counting down the seconds until I could text James back in peace.

I unlock my phone and try to suppress the stupid grin fighting for dominance on my face when I find a reciprocated picture attached to her response. A pink mug with a book flipped upside down on a table.

Morning :)

Followed by a sun emoji.

She had programmed her name as James in my phone but I promptly changed it to Jimbo when I left her parent's kitchen last night.

I tilt my head, trying to make out the book title she's reading. Looks like some kind of art book. I file that information away for later. It's a subtle type of desperation I feel … like I need to absorb every little detail from her life that I possibly can.

Knowing she's also not working today since Orso is closed, I decide to shoot my shot.

> I was thinking of heading to the farmer's market this morning. Want to come?

My heart is beating loudly in my ears as if I'm being hunted for sport and not just fucking sitting in my parked car while I wait for her answer. The bubble indicating she's typing appears, disappears, then reappears again, and I start to sweat.

> Sure! Should I meet you there?

Relieved, I still scoff at her question. "Should I meet you there," I mumble under my breath while I type.

> Of course not, princess. I'll come pick you up. Are you still at your parents?

> Haha, okay thanks! No, I took a cab home last night.

She gives me her address and I pop it into my maps app, shifting into drive. The giddy feeling follows me all the way there.

MY EXCITEMENT TURNS to unadulterated lust when I see James come out of her apartment complex. Her long white skirt trails behind her as she bounds down the path toward my parked car. She's paired it with a barely-there tank top, her hair plaited into two braids, loose pink hair framing her round face.

She's almost reached the car when I realize that maybe I should get out and open the door for her, so I quit my gawking and scamper out the car.

"Hey there, Jimbo," I manage to rasp out while holding the passenger car open. When her peach scent reaches my nose, I practically short-circuit.

Her eyebrows rise but says nothing while climbing in.

"What?" I ask, leaning down to meet her eye. My laugh is too nervous for my liking but I continue to pretend I'm as confident as I appear.

"Nothing," she answers with a similar laugh. Toying with her knitted purse resting on her lap, she adds, "I'm just a little wary of the gentleman act, I guess."

There are so many layers to her answer that I fail to come up with a snarky response. But I refuse to have memories of her shitty boyfriend ruin the moment. So, I lean deeper into the car. I gently raise her chin, my thumb softly stroking her jaw as our lips meet. The kiss is chaste, a slow press of our lips, a simple reminder of who she's with right now.

Me. Not him. *Me.*

When I feel her kiss turn eager, I purposefully pull away, if only to leave her unsatiated and craving more.

"You look delectable," I whisper low, my thumb trailing one last path over her cheek before straightening back up. Her eyes are pinned to mine, her mouth slightly agape, looking like she's still stuck somewhere in the recent past, kissing me. I smile, and head back to the driver's seat, suddenly feeling a lot more self-assured than five minutes ago.

"Why does it feel like everyone knows you here?" James asks, ten minutes into our aimless walk around the farmer's market.

"I used to work here back when I was a teenager, the vendors haven't really changed since then."

"Really?" she says as if not expecting that answer.

I laugh. "Why so surprised?"

"I don't know," she says, her tone light while picking up some organic honey and inspecting the jar. "I guess, I just pictured you a little bit more …"

"Delinquent?"

She turns around, her mouth falling open in amused shock. "That's not what I meant."

"Who says I can't be both, princess?" I ask, chuckling while I avoid her playful shove.

"If you say so," she replies, her eyes full of mirth as she moves onto another stall. I follow, happy to just be here with her—somewhere outside of Orso where we can have an uninterrupted conversation.

I could spend the day simply following her around and still ask for more.

But then I remember.

And my smile falls.

I need to know.

"So … what happened yesterday?"

I pick up a random cucumber and pretend to inspect it, hoping my question wasn't too intrusive. I can't see her expression, but she falls silent behind me until finally, she says softly, "We broke up. It's over."

I feel an evil desire to smile but hell … that loser never deserved her to begin with.

It's not to say that I'm the one who deserves her, but at least now I can soak up *all of her* while the fun lasts.

She's mine—until she finds someone more deserving.

Trying to fix my face as best I can, I turn around to look at her. When I realize I'm still holding the cucumber I quickly throw it back where it belongs.

I almost say *I'm sorry*. But I'm not. So I settle for, "Are you okay?" I reach for her hand but drop my arm before I even make contact, not quite knowing what to do.

Her lips press together and she gives the smallest of shrugs. "I will be?" Her voice quivers and I immediately regret even bringing it up.

My mind scrambles for something reassuring to say. "Have you ever had stroopwafels? There's a booth some-where around here that's famous for them," I blurt out.

Idiot.

James' gaze softens and she laughs. "I don't think I have, no."

"Well," I say, holding out my elbow for her to take. "You're in for a treat, Jimbo."

With our stroopwafels in one hand, and coffees in the other we find an empty picnic table near a flower stand and sit. My nerves slowly wane as I watch her enjoy her snack, noticing how relaxed she looks compared to last night. A small, selfish part of me hopes I have something to do with that. And that same selfishness hopes I can continue making her feel this way.

Because something about James just feels … *right.*

16

JAMES

It's been almost a week since the farmer's market, and although Ozzy and I haven't had the chance to see each other outside of work again, Orso has become a flirty playground for us. Ozzy managing to find me in dark, hidden corners every chance he gets.

It's a slow Sunday night when I flounce down the stairs into the basement of Orso. The bar was out of Rioja so I offered to run down and grab it from the booze room.

My feet have barely hit the bottom step when I hear another pair of feet clamber down after me. Whipping around, I barely have time to register Ozzy before he takes my hand and drags me into the unlocked keg room.

He pushes my back against the cold brick wall, his name leaving my lips in a shocked whisper. Without a word, he buries his face in the crook of my neck and takes a large inhale. I break out in goosebumps, his hands roaming over my hips heightening the sensation. He lets out a long, hungry hum; the vibration dancing over my skin.

"All I want is to consume every little piece of you until

there's nothing left but the taste of you on my tongue," he says, *much* too seriously.

I giggle. "You're so weird," I say, a little breathless, giving him a playful tap on the shoulder. Still, I tilt my head to the side to give him more space for the kisses he's now peppering all over my throat. Molten heat spikes low in my stomach. The thrill of seeing Ozzy this undone is undeniably sexy.

"Oh, princess," he growls, his mouth finding a path up to my jaw. "You don't know how *weird* I can get."

Catching my bottom lip with his teeth, he tugs on it hard while he presses his hips into mine. For a few blissful seconds, while his mouth is on mine, I forget where we are —forget why I was down here in the first place. His hands find my breasts, squeezing and groping hungrily over my black satin shirt. I moan softly and the sound spurs him on.

When his tongue in my mouth starts to feel like me wanting to fall to my knees and do a lot more than just kiss, I manage to come back to my senses and break away. The flush on his cheeks makes my stomach dip but the petulant look he gives me while still trying to hold on to me has me snickering.

"I need to get back," I say playfully, shooing him away. "And you probably do too."

He presses his lips together, straightening his shoulders and closing his eyes as if collecting himself. Smoothing his tattooed hand over his face, his gaze snaps back to mine. "Just you wait 'till I get my hands on you again," he declares, giving me a head-to-toe stare while slowly walking backward before exiting the keg room. A thrilling shiver skitters down my spine, every fiber of my body now anticipating what will come next.

ABOUT AN HOUR LATER, Michelle and I are leaning against the service bar as subtly as we can, waiting for our tables to need us. It's a slow night. I put my weight on one foot, idly tapping the tip of my toes on the floor with the other. Now that Ozzy and I are … whatever this is, I have trouble focusing on anything but that.

As usual, my attention is on the kitchen, staring at Ozzy who's milling around close to the pass, his crystalline eyes fixed on me while talking to Itzel beside him.

"Wait," Michelle says slowly, following my gaze, then back at me.

My attention snaps back to her, now sporting a wide-open smile on her face.

"Is something going on between you and Ozzy?" she asks, low and conspiratorial.

"What? No." My voice is much too high for her to believe my lousy lie.

"Please." She laughs. "You wouldn't be the first one to fall for his cocky bad boy bit. It's a rite of passage really."

I know she doesn't mean it maliciously, and I'm not the one to care about someone's sexual history but something about her comment still stings. My mind drifts back to when the hostess warned me about the kitchen staff—*especially that slut Ozzy.*

My mood sours. Maybe this is a mistake.

"Have you?" I blurt out.

Michell looks at me like I'm an idiot. "Gay, remember?"

"Right," I say, shaking my head. "Duh."

She shoots me a sly smile. Since she already knows about the break-up between me and Zachary, she says,

"Maybe fucking a slutty line cook is exactly what you need." She snickers, waggling her fingers at me. "What's that expression again? The best way to get over someone is to get under someone else?"

I burst out laughing, but don't bother correcting her.

In truth, breaking up with Zachary was a relief.

As if I was finally able to take a proper breath for the first time in over three years.

Only … well.

That isn't why the hallowed sadness lingers …

It's because of the festering wound that I'm still trying to avoid.

The one Zachary and Spencer created six months ago.

At least I gave it a name the night we broke up. I allowed it space to grow, but like vines squeezing my lungs too tightly, it threatens to choke me to death if I don't do something about it soon.

How do I move past this?

Hell, I can't even say the word.

As if the word itself will slice my tongue like a too-sharp blade, and I will bleed and bleed and bleed until my veins dry out and I turn to dust.

I'm not even sure I can heal from it …

How do I stop it from becoming a part of me forever?

The kitchen bell dings, ripping me out of my demoralizing thoughts, and I jump into action, delivering hot plates to my table while I try to avoid the angst sticking to my clothes like cheap perfume.

"STILL COMING with us to Stanley's?" Michelle asks while she grabs her bag out from the locker.

I nod eagerly, stepping out of my work skirt. "I just need to change."

"Great! I'll wait for you out back," she says with a wide smile before she disappears down the hall.

When I first started working at Orso, over a month ago, I was surprised to find out how much the majority of the staff would party on any given day, considering most of us worked, on average, six days a week.

But I quickly learned that letting off steam after a grueling shift was necessary if not mandatory. My coworkers have become friends in a short amount of time. We trauma dump, our version of small talk, between punching orders. And like soldiers, we celebrate surviving another shift by swapping war stories over copious amounts of alcohol.

And the next day, we do it all over again.

Tonight's no different.

Admittedly, I've been a little apprehensive about going to Stanley's after discovering Zachary was cheating on me with Marguerite. She's not the one who bothers me, it's the possibility of seeing my ex there that irks me. But I decided to overcome the unease.

Stanley's is *my* skeezy little bar. And he can't have it.

After I'm done changing, I meet up with Michelle outside and wait for the rest of the crew to join us.

My stomach does a little flip when I see Ozzy in street clothes again, strutting out into the Orso back parking lot, lighting a cigarette as soon as the door is closed behind him.

He's wearing another one of his cropped band tees, a few inches of stomach showing, just long enough to cover his belly button while his black jeans ride low on his hips. The jangle of his keys clipped to his belt loop is becoming Pavlovian, I salivate at the sound.

"Ready, Jimbo?" His tone is a lot less loaded now that we're surrounded by the rest of the staff who are joining us.

I can feel Michelle staring at me, but I force myself not to look directly at her as I give Ozzy a quick nod. I catch him wanting to put his arm around my shoulders but he stops himself at the last second.

I pretend not to notice.

When we get to Stanley's, I spend most of my time talking to Michelle at the bar, while Ozzy plays a game of pool with Alec. Eventually, Michelle dips outside for a cigarette with Gustavo, and as soon as she leaves, I feel a body slide close to mine.

"Do you like to party?" Ozzy says close to my ear.

I turn around to face him and smile. "I thought that's what we were already doing."

"No." He chuckles low, looking me hungrily up and down. "I meant …" he trails off, giving his nose two taps with his index finger.

"Oh!" *God, I'm an idiot.* "Um—"

"What do you say, princess, want to be a bad girl tonight? Really give mommy and daddy something to throw a fit about."

I stay silent for a beat before answering. I've been offered coke before but never did I have the urge to try. There's something about sneaking around and sharing something illicit with Ozzy that gives me a thrill I can't really name. "Why not?" I try to sound as nonchalant as possible as I give him a little wave of the hand meant to say: Lead the way.

His grin turns wicked and I swallow hard.

He takes my hand and brings it up to his mouth while he keeps his darkening gaze fixed on me. Pressing his lips gently on my knuckles, he then covers my hand with his. "Follow me."

He leads me into the back of the bar, pushing a door open that has an *employees only* sign nailed on it.

"Wait," I say, trying to pull out of his grasp. "We're not supposed to go in there."

He laughs. "C'mon, Jimbo. Live a little." He tightens his grip and I have no choice but to follow. He makes one left turn into a small hallway before opening a door to a private restroom.

"Do I even want to know how you know about this bathroom?" I ask, crossing my arms in faux-attitude.

"What can I say," he says with a wink, closing the door and then locking it. "I have friends in high places."

I give him an eye roll but can't hide my smile. "Sure you do."

Slowly crowding me, he pushes me into the sink, trapping me in between his arms. "Jealous are we, James?"

I scoff in disbelief. "Not at all."

Taking my chin in his hand, he smooths his thumb across my bottom lip. "I like you jealous."

My eyes flit back and forth, suddenly finding it hard to catch my breath. "Oh?"

I'm not sure what else to say.

His grin is crooked but he stays silent, his thumb now caressing my cheek. Stepping away, he breaks the tension rising between us.

"Is this your first time, Jimbo?" Ozzy asks while he fishes a small bag from his front pocket.

There's no judgment in his tone so I nod my head without any awkward embarrassment.

"What does it feel like?" I ask hesitantly.

He shoots me a playful look. His smile is almost coy. "Nervous?"

I give him a quick shrug but don't say anything. His heated gaze lingers on me until he looks down, digging one of his keys into the bag. Bringing a small mound up to his mouth, he places it on his tongue. His eyes flit back to mine as he reaches for me, pulling me into a kiss.

There's a slight bitter taste on his tongue as it finds mine, and a small jolt of adrenaline rushes through my body knowing what exactly I'm tasting. His hand snakes to the back of my head, deepening the kiss, a groan tumbling out of his mouth. I don't have time to melt into him before he pulls away, pinning me with a smoldering stare.

"Just follow my lead, okay?" he says, his voice gravelly.

I nod, my gaze now locked on his actions.

Digging the key back into the bag, he brings it up to his right nostril and takes a quick hard sniff. Pinching his nose, he takes another few sniffs and clears his throat.

The fiery look he gives me has all kinds of unspoken words attached to it, and that same tingle zips through me.

Digging his key in the bag again, he holds it towards me. "Ready?"

I nod assuredly. Easy. I can do this. Leaning forward, I mimic what he just did.

The taste hits the back of my throat immediately. It's acrid and bitter and it makes me want to wash it down with another gin and tonic.

I swallow hard, watching Ozzy expectantly, not really knowing what to anticipate.

"Give it a second," he says, his pupils already blown wide. Clipping his keys back on his jeans, he stuffs the bag back in his pocket, his eyes then bouncing to mine. With two quick strides, he pulls me away from the sink and presses me against the wall, kissing me with ardor, sliding his hands up my waist and over my breast. "I can't *fucking* wait to have my way with you," he says, his voice intense and low.

His declaration happens to coincide with the drugs finally hitting my system and a wave of euphoric bliss washes over me like a warm wave. I've never felt anything quite like it—like everything and anything is possible. My head falls back, eyes closing and I suddenly want nothing else but Ozzy to do just that.

"Why don't you?" I rasp, my heart pounding in my chest. My mind feels on fire, my thoughts like lightning in a jar.

I can feel his erection pressing against my thigh, and I'm desperate. So fucking desperate.

But when he hums a no, my brows furrow, and he pulls away once again. His gaze is devious but his tone is serious when he says, "I want you good and sober, the first time we fuck. I want you to remember in vivid detail how I make you scream."

I wasn't expecting him to say that. His words touch a part of me that is much too raw to acknowledge. I don't know what my expression looks like but his face softens and he gives me his hand. "Let's go get a shot, yeah?"

Something about just being around Ozzy, even simply looking at him, relieves some of the ache in my chest. I laugh, trying to snap myself out of it. "Absolutely," I say as I open the bathroom door and lead us out.

Stepping back into the main room, time passes. It might be half an hour. It might be two hours. I can't tell. Time is inconsequential. High off powder up my nose and impassioned kisses shared in secret. Conversation shouted over loud music. Rounds of drinks. Laughter. Camaraderie. Gidiness. Feeling alive. So alive.

And Ozzy.

Ozzy.

Ozzy.

Ozzy.

His smile. Lips. Hands. His words. Stories. His eyes. Watching. Always watching.

I feel so alive.

So ali—

The fall from bliss is a painful and sudden one.

Zachary is looking at me from across the bar. And suddenly the world around me feels bleak. The sounds too loud. My mind too hazy.

His arm is around Marguerite. She's not working tonight. And the smug look on his face tells me he came here to hurt.

He's right.

It does hurt.

But it's not because he's here with her.

He's just an abject reminder. A big red flashing arrow pointing to all the reasons I should have left him earlier. I'm trying desperately not to blame myself for staying.

The memories are penance enough.

I hear Ozzy close by. "You good?"

"I need some air."

I dart through the crowd, now desperate to be anywhere but here.

I feel the tears coming. It would take a herculean effort to stop them, and I'm too tired.

I'm just too tired.

When the night breeze finally hits my face, I gulp it

down but it doesn't help. Sliding onto the curb, I plop down onto the sidewalk.

I feel empty.

"James," Ozzy says softly, crouching in front of me. But I feel lost. So lost. "James, baby, look at me." His hands are on my face, wiping the tears away only for more to replace them. "You can't let him get to you like that."

My gaze connects with his. "It's not what you think."

"What isn't?" His thumbs are still on my wet cheeks, eyebrows furrowed in concern. "Talk to me."

The words form slowly, they slip and slide in my mind. I think I drank too much. But it's too late to bother with the regret coating the inside of my mouth.

"I just." I try to pull away, but Ozzy doesn't let me. "I just want to forget what he did … what he let happen, but I can't." My voice cracks.

I hate myself.

"Do you mean," Ozzy says, studying me. "How he treated you?"

"Yes," I mutter after a long beat of silence. "But also." I take a deep breath. I can't do this. But I have to. Tears spill. "He watched while." I close my eyes. "While I was passed out. Drugged I think. I only remember bits. And … and …" I let a sob slip. "Spencer raped me."

I open my eyes and see my pain reflected in Ozzy's gaze, his face pales, fingers stiffening around my cheeks. It's almost too much to bear but I force myself to look. To accept.

"That fucking piece of shit, do you want me to kill him? I'm going to kill him. I'll kill them both," Ozzy says through his clenched jaw, standing up, tight fists locked against his body. I realize he's gunning for the door. Zachary is still inside.

"Wait! Don't," I urge, managing to grab his hand before he gets too far away. "Please, just stay here with me."

Ozzy's jaw ticks, his chest heaving, still looking at the front door as if deliberating.

But when his eyes land back on mine, he's managed to calm himself down. His expression is so tender that it almost feels meant for someone else.

Because when have I ever had someone look at me like that before?

"Come on," he says, pulling me up onto my feet and into his arms. He kisses my forehead. "Let me take you home."

"I don't want to be alone." The words slip out. I make no effort to take them back.

Ozzy squeezes me closer. "We'll sleep at my place."

17

OZZY

It's two in the morning by the time we get to my place. I left my car in the parking lot of Orso, called us a cab, and texted Alec on our way. I didn't mention James being with me but was relieved when he told me he was heading to an after-party with some of the kitchen crew.

She was quiet most of the ride here. I counted my breaths in silence, hoping it would help quell the burning rage I had inside me. It hasn't much subsided, but I try to focus on James instead while we walk up the stairs.

I can still feel the drugs flowing in my system. I'm wired, clenching my jaw too hard. It's that strange time of the night when the body refuses to wind down even if the party's over.

Only time can fix that problem.

"If you're feeling extra doom and gloom right now, it's normal," I tell her while unlocking the door. "Sometimes the comedown is harder when you don't know what to expect. You just need to sleep it off." I hope I sounded comforting and not like I'm mansplaining cocaine to her.

"Yeah," she answers softly behind me. "I kind of figured."

I open the door and flick the hallway light on. "So this is my place." I scratch my head nervously. "It's not much." My room is on the right, Alec's on the left. The hallway leads into the double living room, one side converted into a dining room, followed by the kitchen near the back balcony.

James lets out a little snort. "You should see my place."

"Oh?" I say, walking into the living room. "No grand piano?"

"I wish," she mutters.

"Or a private studio for your paintings?"

She gives me an unimpressed look. "Are you *trying* to make me feel worse?"

I chuckle and take her hand. "Come on, I'll make you something to eat before we go to bed."

I said that so casually—impressed with my delivery—when inside, my chest squeezes with an ache I can only describe as yearning.

Chill, Ozzy.

I try to muster up a believable lie to help with my nerves while I bring her into the kitchen. I land on: She's just another girl.

But I know in reality, she's not *just* anything.

She's James Ferdinand. And I'm down bad.

"It's okay, I'm not—"

"When was the last time you ate?"

Sheepishly, she answers, "Staff meal."

"That was ten hours ago." I prop her on a stool near the balcony door. "I'm feeding you."

Her shy smile is confirmation enough. I open the fridge and do a quick survey. There's fresh agnolotti that I brought home from Orso yesterday. Noticing we still have some of that white wine we use for cooking, I get inspired.

"You like pasta?" I ask while I take out butter, shallots, garlic, red chili, and pecorino.

Another one of her cute little snorts. "Who doesn't."

I shoot her a smile. "True." Taking a glass from the cupboard, I pour some water and hand it to her. "Here, drink this."

She takes it eagerly. "Why are you so good at this?" she mutters into the glass, taking a large gulp.

"At what? Cooking?" I say distractedly, putting a pan on the stove.

"No." She snickers, and I can tell she's still drunk. "At taking care of people."

"Oh, uh–" I rub the back of my neck. "Oldest of four. I guess it's just in my DNA."

"Oldest of four?" James says with an adorable bewildered look, small strands of pink hair framing her face. "What's that like? I always wanted a sibling."

"It feels …" *Like the biggest responsibility I've ever had to carry on my shoulders.* "Like always having someone on your team. Especially when it comes to the weird shit our parents do, makes you feel less crazy, I guess?"

"Shitty parents," she flatly states, nodding in agreement. "Same."

I burst out laughing, shaking my head while I cut some chilis. "Yeah, something like that."

After a beat, she asks, "You always lived in Marsford Bay?"

"Born and raised." I shoot her a teasing look. "Down in Pecket, far away from where you grew up, princess."

"Never been." By the innocent look she gives me, I can tell she doesn't have a clue how bad of a reputation that neighborhood has. I suddenly realize how wide the chasm is between how we both grew up.

My stomach sinks. I'm just a pit stop for her.

It's inevitable, one day she'll go back to her world. She doesn't belong here. Especially with a guy like me, a line cook from the wrong side of the tracks who can barely make ends meet.

We both fall silent while I finish cooking the pasta. She studies me the whole time, and I find it hard to deny how calming it feels to have her here in my kitchen, watching me cook.

Ten minutes later, I grate some pecorino over the pasta and hand her a bowl. Her face lights up when she takes it, still sitting on the stool. "Thank you," she sing-songs, a pleased hum leaving her lips when she takes her first bite.

"Good?" I ask her, taking a mouthful from my own bowl while I lean against the counter.

"I could get used to this." Her eyes crinkle in delight.

I smile down into my pasta.

Me too.

———

AFTER WE FINISH EATING, I dump the dirty dishes in the sink and show her to my bedroom. She stands in the doorway, a shy smile on her lips. While she surveys the space, I busy myself with picking up some clothes off the floor, stuffing them in the closet, and then de-wrinkle the duvet with a quick snap of my wrists. I give her a thin-lipped smile when I'm done, suddenly—and somewhat painfully—awkward as I wait for her to say something.

"I'm just going to go to the bathroom first," she says softly, pointing her thumb behind her.

"Sure, it's the door before the living room on your left."
In my head, it feels like I'm babbling, and I cringe. Something about James makes me horrifyingly self-aware and I'm struggling to keep up the casual fun-time Ozzy that usually comes so naturally to me. "Anyway, I'll be here," I tell her while she turns into the hallway.

I close my eyes, my head falling back toward the ceiling. *Just shut the fuck up.*

For a second, I'm paralyzed, not knowing if I should just stand here until she comes back. After a quick mental flogging, I tug my shirt over my head and take off my jeans. I climb into bed in just my boxers and wait. After realizing that just sitting there, staring at the door makes me look fucking crazy, I quickly snatch my phone from my jeans pocket and resume a casual pose, forcing myself just to scroll online until she returns.

When she does, I notice she's washed her makeup off. There are a few strands of her hair stuck to her temples as if she splashed some water on her face before pulling her hair into a ponytail.

"Classic boys' bathroom you got there, salad boy," she says with a sardonic smile.

I grunt a laugh, my nerves less prickly now that she's back. The slightly degrading dig, paired with that nickname, shoots a shiver up my spine but I ignore it when I realize she's toying with the hem of her summer dress.

"Do you want a shirt to sleep in?"
Idiot, should have thought of that earlier.

"Those crop tops you wear won't fit me," she says with a taunting curl of her lip, one eyebrow raised while she waits for me to answer.

"I do *own* full-length shirts, Jimbo," I shoot back while I scramble out of bed. I riffle through the middle drawer of my dresser and find an old band shirt for her to wear. "Here."

She takes it, muttering a small thanks. I realize that her hesitation might have to do with me watching her undress. "Sorry," I blurt out. "I'll give you some privacy."

Before I have time to turn around, her steady voice reaches my ear. "I don't want you to."

I freeze in place, swallowing hard. My eyes flash to hers, studying her face as if trying to solidify that what I heard her say was not just me imagining things. Her smile is vulnerable but the hesitation I saw earlier is gone, replaced by a serious but hungry gaze.

Slowly she tugs on the stringed bow on her chest. Her dress gaps open, the full curve of her breasts revealing a purple lace bra. My balls tighten and I lick my lips, ravenous. One by one, she pushes the straps off her shoulder, pushing the fabric down over her full hips. The dress falls to her feet, leaving her in only a bra and flower-patterned cotton panties.

I'm losing my fucking mind just looking at her. My gaze roves down her body, to her soft stomach that I'm desperate to feel and grip under my hands. I pause on her left thigh, my eyes flitting back up to her face. "A secret tattoo, princess?" I ask with a side grin.

"Not secret," she answers while tugging my shirt over her bra. "Just hidden."

The hem falls just below her hips, the material stretching over her tits, panties still peeking out. I take a step toward her. My hand curls around her neck, tilting her chin up with my thumb while I caress her thigh with the other. "I like it," I rasp before I kiss her gently on the lips.

I like you.

She pushes a soft hum into my mouth and I swallow it

whole, starving for more. But I hold back, coaxing her to bed and under the covers instead. The last thing I want is for her to feel pressured after what she confessed to me earlier.

All I want is for her to feel safe.

In *my* arms, and *my* bed.

I turn off the light, the city glow still peeking through the half-open curtain, and pad over, joining her under the duvet.

I find her curled on her side, her hands in loose fists near her chest, facing me. I pull her leg over mine, our bodies tangling together, my arm snaking around her waist. The smooth silk of her skin against mine is everything I've ever asked for and more.

"How are you feeling?" I whisper.

She's silent for a few breaths. "Better," she finally says.

"Good." I kiss her warm cheek, her hair tickling my nose. "Better is good."

I listen to her breathing soften into a dreamy cadence and I can hardly believe James is here, falling asleep in my arms. The sense of contentment that follows feels almost other-worldly in nature, and it stays with me until I, too, fall asleep.

18

OZZY

The dip of the mattress wakes me up, and it takes me a second to remember that James slept over last night. My head pops up from my pillow. The vision of her sleep-mussed and so delectably sweet as she climbs back into bed has my heart pitching over a cliff.

"Morning," she whispers.

I blink, silently taking her in. Her blue gaze is slightly coy, perfect pink lips pursed together. I can't help myself. I grab her wrist and pull her down, my body half over hers as I bury my face in the crook of her neck. I'm instantly hard but try not to grind against her, desperately trying to keep *some* level of decorum. She giggles loudly when I take in a large inhale, pressing kisses into her warm skin.

"Morning, sweetheart." My lips continue to caress her throat. "Where did you go?"

"Just freshening up," she says a little breathlessly.

Humming in acknowledgment, I give her one last kiss before rolling off her and jumping out of bed. "I should do the same." I stretch my arms over my head. I'm definitely a little hungover but it's nothing I'm not used to. "Do you want coffee? Are you hungry? I can make you something."

She watches me with a small smile, cheeks rosy as she pulls the covers up her chest, still wearing my shirt from last night. "I thought we could just ..." Her gaze dips down to my boxers and lingers on my erection. "Stay in bed for a bit."

I fall silent, studying her demeanor. I question if she meant what I think she meant but her loaded gaze is certainly speaking volumes. "Really?" Realizing I said that with way too much zeal, I clear my throat. "I mean yeah, we can stay in bed." I point a thumb toward the door. "Be right back." I act casual but as soon as I'm out of the bedroom, I dart into the bathroom and lock the door behind me.

Trying not to hyperventilate about having James in my bed, I lean my hands on the sink while I stare at myself in the mirror. "Ok, this is it," I mutter out loud.

Well, maybe.

I don't know.

This *might* be it. The implications are there. Right? My shoulders sag and I let loose a large sigh, rolling my eyes at my own reflection. "You better not fuck this up," I tell myself, pointing a finger at the mirror. Feeling ridiculous, I snap myself out of it. Hurriedly, I brush my teeth, pat some water into my messy curls, and run back into the bedroom.

James is on her phone but looks up at me, beaming like the morning sun, when I join her back in bed.

"You're so fucking beautiful," I say in awe, pulling her into a kiss. It's slow and sweet, her lips perfect on mine. But before it gets too far she pulls away and looks at me sheepishly.

Worried, I ask, "What's wrong?"

"Nothing. It's just …" she trails off, looking down at my hand holding hers. "I'm just a little embarrassed about last night." She looks back up at me. "This is supposed to be fun and casual and I made it … just too much, and I'm sorry."

"Don't be sorry," I rush to say, smoothing my hand over her arm. "There's nothing to be sorry about." But my mind is snagging on fun and casual. I chew on my lip, gathering my thoughts but end up just blurting out, "Fun and casual huh?" I try to sound nonchalant but instead sound like a sad puppy. I hide the cringe currently making my skin itch.

Jesus Christ.

"Well." She straightens herself up, her eyes drifting shyly from me to the bed and back. "I just mean, that I'm fresh out of a three-year relationship, and you—well …" She laughs, her nerves obvious. "From what I hear, you're not the relationship type. I think what I mean is that I just want to have some fun for once." She gives me a noncommittal shrug of the shoulder. "We can be something like …" She pauses. "Friends with benefits?"

I hide the sting of her words by cutting the tension with a playful laugh. But there's nothing about what she just said that I find amusing. "Friends with benefits? Sounds like we're in high school," I say, hoping my tone sounds teasing, and not like how I feel inside.

Which is: Disappointed, pushed to the side, and maybe a little hurt.

And who the hell is she talking about me with?

She lets out a small huff, acting as if she's offended, suppressing a smile and crossing her arms. "You know what I mean, Ozzy."

I let her words stew in my head until I decide what to make of them. "Okay," I say as I fling the covers off her body, moving down so I'm kneeling in between her legs. If *fun* is what she wants from me, then that's exactly what I'll give her.

"Okay?" she parrots, her eyebrows slightly raised. I grab her calves and tug hard, making her slide onto her back. "What are you doing?" she shrieks with laughter.

I give her a look that I hope conveys all the dirty things I want to do to her and simply say, "Redeeming my benefits." I pause, my hands smoothing up her legs and thighs. "Yes?" I coax.

"Yes," she answers coyly, biting her index finger between her teeth.

I quirk a dark smile, tugging on the hem of the t-shirt she slept in. "Take my shirt off."

Her movements stutter but she regroups fast, pulling it over her head. She keeps it in her hands for half a second, as if still trying to cover herself with it but then finally drops it on the floor. Her expression turns serious, and I don't let myself overthink it. I remind myself that I'm the kind of person who easily chases the instant gratification sex can usually offer.

Especially with someone as delicious as James.

My hungry gaze travels over her chest and down her body.

I let my fingers trail over the top of her panties, barely a touch.

"I've been dying to see that perfect pussy of yours since I first had a taste."

I hear her breath hitch, and I lick my lips, swallowing hard.

"I've never done anything like that before," she whispers, and I know she's talking about the Snickers dare.

My eyes flick to her face. "Did you like it?" I let a finger dip just half an inch under her panties, my cock hardening against my boxers. "Doing something that felt wrong … dirty … for me."

Her chest begins to rise faster. "Yes," she whispers. "I did."

I bring my finger back out and circle her clit over the soft cotton fabric.

"You like being bad for me, baby?"

She nods slowly, her legs falling even wider open, eyes focused on me. I press a finger over her pussy, pushing her panties into her entrance. I circle the wet spot it made and give her a mocking grin, followed by a few tsks. "Bad girl, already so wet just from the thought."

"Ozzy," she whines. It's greedy and full of need and it only makes me want to fuck her that much harder.

"Take that shit off," I say, pointing to her bra with my chin while I forcefully tug her panties down her legs. "I want you naked and covered with my cum by the end of this."

"Yes, chef," she says while unclasping her bra. A pleasurable shiver wracks my body at her calling me that and I groan out loud.

Her teasing smile tells me I'm pushing all the right buttons and she's as eager as I am to jump into the deep end.

Her tits bounce down ever so slightly when she takes off her bra, nipples peaked, and the perfect shade of pink. This time she lets the bra fall with a pinch of her fingers and a lot of arrogance.

I want to eat her alive.

I match her arrogance, pushing my boxers off and slowly palm my dick. I watch her eyes widen and can't help but flash her a cocky grin.

"What's wrong, princess?" I lick the palm of my hand before continuing to idly stroke my cock. The question is rhetorical. I'm used to this expression by now.

"I just don't ..." She licks her lips, her eyes fixed on my cock. "I don't think it's going to fit."

I chuckle darkly before answering. "Don't worry, baby. You'll be begging for every inch of me by the time I'm done with you. Now, turn around, and get on your hands and knees. Let me see that dripping cunt."

It takes her a second before my demand registers, her gaze slowly making its way up to my face. I don't know what she sees in my expression but the way she comes back to life and scrambles into position almost makes me want to laugh. Except, when I finally see her splayed wide for me, humor is the furthest thing on my mind.

I hum my approval and squeeze her ass, gripping her cheeks open and licking her from cunt to asshole. My eyes damn near roll into the back of my skull.

I'm fucking starving.

And the goading moan that falls out of her lips is damn near breathtaking. Her pussy is so pretty and pink, all I want is to eat it for breakfast, lunch, and dinner.

I massage her ass while my tongue circles her tight hole. Her quickening breaths spur me on. I ignore my raging hard-on, edging myself as much as I crave to edge James. Desperate to see my teeth marks on her tender flesh, I bite the soft skin of her ass as if taking a bite of the ripest apple. She hisses, then mewls but doesn't pull away.

Greedily, I continue. Hardening my tongue, I push it into her asshole, just enough to breach the tight muscle. Her moans are devious, devilish, and I need more. So much fucking more.

"I'm fucking *weak* for your taste, baby," I say after

pulling back and sitting on my heels. My hand to her pussy finds her soaking wet, two fingers pushing into her. "I'll have devoured every part of you by the time I'm done," I say.

"*Yes, yes, yes.*" Her voice aches with need, my fingers still pumping in and out, the sound of her desire evidence enough. "Fuck me," she pleads, followed by a desperate little whine. "*Please.*"

She gives me tunnel vision.

The very thought of her sends me spiraling.

James. James. James.

I turn as desperate as the sound of her voice.

Reaching over to the bedside table, I open the drawer and grab a condom. With a click of my tongue, I say, "I'm not just going to fuck you, baby." Ripping the wrapper open, I roll the condom over my cock. "I'm going to make you forget any other man exists."

The look she gives me from over her shoulder is so full of heat that it burns permanently into my mind. I smooth my palm up her arched back, fisting her hair at the nape. Her mouth falls open on a gasp and I lean down, licking her neck, my teeth catching her earlobe. I slide the tip of my cock over her pussy, slick with her arousal, and start to slowly push in.

"Relax for me baby," I groan. "Let me in."

"Slow down, Ozzy … so big," she says breathlessly, sounding a little bewildered. "I need more time." Still, I feel her try to push into me.

I let out a small hush. "I thought you were my bad girl," I rasp. "I have to move, you feel too fucking good." Desperation tinting my words, I caress a hand up her thigh and over her ass. "I know you can take it."

Straightening back up, I look at where we meet, her

pussy stretching wide around my cock. I've never seen something so fucking erotic in my entire life. I dig my fingers into her plump ass, one thumb putting pressure on her asshole but I don't push all the way in.

When I sink another inch into her tight cunt, the pleasure is damn near excruciating, and the last threads of my self-control are fraying. I'm like a tightrope threatening to snap in two.

She feels too good. Too fucking right.

"That's it," I coo. "Just like that. *God*, you feel so good, James. So fucking perfect."

I give her ass a hard slap, and she moans loudly just like I hoped she would.

I feel her reach down to play with her clit, her fingers intermittently slipping down to stroke the base of my cock, my balls tightening at the sensation.

Normally, I'd give it a few more pushes to adjust but I can't help but bottom out. Immediately, I pull back out to the tip and slam back in, this time in one hard thrust.

When my name tumbles out of James' lips, I almost come on the spot. It's a pure kind of bliss, a kind that only exists when her moans fill the space between us and I'm balls-deep in the prettiest fucking pussy I've ever fucking seen.

James' voice rises thrust after hard thrust. Until she's almost babbling, her fingers still stroking her clit. "I'm coming," she whimpers, her voice sensual, her tone like honey. "Don't stop, don't fucking stop." Her words are dripping in need as I piston into her, skin slapping on skin. I'm so fucking close myself, but will myself to stay on the edge as James topples over it. Her pussy squeezes around me as she comes with one long moan.

As soon as James relaxes around me, I pull out. "Get on

your back, baby. I want you to watch while I paint your skin with my cum."

Ripping the condom off, I throw it somewhere in the room, not caring where it lands. Now facing me, her cheeks and chest are flushed, pink hair disheveled, looking thoroughly fucked—and she looks more beautiful than ever.

Her eyes are hooded but intent as she studies me and it only takes a few more pumps into my fist before thick white ropes of cum land on her stomach, my orgasm slamming into me. The pleasure of having James under my touch is so powerful I nearly double over.

"*Fuck James,*" I say in awe, my fingers spreading my cum all over her stomach as if I'm trying to push it into her skin, needing for her to have a piece of me living inside of her. "You're so beautiful it hurts."

She laughs almost shyly and my eyes find hers. "Don't get shy on me now, sweetheart." Needing to hear her laugh again, I add, "Not after I've literally eaten your ass."

"Ozzy!" she shrieks, slapping both of her hands on her face. "Why do you always have to be so crude."

I bark a laugh, squeezing her thigh and giving it a soft tap. "Because then I can watch you squirm. Win, win if you ask me." Jumping out of bed, I add, "Wait here. Don't move."

I pin her with a stare to show that I'm serious, and she nods, her expression playful. Running out of the room stark naked, I dampen a hand towel with warm water and bring it back to the room. "Let me clean you up."

I don't give her time to protest or tell me she can do it herself, and clean off her stomach while pressing kisses over the clean, damp skin.

"Thank you," she says softly, the coyness back in her tone.

I give her a quick wink, the towel discarded on the bedside table. "Anything for my Jimbo."

Her giggles are addictive as I lay back down beside her, pulling the covers over us, my body curling around hers.

James falls silent, and I can tell she's busy having too many big thoughts. "Maybe I should go …" she says tentatively.

I squeeze her even closer and kiss her on the lips. "Who said friends can't cuddle after sex?"

Fuck whatever rules she thinks she needs to abide by.

She gives me an amused eye roll and smiles.

Her nose burrows into my neck, followed by a long pleased sigh.

It's answer enough.

A few minutes later, she falls back asleep and I stay awake watching her, already dreading her leaving my bed.

God, I'm fucked.

19

JAMES

It's early afternoon by the time I wake back up. I'm snuggled into Ozzy's side as if there isn't any other place I'd rather be. A pang in my heart reminds me that this is temporary and I shouldn't get too comfortable. I'm not special. Ozzy's bound to move on to a new flavor of the month soon enough.

Although the way I catch him watching me sometimes—it's hard not to romanticize the look in his eyes, especially after what we did this morning.

God, that was … unreal.

And unlike anything I've ever experienced. I can feel the twinge between my legs, I'm definitely sore, but it somehow only makes me crave Ozzy's depravity even more.

Something about him just makes me want to stop caring about how I'm supposed to look or act while having sex, and just seek pleasure for what it is—carnal satisfaction.

Pure and wanton.

Peering up at him from my position, I find him sitting upright, leaning against the headboard, busy writing in the margins of a frayed book. It looks battered like it spent quite some time in the bottom of a backpack getting knocked around, masking tape all over the spine keeping it together.

"Hey, sleepyhead," Ozzy mutters softly, his gaze sliding to find mine, and the familiar curl to his lip makes my stomach flip.

Realizing I'm still naked under the covers, I push myself up, keeping the duvet wrapped tight against my chest as I rake my fingers through my hair in a vain attempt to comb it into compliance. "Can't believe I slept that long."

"You probably needed it," he says, sticking the pen into his open book and closing it.

"Didn't mean to overstay my welcome," I mutter sheepishly.

Ozzy's eyebrows dip. "Who says you overstayed your welcome?"

"Well I just mean …"

I trail off, the earnestness in his expression feeling like a punch in the gut.

If he had wanted me gone he would have told me.

It slowly dawns on me that Ozzy is not Zachary.

It feels like a silly thing to suddenly realize.

Of course, Ozzy isn't my ex. They're nothing alike.

But there's a gaping, aching part of me that doesn't understand that yet.

My brain still reacts the same to Ozzy as it did with Zachary.

I'm having to undo years of learned behavior from my time with him. Years of walking on eggshells. Years of being on constant defense, no matter my innocence. My impulses—those knee-jerk reactions that still seem to have control over my decisions—don't seem to care that I'm no longer with Zachary. I'm like a well-trained pony, eager to please, eager to do as I'm told for fear of getting punished.

I don't want to finish my sentence, unwilling to admit my entire train of thought. Why do I always have to get so damn depressing?

My gaze lands on his book. "What are you reading?"

Ozzy blinks, looking slightly surprised at the change of subject but indulges me.

"Just a memoir," he says, chucking the book on the bedside table. His demeanor has shifted, almost looking shy now that I've moved the attention to him.

I let out a small disbelieving laugh. By the state of it, it doesn't look like just a book. Reading the name on the cover, I ask, "Marco Pierre White? Who's that?"

When he peers down at me, there's a shine to his eyes as if he's about to talk about a subject he's really passionate about. "He's kind of a badass in the cooking world. Was the youngest and first British chef to ever receive three Michelin stars." Ozzy twists himself towards me, his face lighting up, and my heart warms at the sight. "But what's so cool about him is that when he retired he gave those stars back. That was unheard of—said that if he wasn't behind the stove there was no point in keeping them. What mattered most to him was the judgment of his peers. The ones who knew what it meant to give yourself entirely to the kitchen."

He's beaming. And I fight the urge to kiss him.

"So Orso is more than just a job for you?"

"Sometimes it feels like it's my entire life," he says with a dry chuckle. "But yeah, I mean …" He drags a hand through his messy curls. "I started as a dishwasher. I didn't have any dreams back then. I just needed the money. But now, I couldn't see myself doing anything else."

"Would you want to open your own restaurant one day?"

"Wouldn't that be the dream," he says as he rolls out of bed, a pair of briefs hanging low on his hips. It's subtle, but there's bitterness to his tone. He's quick to change the subject while stepping into some jeans and a cut-off t-shirt. "You feel like going out for lunch? I know a great diner over on Dunford."

I can't help but feel like I've said something wrong, and I immediately start to feel guilty. There's a large part of me that wants to apologize, but I force myself not to.

Instead, I smile and nod. "I just need to get dressed—"

His phone rings beside me in bed, and without much thought, I reach for it. The name *Sophia* flashes on the screen while he reaches over to take it out of my hand. "I'm sorry, I didn't mean to—" But I stop in my tracks not sure what to say.

"It's fine." He flashes me a grin and points to his phone. "Do you mind if I take this?"

"Of course not," I say hurriedly, hoping my voice didn't come out squeaky.

"I'll wait for you outside."

I stare at the wall for a few seconds, chastising myself for having jealous feelings about whoever this Sophia is. They must be close if she calls him out of the blue like that. Shaking my head, I refuse to sit with whatever theories my mind is trying to come up with.

Ozzy's a free man. And me being naked in his bed doesn't change that fact.

I find my dress rumpled on the floor, my panties nowhere to be found. I decide to wear Ozzy's t-shirt overtop my dress, twisting a small knot so it hugs my waist. I don't dwell on the fact that wearing his shirt out might be a small show of claiming him as mine. And how his shirt smells like fresh laundry but his cologne lingers, hints of blackcurrant and tea. It's warm and cozy and I hate how it makes me feel. But I don't hate it nearly enough to take it off.

Leaving the bedroom, I spot Ozzy on the balcony, having a cigarette and talking animatedly on the phone with a large grin on his face. I stand awkwardly in the living room waiting for him to finish.

"Hey new girl," someone says behind me.

I jump, swiveling around, mortification burning my cheeks.

"Alec!" I say way too loudly. "I didn't know you were here."

I don't know what to do with my hands, crossing my arms but then immediately dropping them to my sides.

Oh my god, this is so embarrassing.

"Just got back," he rasps, his disheveled and ragged look confirmation enough. Nothing about his demeanor seems at all fazed to see me here, and I'm too frazzled to question whether that's a good or bad thing. He stretches his arms high above his head, yawning long and loud. "Anyway, goodnight."

It's two in the afternoon but I mutter a soft *goodnight* back as I watch him slink into his bedroom. Hearing the patio door open and shut behind me, I turn around just in time to catch Ozzy taking me in. His gaze is slow and full of gluttonous hunger and I forget all about the awkward run-in I just had with our coworker.

Ozzy clears his throat. "Ready, Jimbo?"

WHEN WE GET to the diner, Ozzy is greeted like a celebrity. The interior is outdated but charming, the whole place decorated in chrome and baby blue, with two rows of booths lining opposite walls. He waves to the staff with familiarity and warmth while we walk to a booth facing the window, making a point to introduce me to everyone as if it's the most important thing he's ever done.

"Alec and I come here a lot," Ozzy says with a smirk, instructing me to sit down first. Sliding into the booth, I expect Ozzy to sit in front of me, but instead, he follows me in, nestling against my side.

"What are you doing?" I say with a giggle.

"What?" he asks me all too innocently. A lock of brown hair falls into his piercing blue-green eyes, and he brushes it away with a quick head flick.

"Usually people face each other," I tease.

He pushes himself even tighter against me, whispering in my ear. "It's much easier for me to keep my hands on you if you're next to me, baby." Proving his point, he slips his hand in between my thighs under the table. "I know you're not wearing anything under that dress."

A small gasp escapes me. But inside I'm ablaze with his hand burning up my thigh. "How would you even know that?"

His voice lowers, like soft silk to my ear. "I have your panties in my pocket, princess."

I slap him away, chiding him because I can't think of how else to react. "Ozzy! Where's your sense of decorum?"

His chuckle is low as he straightens in his seat. "What made you think I had any."

I return his laugh, my gaze lingering on the curves of his face, and the small scar on his lip that somehow just enhances his appeal.

I never knew playfulness could be so sexy, that laughter could be such an aphrodisiac.

When the server comes up to our table to fill our mugs full of hot coffee, she's just as friendly to Ozzy as everyone else. His presence seems to make people light up, like the entire world is simply grateful to have him around. Just being a simple bystander, and witnessing what I can only describe as the *Ozzy effect*, touches me deeper than expected.

I suddenly feel like crying. But this feeling isn't full of melancholy, no, it tastes like relief. Like I never knew someone like Ozzy even existed.

I clear my throat. *Crap.*

"The usual?" the server asks.

When Ozzy turns to me, I force an easy smile, trying to hide the emotions I'm sure are lingering in my gaze.

"You trust me? I promise you won't be disappointed," he says.

There's a pause before my answer. Recalling how many times people have called me a picky eater because of my food aversions. But there's a gentleness to his gaze that keeps me hopeful. "Of course," I answer.

His eyes brighten, then he turns to the server and nods enthusiastically. "Two of the usual, please Diana, thank you."

She returns the nod, with a closed-lipped but warm smile and walks to the next table.

"So, what did you order for us?"

Ozzy's smile widens, and *my god*, if I could spend the entire day watching him smile I would. "That's a surprise," he says, taking my hand in his, the small stick and poke smiley face tattooed on his thumb mirroring the man himself. He kisses the top of my knuckles as if it's the most natural thing in the world. "Hope you're hungry."

"Starving," I reply, making no effort to remove my hand from his.

I feel Ozzy stiffen beside me. But I don't have time to ask him what's wrong before his arm flies out of the booth, intercepting the young-looking guy walking past us. Ozzy's fingers lock around his wrist.

"Shouldn't you be in summer school?" Ozzy's question is practically a growl.

So, not strangers then.

He rips his arm out of Ozzy's grasp and sneers. "Fuck off."

When he walks away from our booth, Ozzy jumps up, his fists tight, shoulders tensed. "I'll be right back," he mutters quickly before following the other guy outside.

Luckily, the large windows I'm facing allows me to inconspicuously spy on them while I sit in the booth and wonder how they know each other. Similar hair and height, familiar traits. Brother maybe? I vaguely remember him telling me about his siblings before. Their interaction seems heated.

The only times I ever see Ozzy this serious is in the middle of a busy service. But there's a pained expression etched into the lines of his face that normally isn't there. Despite the frustration written on his face, I can still see the care in his eyes.

They must be family.

Eventually, the younger one storms off, and I watch Ozzy let his head fall back toward the sky, his fist rubbing against his forehead. He smokes half a cigarette and then walks back in.

"Sorry about that," he says, sliding into the booth across from me this time. Before having to ask, he adds, "That was my younger brother, Huxley." He rolls his eyes. "He's seventeen and always in trouble. I haven't seen him in weeks."

I study Ozzy's demeanor trying to gauge his mood before speaking. If anything he looks tense and distracted. "Does he still live with your parents?"

"My dad, yeah. And my other two siblings," he answers carefully as if chewing on his answer. The silence between every word he speaks tells me he would rather leave this subject alone. He can barely match my gaze and I squirm in my seat not quite knowing what to do or say.

Thankfully, our food arrives not long after, releasing us from the awkward tension his brother created between us.

Ozzy perks up. "This is called a Portuguese breakfast." His usual amusement is back in his eyes while he takes his time to explain everything on my plate, from the linguica sausage to the shrimp cake and my stomach rumbles at the sight.

"Looks delicious," I say before taking my first bite.

"If it's not, don't tell me. You'll hurt my feelings," he says with a wink and I snort out a laugh.

We spend the rest of the time eating and chatting, the heavy topic of his family seemingly forgotten. Soon enough, he springs back to the flirty Ozzy I'm used to, and eventually slides back into the booth beside me on his way back from the bathroom.

"Where to next?" he says after he pays for the bill. I told him that friends should split the bill but the look of disgust on his face told me that was one thing he wasn't going to budge on.

"Well, I kind of need to go home. I should really change out of these clothes," I say while looking down at my wrinkled dress.

I don't necessarily want this to be the last of our little day together but all good things come to an end. Ozzy pulls me to my feet and gives me a quick kiss on the lips. "Your place it is, then."

I must be giving him a look because he asks jokingly, "What? I'm not invited?"

"No. I mean, yes." I regroup, trying to keep my stuttering to a minimum. "It's just, we've spent the day together. Are you sure you're not sick of me yet?" I add a little laugh at the end, hoping my insecurities aren't too glaring. I guess I'm just not used to people *choosing* to spend time with me. Not like this anyway. Like I'm the most important part of his day.

His gaze sears into mine as he places his hand on the small of my back, pulling me into his hips. "Oh Jimbo," his voice low and dark, "Not even close."

20

JAMES

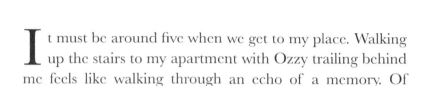

It must be around five when we get to my place. Walking up the stairs to my apartment with Ozzy trailing behind me feels like walking through an echo of a memory. Of when Zachary helped me move in, his petty remarks still stuck in the corners of the halls like some kind of permanent cobwebs.

Sometimes I wish I wasn't so quick to remember the past.

But it's just the way I am. And I don't think I'll ever change.

Today, I choose not to dwell on the memory. Especially when the present looks, smells, *feels* like Ozzy. I simply acknowledge it and continue to climb up the steps.

When I unlock the door, he strolls in, looking around, hands on the back of his hips, and whistles. "Reminds me of my first apartment."

I cross my arms, a side-smirk on my lips. "That sounds like an insult."

Ozzy barks a laugh. "Not at all." He plops himself on

the ratty couch looking almost more comfortable here than I am—despite having lived here for months now. "Everyone needs to start somewhere. You're just paying your dues."

"Yeah well," I mumble while walking up to the couch. "I'm so broke I can barely *pay* those dues let alone my real bills."

I shriek out a laugh when Ozzy pulls me down to the couch, pushing me onto my back. Undulating his hips over mine, he whispers in my ear. "Is your roommate home?" I shake my head. "Good," he rasps, pulling me into a kiss.

His tongue is so soft, tracing my lower lip, so unlike his hard body grinding against mine. It slips into my mouth, hungry, needy. He groans and my skin pulses with need. But after a minute-long freefall, I gently push him away, gasping for air. Straightening back up, he settles into the opposite corner looking like the cat who got the cream.

"I should shower," I say, slightly out of breath.

"Great," he says with a clap of his hands, jumping up from the couch. "I'll come with."

"No." The word morphs into a giggle. "There's nothing sexy about my shower, trust me."

I stand up and lead us to my bedroom. Aside from the bed and furniture I bought when I moved in, like the desk near the closet and the dresser stuffed full of clothes, it's still pretty bare. The apology for the sad state of my room is on the tip of my tongue, but I swallow it back down. I don't have anything to apologize for.

"Give me fifteen minutes, tops. I'll be right back," I tell him while I gather a change of clothes and my towel.

"Hurry back." Ozzy gives me a quick slap on the ass and I yelp in surprise. The sound of his laughter follows me into the bathroom.

I shower as fast as I can, keeping my hair up in a bun

and out of the water. After drying off, I step into white cotton shorts, chosen specifically because they ride up my ass, and a tank top, no bra.

When I walk back into the bedroom, Ozzy is crouched down, looking at some canvas paintings I have out on display and leaning against the wall near the window. I freeze, an intangible kind of embarrassment dripping over me, like a cracked egg spilling over my head.

I brace myself for the inevitable teasing comment about my art. An innocuous kind of belittling that feels like a thousand paper cuts on the skin.

Ozzy's head lifts when he hears me walk in. The expression painted between his raised eyebrows, the glint in his eyes, the dip of his open mouth makes me stop in my tracks.

It's almost like … admiration.

"You painted all these?" is all he says, his tone clear but soft.

I clasp my hands together, looking down and then up while I pick at my nails. "Yeah."

He stands up, dusting off his knees, and steps towards me. "Those are amazing, James. I mean," he says, raking his fingers through his curls. "I never had a doubt that you'd be talented, but those are like …" He waves towards the canvases. "*So fucking good.*"

The reflex of minimizing my artistic skill is second nature. Even if, deep down, I *know* I'm that good. Instead, I blurt out, "Can I draw you?" My voice turns shy when I add, "Please?"

There's coyness in his responding smile. "What?"

"Sit down, I want to draw you," I say, a little more demanding this time.

"Alright," he says with a grin. Tugging on the bottom

hem of his shirt with both hands as if straightening a suit jacket, his chin slightly raised, eyes glimmering with mirth. "But if you draw me, I'm posing in the nude."

"Okay," I say immediately, lifting a shoulder in a shrug, completely unfazed.

He seems a little surprised but tries to hide it.

I laugh. "What? You think you're my first nude model?" I scoff. "Please, salad boy, don't make me laugh."

His smile turns devilish. "Fine, then."

I only have time to blink once before Ozzy grabs his shirt by the back of the neck and tugs it over his head in one continuous swoop. He pins me with a dark gaze, while I listen to the sound of his studded belt unfastening as he side-steps out of his jeans. His movements are hurried, eager, and he ends up tripping over his own feet but catches himself. We both stifle a laugh. When his socks and boxers finally end up on the floor next to him, my eyes immediately flick to his cock.

It's as impressive as I remembered, even when he's not hard.

He clears his throat, and my gaze jerks back up to his face. The proud little smirk he's sporting makes me want to give him a little smack in the face but I say nothing.

"Where do you want me?" he asks.

Standing over me, with your cock shoved in my mouth.

Maybe I'm more fazed by the sight of Ozzy naked than I care to admit.

"You can sit on the bed, I'll be right back," I tell him before dipping into the hallway and into the kitchen to grab a chair. When I return, Ozzy has positioned himself lying on his side, one knee up and an arm holding his head. I burst out laughing. "You're an idiot."

"What?" Ozzy says, acting confused but clearly joking as he sits back up.

Before sitting down, I link my phone to my speaker and press play on a recent 70s playlist I made. Grabbing my sketchpad and a charcoal pencil, I sit a few feet away, facing him.

I carefully instruct him on how to sit. Legs parted. Feet firmly planted on the ground. Shoulders straight but relaxed. Left arm slightly behind him, his palm splayed on the mattress holding up his weight.

By the time I tell him to place his other hand loosely over his right thigh, we've both lost our smiles. It's also hard to ignore the erection slowly forming between his thighs while I finish up my instructions.

His serious gaze studies me while I study him back. "Now hold still," I say, my voice lower than usual, so as not to disturb the tension beginning to buzz between us.

It's a privilege to have Ozzy like this. Relaxed and unguarded. So open to share this experience with me. I'm also free to let my eyes wander aimlessly over every curve, every dip of his body. A collection of tattoos I haven't had the luxury to linger on yet. Aside from obvious cooking ones, like a butcher knife near his hip and a pig's anatomy on his left thigh, there doesn't seem to be any rhyme or reason to most of them.

Which somehow just makes sense for Ozzy.

I fall into a rhythm, letting my hand draw the lines of his body over the rough sketch paper. The scratches of my charcoal pencil are the only sounds aside from the music playing in the background.

My eye catches on the twitch of his hand.

My hand freezes as my gaze lands on the crook of his thigh, his hand slowly curling around his now-hardened cock. "Don't stop," he says. The note of desperation in his tone makes it feel like I've been physically touched, heat pooling low in my stomach.

Forcing my hand to move, my eyes intermittently look down at my sketch then quickly back up while Ozzy starts to fuck his fist in long, languid strokes. After a few pumps, he tilts his head forward. Lining his mouth directly above his cock, he lets a long spool of spit fall on the tip, his thumb smoothing it over the skin.

I lick my lips, my heartbeat racing as I listen to his breath catch. He lets out a low groan, his eyes fluttering shut, his head falling backward and I have the sudden urge to pause the music so I don't miss a single sound he makes.

The curve of his stretched throat is as erotic as his thick cock pumping into his squeezing fist, and I feel lightheaded. Intoxicated. Drugged up on this vision of Ozzy masturbating in front of me.

I suffer through another long minute, desperately trying to concentrate on the sketch on my lap while Ozzy continues to fuck himself. Until I begin to hear and notice tell-tale signs of him nearing the end.

A pitch of his hips. A hiss.

His movements getting jerkier.

The long bite of his bottom lip.

I throw the sketch pad on the floor beside me, on my feet in seconds, falling to my knees just as quickly.

"Let me taste you," I say, echoing the same hunger he's used with me. My hands smooth up his thighs while my mouth falls open, tongue splayed out.

"*Fuck*, baby," he rasps, his free hand stroking my cheek, his eyes hooded and glazed.

When I feel the first spurt of cum land on my face, I close my eyes, basking in the lewd sounds of Ozzy coming.

What I don't expect is for him to grab the back of my neck and slam his mouth against mine, the taste of him on my lips, now on his. I push myself up on my knees, chasing his burning kiss.

Hungry. So fucking hungry.

Pulling away, he gives my cheek a long lick with the flat of his tongue and kisses me one last time. With his hand still firmly around my nape, he gazes down at me.

I've never seen such pure adulation in someone's eyes.

"You're fucking perfect," he says.

21

OZZY

I t's gearing up to be a busy Friday, the books are full and
my prep list is a mile long. I have at least three hours left
before the restaurant opens, but my anxiety levels are at an
all-time high and I'm on my second cup of coffee since I
clocked in an hour ago.

Doesn't help that I was already on edge when I walked
into this fucking kitchen.

After I left James' place Tuesday morning, Sophia
texted to tell me Charlie was caught stealing other kids'
snack money at the public pool, and he's now banned for
the rest of the summer.

There goes free day camp.

I can't have Soph be responsible for him for the next
month until school starts again, and I obviously can't
depend on our piece of shit dad, so I've been spending
most of my free time at the house, keeping an eye on him.

James hasn't worked since Sunday, which means I
haven't seen her in four days and I'm about to jump out of
my fucking skin.

Four days … that should be nothing.

I've never craved someone this bad. Thank fuck, she has a shift tonight or I would've shown up on my hands and knees at her doorstep. Spending the whole day with her on Monday was perfect, except for the resulting void it created from not having her around.

That was especially jarring.

We've been texting. But it's just not the same. Not when being with her in person is like listening to your all-time favorite song on repeat.

Speak of the devil, my phone buzzes in my pocket. I fish it out hoping it's James, even if I'll be seeing her in a couple of hours. My stomach flips when I read her name on the screen. Swiping my phone open, I realize it's a video that she's sent me, followed by a text that says:

Do not watch around other people!!

My attention zeroes in on the video's thumbnail.

Holy fucking shit.

Slamming my phone screen down on the cutting board in front of me, my head falls backward as I close my eyes. I mutter a half-crazed prayer of gratitude, while I swivel my head around, making sure no one in the kitchen is peeking over my shoulder.

I promptly head for the back door.

"I'm going for a smoke," I yell out to no one in particular, speed-walking and eyes down. Near the dumpster, I uncurl the death grip I have on my phone and pull up James' video, making sure the volume is almost all the way down. I should have grabbed my fucking headphones from my bag.

It starts with her smiling at the camera while she places

it down, centering her bed in the background. Her pink hair is down, framing her perfect face, blue eyes bright and shining as if we're sharing a secret. When she backs up to reveal her body, I almost squeal like a schoolgirl.

She's wearing a lavender lingerie set, her full breasts practically spilling out of the lace bra. I groan, closing my eyes for a split second, and rub my forehead, the cigarette still lit between my two fingers accidentally singeing a few hairs in the process.

I curse under my breath.

I can't believe I'm watching this beside a fucking dumpster.

My gaze lands quickly back on the video.

James settles herself on her back in the middle of the bed. I lick my lips. She trails her hand up her thigh, over the lavender thong, and then up her stomach. My grip tightens around the edges of my phone. She palms her tits with both hands. I'm fucking sweating. Her gaze lands on the camera. It feels like she's staring straight at me. I take a large pull of my cigarette. She picks up something on the mattress beside her. At first, I can't make out what it is until I hear the buzz.

Oh *fuck*.

It's a small, pink vibrator. And I've never wanted to be a man-made thing so much in my entire life. Especially when she starts to circle it around her clit over the lace.

The back door slams open, and I nearly fling my phone into the bushes.

The dishwasher on shift pokes his head out. I turn my screen black.

"Fuck off Peter, I'm busy!"

He looks sheepish. "Sorry Oz, uh, Elle is looking for you. Says it's urgent."

I press my lips together. Of course.

"Fine," I grumble. "I'll be right in."

He gives me a nod and disappears. Hurriedly, I try to conceal the semi currently in my pants, before shooting James a quick text.

> Little tease. Just you wait till I get you all to myself again.

I head back inside to find Elle, while the half-finished video burns a hole in my pocket.

A FEW HOURS LATER, I've finally gotten through most of my prep list, my phone still weighing heavily against my thigh. James never replied to my message. Obviously, it's a deliberate move, and it's working wonders because I'm about ready to explode.

But for now, I keep my focus on anything else but her. It's my turn to cook the staff meal. On the menu for today, is a kitchen sink pasta which consists of whatever ingredients I have on hand that need to be used.

Front-of-house staff start trickling in, some of their hellos are chipper, some more muted as they pass the kitchen to get to the staff room to change.

"Afternoon, chef."

James' voice is sunny, upbeat, and so *fucking* delectable I could cry.

Instead, I quirk a smile but don't look up. "Afternoon, lavender."

Finally catching a glance of her as she walks away I notice the strap of her bra under her white tank top is fucking *lavender*.

Must be the same one as in the video and it takes me everything not to abandon my post and follow her into the staff room.

I'm simply biding my time—I know exactly what I have planned for her.

Ten minutes later, most of the wait staff are busy filling salt shakers or whatever side job they've been assigned when I ring the bell, signaling that the staff meal is ready.

A collective mutter of half-cheers can be heard throughout the dining room. They file in one by one serving themselves a plate, thanking me, then heading back out to sit around the bar.

When it's James' turn, she can't keep from smiling, but I say nothing.

She thanks me, I give her a nod and she walks out, settling beside Gustavo at the bar.

But before she has time to take her first bite, I yank my phone out of my pocket and text her.

> Dry storage. Now.

22

JAMES

My fork hovers somewhere in between the plate and my mouth, my heart jumping into my throat when I see a notification that Ozzy has just texted me. My body flares, my gut instinct telling me I should read it immediately. I give the pass a quick look, but Ozzy's nowhere to be found.

Dropping my fork back on my plate with a clink, I bring my phone to my lap and bite my lip in anticipation while I unlock the screen, trying to be as subtle as I can.

Dry storage. Now.

Oh shit.

The effect is immediate. I'm so turned on right now, I can barely manage to breathe air into my lungs. I don't know what he has planned for me but that little threat he sent after my video still pulses decadently inside of me.

I mumble something to Gustavo beside me about needing the restroom. Walking into the kitchen as casually as I can, I hope no one is paying too close attention to what I'm doing—being that the restrooms are actually on the other side of the restaurant.

When I'm sure I'm out of sight of my coworkers, I scurry to the dry storage. My heart beats wildly with exhilaration. I'm not even halfway into the dark space, when Ozzy yanks me inside and slams me into the wall beside the metal shelving full of canned San Marzano tomatoes. They rattle just like my spine. But it doesn't hurt, it only unlocks that desperate and needy part of me that only Ozzy seems to sate.

My mouth falls open on a gasp, the air pushed out of my lungs. Ozzy's greedy hands are everywhere, digging into my breasts, my hips, thighs, groping my ass. It's as if he can't bear the thought of leaving a part of me untouched, and I feel the same, my hands as heated and hurried as his.

He catches my bottom lip with his teeth and tugs forcefully, kissing me with such possessive heat that I forget where we even are. There's only him and I and this smoldering, brazen moment between us.

"You thought you could send me that video and I wouldn't take advantage of you," he says in between ravaging kisses. "Huh princess?" His hands knead my ass, pushing my skirt up with his leg in between my thighs. "You think I'd see you in that pretty little lavender set and not want to immediately fuck your brains out?"

My giggle is mischievous, while I chase his lips with mine. "Maybe that was exactly my plan, salad boy." Both our hands are frantically pulling at each other's clothes, eager to fulfill every threat we're flinging at each other. "Maybe all I wanted was to use you, ever thought about that?"

He tugs my thong to the side and plunges two fingers

inside me. My moan is full of shocked delight, my head falling back onto the wall. His mouth tickles my ear. "You can use me as much as you like, baby." His fingers sloppily pumping in and out. "As long as I get to fuck your perfect pussy in the process."

Sliding his fingers out, I whimper at the loss. He shoves my thong down my thighs.

"Take those off," he orders while pulling a condom out of his pocket. "Give them to me."

His commanding tone is so intoxicating that I'd do anything he asks me.

I hand him my thong and he stuffs it in his pocket while tearing the foil wrapper of the condom open with his teeth. He pushes his pants down just low enough for his cock to spring out. Thick, veiny and so fucking enticing.

He then takes my hands and guides me to his cock. "Hurry up and put this on me, so I can rail you against this wall." There's a tremor in my touch while I slowly roll the condom over his hard, throbbing shaft, our burning gazes locked on one another, our chests rising almost in sync. I can barely handle the anticipation. His hand clasps around mine, our fingers curling at the base of his cock. "Bad girls get their pretty cunts stretched and don't make a sound, understand?"

I swallow hard, hiking my skirt over my hips, exposing my pussy to him. "Yes, chef," I say with a hint of a taunt, but inside I'm a shaky mess of adrenaline.

His eyes are hooded as they dip down and then back up, his hand finding me even more aroused than before. He slides only one finger inside this time as if toying with me and then says, "Open your mouth."

I lick my lips and then let my jaw fall open. As soon as I do, he shoves my thong into my mouth. I don't even have time to react before he's lifted me against the wall, both thighs around his hips as he notches himself at my entrance, pushing the tip inside with a slow but deliberate force. I can taste my own arousal on my thong, the cotton fabric getting drenched with my own saliva, my sounds muffled but seeking to be heard.

"Take a deep breath," he rasps, darkened eyes still fixed on me, his deviant grin promising nothing but debaucherous pleasure.

When my lungs are full on an inhale, he slams into me, his hips pinning me against the wall. My moan resembles more of a scream, the mix of pain and pleasure making me squeeze my thighs even tighter around him. Ozzy slams his tattooed hand over my mouth, the thong still balled up inside.

He coos while shushing me. "Not a sound, remember?" He slides his cock out and thrusts back in, his chef jacket straining against his chest. "Or maybe my dirty little princess likes the idea of someone walking in on us?" he says followed by a dark chuckle, his hips now setting a punishing rhythm. "I wouldn't stop fucking you even if they did."

His words are laced with fantasy and I latch on to them, my thoughts ablaze with the idea of us getting caught. I can feel myself getting even wetter. My muffled whimpers burn my lips as Ozzy pistons into me, over and over, hard and unforgiving against the wall.

My nails dig into his shoulder while my other hand trails down to where we connect, my clit swollen and sensitive. I mindlessly circle it, chasing the pleasure already building at an alarming pace and it makes me squeeze around Ozzy's cock, my muscles fluttering with mind-numbing arousal.

The tick of Ozzy's jaw and the groan he tries to contain behind clenched teeth make me believe he's teetering on the same all-consuming edge as I am. "Let me feel you come all over my cock, baby," he manages to bite out. His finger touches his lip, reminding me to stay quiet. "Can you do that for me?"

I furiously nod my agreement, feeling crazed, needing to come so badly I think I might cry. A few more desperate strokes over my clit, paired with Ozzy's cock splitting me open, manages to do just that. I bite down on my thong, my eyes rolling into the back of my head as the orgasm ripples through me like shock waves to the chest.

Ozzy's head falls into the crook of my neck, his breathing heavy and shallow as he pumps into me a few more times before stilling, his hips pushing me even harder into the wall. For a few seconds, he doesn't move, his mouth simply pressing into my skin. I'm sure he can feel the erratic beat of my heart against his lips.

As we both try to catch our breath, he lets me slide back down to the floor, and quickly pulls his pants back up with the condom still on. He then delicately takes my thong out of my mouth, while I smooth my skirt back down. Thinking he's going to hand them back to me, I open my palm. But he stuffs them into his pocket with a wink.

"Seriously?" I ask with a raised brow. "You're going to make me work commando?"

He barks a laugh, cheeks flushed, hair mussed, and looking prettier than ever. "If I had any say in it, you'd never wear panties again, sweetheart."

I roll my eyes, smiling like a fool.

Grabbing my neck with one hand, he kisses me. It's quick but passionate, and I'm left breathless all over again.

Afterward, he reaches over for a can of tomatoes. "Alibi," he deadpans. I giggle but don't say anything. "I'll go out first," he adds, his thumb stroking my cheek and bottom lip. "Have a good shift, yeah?"

I nod, my smile still wide against my cheeks. He nods back, eyes sparkling, and leaves.

I make a quick pit-stop at the restroom, hurriedly fixing my hair and my smudged mascara before returning to my cold plate of pasta. Checking my phone, I realize I don't have any more time to finish my staff meal.

Worth it.

Shoveling a few bites into my mouth near the dish pit, I scurry to finish my side jobs before Orso opens for the night.

23

JAMES

We end up getting slammed. My section is so packed that it feels like I'm constantly multiple steps behind. Customers wave me down for such inconsequential demands that all I want is to scream in their faces. The vibes feel off, more rowdy, aggressive even. Most of the wait staff blame it on the full moon.

Even if only a handful believe in astrology, no one can deny the effects of a full moon weekend. Without fail, customers will turn into snarling, snapping hellhounds and at least one of us will end up screaming in the walk-in fridge.

At least this time, I'm not the one crying in the back.

I think my little romp with Ozzy pre-service helped me coast through the worst of it.

Now, it's after midnight and I'm sitting at table 56, rolling cutlery. After a month and a half of working at Orso, it's become muscle memory. I stare into space, my feet throbbing, wondering if I should go out or just go home, order pizza, and eat it in bed.

I can't help but wonder what Ozzy's doing tonight. I don't automatically assume he'll want to hang out, but I can't deny I'd want to.

It's only been two weeks since my break-up with Zachary, and a week since I last saw him at Stanley's. Am I moving too fast with Ozzy? Even if we *are* just friends, he's still a distraction from my problems. Maybe I should be taking this time to learn how to be single and really embrace my independence.

But it's hard to focus whenever he's around.

Like a magnet, my eyes land on the man in question. He walks up to the bar where Elle is sitting, busy talking to Itzel. His chef jacket looks rumpled like he's gone through the wringer himself tonight. While they exchange some words, Ozzy pushes his blue bandana off his forehead, letting his curls fall loose. He spots me, his eyes lingering for half a second before focusing back on Elle and my stomach can't help but do a little swoop.

I go back to rolling cutlery and unbutton the top of my black shirt, suddenly feeling a little hot. I must have zoned out for a second because I startle when Ozzy pulls up a seat and sits down in front of me.

"Managed to survive your shift, Jimbo?" he asks with the usual curl of his lip, the small dimple appearing on his cheek.

"Barely," I groan, letting my body fall onto the chair behind me. He keeps his smile while he falls silent, staring at me. "What?" I eventually say.

He shrugs. "Nothing. I just like staring at you."

Warmth spreads behind my chest and I turn shy.

As if breaking out of a spell, he gives his head a little shake and straightens his back. "Anyway, I just wanted to tell you that I'm staying late tonight."

My eyebrows dip. "Why? The kitchen's been closed for over an hour."

He sighs, drumming the table with his fingers. "The rush never stopped and we ended up using absolutely everything so someone needs to stay to prep overnight." He looks at me with slight defeat and presses his lips. "I volunteered."

"So you're just going to be here by yourself?"

"Yeah," he says casually. "I've done it before. If Elle is gone then I just wait for the night porter to show up before leaving since I don't have the keys."

"I can keep you company," I blurt out.

Shit. I hope that didn't sound too desperate. Although I'm exhausted, hanging out with Ozzy sounds more inviting than sitting alone in bed with my thoughts.

"Really?" There's a flash of vulnerability in his gaze but it's gone as fast as it appears. It almost feels like he's surprised I'd choose to stick around and spend time with him.

"Yeah, why not? I don't have anything better to do."

He presses his hand to his heart. "I'm touched."

I burst out laughing. "That's not—you know what I mean."

He winks, his hand finding my calf under the table, giving it a little squeeze.

"Come find me when you're done," he says before standing up.

I smile as I nod, finishing another rolled cutlery. My eyes are still tracking Ozzy when my phone buzzes on the table. A quick look makes my stomach lurch.

It's Zachary.

Why the fuck would he be calling me?

We haven't talked since my birthday party. God knows

what he'd want if I picked up. Nothing good would come out of us speaking. I let it ring, a sick sense of dread scalding up my throat. When the call finally ends, I delete the missed call and pretend it was just a glitch in the matrix. Nothing more.

———

AN HOUR AND A HALF LATER, I'm sitting on a bar stool near Ozzy's prep station while he finishes slicing up the last of the wonton wraps into chips to fry. Elle left an hour ago, and the night porter isn't scheduled for another half hour so it's just us in here for now. I've never seen Orso so quiet, like a wild beast slumbering for the winter.

"Jamie! I know you're in there!"

The indignant voice pierces the silence like a rusty knife.

Ozzy and I freeze, his quizzical gaze slicing into mine. He might not immediately recognize the voice but I do. My eyes go wide while I stumble to my feet, knocking the stool over.

"Oh my god, it's Zac—"

I don't have time to finish my sentence before my ex stumbles into the kitchen like a raging bull.

How the hell did he even get in here?

Then I remember Ozzy propped the back door ajar when he last went for a smoke.

Years of being terrified of Zachary's erratic actions sink back into me like cement, and I can't move. Not one step. I can only watch, horrified.

"Jamie …" I can tell by the glazed look in his eyes and how he slurs my name that he's been drinking.

"Wh—" My voice cracks with nerves, and I close my

eyes for a small breath, swallowing hard, then pin him with my stare. "What are you doing—how did you even know I was here?"

His lip curls into a snarl, eyes narrowing. "Stupid bitch, too dumb to realize I permanently shared your location with my phone when you were sleeping."

His insults are sharp, but somehow, this time, they don't cut into my skin.

I feel Ozzy shift behind me but I hold out my hand, signaling him to stop.

Zachary takes a step forward, and I take a step back, my heart hammering.

"Please leave," I say as forcefully as I can muster.

"Jamie," he whines, his demeanor shifting on a dime. "I need to talk to you, I miss—"

"That's enough, buddy." Ozzy steps in front of me, blocking me from Zachary's path. "She told you to leave, so *leave*." His tone is neutral but still manages to sound ice-cold.

Zachary stumbles backward as if pushed, looking genuinely shocked that someone would cut him off while he was speaking. His lip lifts into a snarl. He tries to meet my gaze behind Ozzy, but I look down at the floor. I feel nauseous, I can't bear even looking at him.

He starts to chuckle. It's dry and menacing as it ripples over my skin like unwelcome goosebumps. "So what? You're fucking this loser now? I mean, look at him," he spits in disgust. "I knew you were a disgusting slut, but I never thought you'd sink to this level."

"That's it," Ozzy hisses, taking another menacing step toward Zachary. "You aren't going to speak to her like that in front of me."

Zachary smirks while Ozzy walks towards him, probably thinking because he has a few inches over him, he'd beat Ozzy in a fight.

Ozzy places a hand on Zachary's shoulder. He tries to shove it away but Ozzy is faster, grabbing him by the collar and dragging Zachary to the fryer. There's a scuffle, and it happens so fast that my brain lags trying to decipher what's going on.

I hear Zachary scream.

It's blood-curdling and my hands fly to my face in shock, covering my mouth.

I realize then that Ozzy has plunged Zachary's right hand into the fryer. I hear the hot oil sizzle before Ozzy grabs him by the back of his shirt with both hands. He pulls him away from the kitchen while Zachary whimpers, his left hand holding the mangled skin of his right. His feet skitter and slip on the floor while Ozzy drags him out the back door.

Needing to see how this ends, I follow them out into the parking lot. Ozzy shoves Zachary onto the pavement and spits on him.

Zachary is a blubbering mess, eyes wide. "You're fucking crazy." He repeats it a few times under his breath as if stunned. But his gaze is etched in terror as if he can't even comprehend that someone could physically harm him.

Ozzy takes a menacing step toward him, and he skitters backward on his ass.

"If you think that was bad, know that James told me what you and your friend did to her. And if you ever so much as *think* about her, or tell a soul what happened tonight, remember that I can make what I just did to you look like child's play next time."

Zachary lets out a small sob in response, snot dripping

down his face. He nods profusely while pushing himself up with his uninjured hand

He doesn't dare look at me before slinking away.

As soon as he's out of sight, Ozzy turns to me and drags me back inside, slamming the door behind us. He yanks me into his arms.

I realize I'm shaking.

Letting me go, he cradles my face with his hands, peering into my eyes. "Are you okay?" His words sound so tender that I crack. I shatter like fragile glass and begin to sob.

He tugs me back into his arms and I don't fight it, melting into his embrace while I try to gulp back my tears, but it's futile. "I'm fine," I mumble into his chef's jacket. "I'm fine."

I repeat the words over and over again, hoping that saying them might prevent the dark hole hovering above me from swallowing me up.

"You're safe," he says into my hair, squeezing me into him as if terrified to let me go. "I'm so sorry, James. I shouldn't have done that in front of you. You shouldn't have seen that."

I'm still shaking. Freezing but also so numb. "It's not that … I don't care that you—I just …"

The words just don't seem to form. Ozzy softly shushes me, trying to calm me down and have me take a deep breath. I do, and the familiar scent of blackcurrant and tea from his cologne manages to ground me somewhat.

His lips graze mine and I slowly feel less cold. I grab hold of his jacket near his waist, pulling him into me hard. The adrenaline still pumping through our veins adds urgency to the kiss, our lips wet with my tears. I want to lose myself in this feeling, but eventually, Ozzy gently pushes me away. His expression racked with concern.

"Come on, let me drive you home," he whispers.

I shake my head, my gaze fixed on his comforting blue-green eyes. "Can I stay with you?"

His face softens. "Of course."

24

JAMES

I wake up in Ozzy's arms. I barely remember him bringing me to his place. By then, I was just a blur of heightened emotions, but I still fell asleep quickly when he curled his lithe body around mine in bed. But first, I made sure to turn off my locations on my phone.

I should have known …

Should have suspected Zachary wasn't above tampering with my privacy.

I lay still, pretending to be asleep as I focus on Ozzy's chest rising and falling against my back. His warm body next to mine feels almost … too good to be true.

It's a confusing feeling.

Last night left me fragmented.

Zachary got what was coming to him—Ozzy didn't do anything wrong.

But there's a hard pit burrowing a hole through my stomach, nonetheless.

I can't seem to pinpoint the root cause of it. Maybe I just need time to process.

Not only about what happened yesterday, but everything that happened with Ozzy *and* Zachary leading up to
now. I've become an accumulation of bad experiences
which makes this unnameable guilt tighten around my
throat—I'm not even sure where it's stemming from. My
emotions feel muddled and everything is feeling all too
much.

I just need some time alone to figure it all out.

Carefully, I pull the duvet off of me and lift Ozzy's arm
away before sitting up. He stirs but doesn't wake up. I'm
wearing another one of his shirts again. I consider wearing
it home but decide against it, leaving it neatly folded on the
bed. Finding my work clothes on a wooden chair in the
corner of the bedroom, I put them on.

I'm combing my hair with my fingers, getting ready to
leave, when Ozzy wakes up. He rubs one sleepy eye while
pushing himself up in bed.

"Everything okay?" he asks, his voice groggy and
hoarse.

Is anything ever okay? "Yeah," I answer with a soft, closed
smile. "It's getting late, I just need to get home before my
shift tonight."

"Let me drive you." Flinging the covers off, he jumps
out of bed, but I stop him.

"No, it's fine," I say quickly. "I feel like walking."

"That'll take you over an hour ..." There's a subtle
change in his expression, it's so minute I can barely make it
out. He looks younger then, standing in the middle of his
room as if I'm deliberately abandoning him.

I look away.

I pretend to look for my tote bag.

"I like walking." My smile is forced, and I feel like I'm

unintentionally making this awkward but I can't make myself stop.

Ozzy begins to move forward but stops himself. His chest is bare while he rubs a hand over the top of his opposite bicep as if in a nervous tick. "Okay, then." He crosses his arms but then drops them immediately.

His tone holds no malice, it's just a statement. I know he's just following whatever bleak signal I'm giving off right now, but it hurts nonetheless. Tears prick my eyes. I blink them away.

God, I'm a mess.

I try to leave on a hopeful note. "See you tonight?" I ask since I know he's also working later today. His smile is warm but muted when he nods.

I want to kiss him goodbye.

Instead, I give him a little wave and leave him standing there.

I WALK the first ten minutes in complete silence. My thoughts are so broody, I can barely stand myself, let alone be in my own company. My phone buzzes somewhere inside my purse, snapping me out of my downward spiral. By the time I find it, lodged between my wallet and makeup pouch, I've missed the call.

Seeing who called, I realize I wouldn't have picked up anyway.

My stomach sinks when my phone dings with the notification that my mother has left me a voicemail. I have a suspicion this might be about Zachary, and my breath hallows with anxiety, hoping he didn't say anything that would incriminate Ozzy. Letting out a shaky sigh, I take my earphones out of my bag to listen to what she's got to say.

"James, dear," she says, her tone is curt but worried. "I just got off the phone with Bethany Garret—her poor boy. Why didn't you tell me Zachary had a *firework* accident last night? Imagine how mortified I was not knowing he was *injured*." She sniffs. "Anyway, I'm sure you know he's flying to their house in Turks and Caicos to convalesce." An icy pause follows until she speaks again. "I would *appreciate it* if you would inform me of these things next time," she grits, between, what I can only imagine, are clenched teeth. Before hanging up, she adds, "You better answer next time I call."

Relief washes over me. Deep down I knew Zachary wouldn't dare retaliate. Although a large part of me feared him when we were together, I always knew he was spineless.

It's much easier to prey on the weak. They don't typically fight back.

And last night he finally got a taste of his own karmic medicine.

Deciding I don't want to be left alone with my thoughts for the rest of the walk home, I delete my mother's voicemail and dial Connie's number. We haven't talked since Zachary and I broke up two weeks ago and, well … there's a lot to catch her up on.

She picks up on the second ring, out of breath, and tells me she's out for a morning hike. At least hearing her voice makes me smile. On days like these, I wish I could just head over to her place and curl up in bed with her while she shows me cute cat videos to make me laugh.

We end up talking the rest of the walk home, Connie periodically squealing anytime I mention something Ozzy did or said. I omit the part where Zachary showed up. I don't want her to worry, but I still feel guilty keeping it from her.

When do I *not* feel guilty?

The feeling seems to have always been a part of me, even when I was a young child. Maybe it's about time I shed another skin, relieve myself from the constant ache of feeling guilty for everyone else's actions, or that nagging feeling of never being good enough.

Finally home, I let myself fall into bed, Connie still on the line.

"Don't you think things are moving too fast though?"

She pushes out a laugh. It sounds more like a squawk. "Says who? The dating police? You're just having fun. It doesn't need to be that deep, Jamie. "

I roll my eyes. "Fine. I guess you're right."

"I know I am. Anyway, I've got to go. I'm meeting someone for coffee. Send me pictures of this Ozzy guy okay? I need a visual."

I scoff. "That's going to be hard, he only posts pictures of food."

She cackles into the phone. I tell her I'll try to sneak a picture next time I'm with him, and then hang up.

Staring at the ceiling, I go over what Connie and I talked about, trying to sift through my rational and irrational thoughts. It's a hard task. My feelings are always a complicated mess.

There's no denying my relationship with Zachary was a large influence on the person I've become today. He's the blueprint I compare everything to. He was my first real boyfriend, and even if deep down I knew that his actions were manipulative—abusive—I still don't know what healthy looks like. I continue to experience life through the distorted lens of my past.

It's toxic, and damaging, and—and … I don't know if I'll ever manage to move on from what he did to me. What Spencer did to me.

How can anyone move on from … rape?

I can barely think of the word without wanting to curl up into a ball and sleep the shame away. How do I come to terms with knowing that the version of myself who existed before, died that day? That the person who's here, feeling the tears rolling down my face, isn't anyone I truly recognize.

She's a hollow, empty version of who I once was, and who I hoped to become.

Life isn't fiction. There's no satisfying revenge I can exact.

There's only this. The uncomfortable and painful reality of simply existing. I'm left to revive whatever pieces of my soul they left behind when they were done with me.

Who will ever bother to love me like this?

Cracked. Defective.

Broken.

Just too fucking much …

And just not worth the time.

I let out a long sigh.

Great.

Connie tells me to just have fun, and the first thing I do when we hang up is spiral into a dark pit of despair. Classic James.

Pushing myself up, I grab my sketchbook from beside the bed.

I need to get out of my head.

The sketchbook opens to the last thing I drew.

Ozzy.

It's a rough sketch, barely halfway finished, but my heart feels like it's being squeezed by a fist just looking at it. The memory attached to it is so vivid, I can taste it. I can feel his skin, the coarse hair on his thighs, against the tip of my fingers.

It reminds me of what it's like to be in his presence.

Of how desirable he makes me feel with just a look.

A touch.

Then, I know.

That whatever *this* is between me and Ozzy, I want to chase it for as long as I can.

25

OZZY

"Can we talk?"

James looks shy under the moonlight as we stand outside of Orso. The way she's gripping her tote bag over her shoulder with both hands makes it seem like she's not sure what to do with them while she waits for me to answer.

We barely talked during our shift, barely a glance if it wasn't work-related.

With the way she left this morning, I'm giving her space. As much as I have the innate urge to, it's not my place to comfort her if she doesn't want me to.

Especially with what happened last night.

I somehow managed to suppress the gleeful satisfaction I felt when maiming that piece of shit in front of her. If I had my way, I'd be dunking his friend's face in the oil next.

But what I do regret is having James there witnessing it.

I move away from the dumpster and flick my cigarette further into the parking lot. "Of course we can talk, Jimbo." Knowing someone is bound to interrupt us if we stay here, I ask, "Did you clock out? I can drive you home."

She nods and worries her bottom lip. "Yeah, I'd like that."

"Just give me a sec. Meet me by my car." I run back in for my bag, having already changed into a pair of dickies, a cropped red shirt, and my patched vest before I stepped out for a smoke.

James looks so pretty waiting for me by the car. It's a balmy night, and her long floral skirt is a slinky little thing as it drifts in the night breeze. The slit up her left leg makes me want to push her against the car and drag my palm along her thigh. But I resist the heady temptation, unlocking and opening the door for her instead. She gives me a sheepish thank you and climbs in. Jogging to the driver's side, I get in and start the car.

"Listen, James," I say as I turn the wheel and reverse my way out of the parking lot, my arm around the back of her seat. "I want to apologize for yester—"

She cuts me off. "I don't want your apology, Ozzy." She rests her elbow atop the open window and cradles her head with her hand. "You didn't do anything wrong, he deserved it, and actually …" her voice trails off as if losing herself in thought, and I wait in silence for her to finish her sentence. "I actually wanted to apologize to *you*."

I scoff. "What for?"

She turns her head to look at me and I peek a glance while I drive, curious to see what emotion is painted on that beautiful face of hers. I think I see worry in her blue eyes.

"This … thing between us," she says, waving her hand in the space between the two seats. "It's supposed to be fun. It's supposed to be this casual thing and—well it's only been two weeks and you've seen me cry *multiple* times, not to mention the weird constant drama with Zachary." She huffs, looking out the car window. "It's embarrassing," she mutters. There's silence, then she adds meekly, "I wouldn't hold it against you if you're losing interest."

At that, I laugh. "Losing interest? Jimbo, baby. Why do you think I'd be losing interest?"

She sighs dramatically. "Because how is this any fun? I'm just …" She crosses her arms in protest. "Depressing."

I reach over and give her thigh a little squeeze. "You're the one who said this needed to be fun and casual. I just said I wanted to hang out with you. Cut yourself some slack."

She pauses, and I peek another glance at the passenger seat. It looks like she's mulling something over by the way she's chewing on her inner cheek. "Can we start over?" she asks.

"Start what over?"

"This. *Us,*" she says with another emphatic wave of her hand. "Let's make a deal." She turns in her seat to face me, and I take the time to study her as the car idles at a red light. Her face is bright, eyes sparkling as if excited about whatever she's about to offer up. "From this day forward, we leave the personal shit at home. No more drama. Nothing serious. Just fun, casual … sex," she says with a playful smile and hard nod.

She brandishes her hand toward me, and I look at it dumbly. My gaze slides up to meet hers. "You want me to shake on it?" I say with a laugh.

I'm not about to break her spirit, biting back the urge to tell her to go fuck her rules.

I'll just go with it for her sake.

But then I have an idea.

"Fine," I say, holding off on the handshake. "But I have

a rule of my own." The light turns green and I turn on Willet Street making my way into her neighborhood.

"Okay, that's only fair," she says with a somewhat haughty air. "What is it?"

I lick my lips, holding in a smirk before I answer. "From now on." I reach back over and graze her leg with the back of my hand. Then my fingers brush her naked thigh, dangerously close to her sweet, perfect cunt. "No condoms."

She lets out one single shocked laugh, but I don't miss the subtle opening of her legs. "Okay," she says, elongating the last part of the word for emphasis, clearly chewing on what I just said. Then she counters. "But, no condoms means no fucking anyone else."

"I'm not fucking anyone else, princess," I answer immediately. "Are *you*?" I mean it as a flippant joke. God, I hope it's a joke.

"Me?" She laughs. "I'm not the one with the slutty reputation."

Finally at her place, I park the car on the street, my hand still on her thigh. Her comment stings. The label never bothered me before, but hearing James describe me as just that makes me wonder if that's all she sees me as. Someone who can get her off.

I sit with the feeling for only a split second and then shake it off. There's not much I can do about that now. Turning towards her, I cradle her pussy with my palm for just a few seconds.

My voice turns deep, and slightly mocking. "I don't remember you complaining about my slutty reputation before."

Her eyes go wide, the tiniest of breath hitching in her throat.

I want to devour her whole.

Her blue eyes rove over my face, studying me until finally, she whispers, "Okay, deal." And then adds, "But I don't want anyone knowing about this at Orso."

The sting returns, like salt in an open wound.

Does she not want to be seen with me?

I'm usually a fan of sneaking around but with James? All I want is the world to know that I'm with her. Although —our relationship clearly means a lot more to me than it does to her. Am I being delusional? Maybe. But if it allows me to spend time with her, then I'll gladly stay delusional.

For a loaded moment, we stare at each other.

"Deal," I finally say, holding my hand out for her to shake.

She does and then the car falls silent.

Leaning my arm over the steering wheel, I wait for her to say something.

"Are you …" She clears her throat. "Do you want to come in?"

"Can't tonight," I say as gently as possible. I avoid telling her I need to check up on my two younger siblings. Fun and casual doesn't include my family bullshit.

She looks disappointed but composes herself quickly. "Okay. See you Monday maybe?"

I smile "See you Monday."

She returns the smile. "Thanks for the ride," she says, giving me a quick kiss on the cheek before climbing out of the car.

"Anytime, baby."

She waves goodbye and I give her one back. I stay parked until she enters her building and only then do I drive away. Visions of pink hair and blue eyes follow me all the way home.

26

OZZY

Two days later, I roll over in bed, my head throbbing with a hangover. Groaning, I push a palm into my eye and pat for my phone on the bedside table. Seeing the time, I curse under my breath. It's almost noon. I didn't plan on sleeping so late on my only day off.

I was hoping to see James today since it's Monday.

She didn't work last night, and I can't pretend that I didn't miss her. After work, I went out with Alec to a bar I can't remember the name of and missed her even more after a few pints of cream ale. In the bar bathrooms, the red lights cloaked the space with a crimson hue. I couldn't help but think it would make a nice backdrop for a picture, and after a few Fernet shots, my inhibitions were low enough that I ended up sending a far too serious selfie to James.

Now in the harsh glare of the morning sun, I'm nearly drowning with mortification at the thought. Although, it must not have been that embarrassing because despite it being late, James reciprocated with her own selfie, hers a lot more alluring than mine—nude from the waist up, her arm banded over her naked tits. I jerked off to it as soon as I stumbled back home.

Sitting upright in bed, my feet planted on the floor, I lean my elbow on my thigh, and check the unread text from James.

> Morning! I'm having a park day today.
> Join me?

I grin. Pleased by James' initiative.

> Morning Jimbo. Sounds like a plan to me.
> Want me to come pick you up?

I stand up and head for the shower, my phone pinging in my hand on the way.

> I'm already here. :) It's Dulford Park near
> my house. I'm next to the community
> garden, you can't miss it.

> Sounds good. I'll be there soon.

I WISH I knew how to paint. For the image of James in her blue summer dress, sitting on a blanket with the sun's rays bouncing off cotton candy hair, makes me want to spend countless hours immortalizing her likeness.

Instead, I do the next best thing and stop walking before she notices me, taking a few pictures of her from afar. When I'm done, I resume my way toward her. She's busy focusing on a sketchbook in front of her, paintbrush in hand, concentration creasing the space between her brows.

She smiles brightly when she finally spots me, but

there's a greedy part of me that wishes I'd stayed unnoticed so I could spend my day just staring.

"Hi," she says softly, her lips glimmering with gloss. Looking up from where she's sitting, her eyes slightly squint behind the sunglasses perched on her upturned nose. They match her dress, the lenses blue but transparent, with a small gem-encrusted heart at the bottom right.

"Having a good day, princess?" I ask as I kneel down beside her, kissing her on the cheek before settling on the blanket.

She dunks the brush into a small plastic cup full of water and leans back on her hands.

"Better now that you're here," she says with a coy smile, looking up at the sky.

A warm trickle of relief flows through my veins at hearing those words, followed by a flurry of butterflies deep in my stomach. I didn't realize I needed to hear her say that so badly. Our last conversation had left me insecure, making me wonder if she even really liked me.

"Is that so?" I watch her long hair fall off her shoulder, loose against her back. I lean over, idly twisting a strand around my finger. "Miss me?"

Her smile grows wider. "Like how you missed me last night?"

My hand falls to my lap. "What do you mean 'like how I missed you last night'?"

Her laugh is effervescent but I start to sweat. "You don't remember?"

"Remember what?" *Jesus fucking Christ*, what the hell did I do? Did I really drink that much?

"You called me when you were out."

I fall silent. Her words have unearthed a vague and hazy memory of me on the phone while I smoked a cigarette outside the bar. But what was said during that conversation is anyone's guess. "I called you," I repeat.

"Yeah," she replies, tonguing her cheek, her eyes slowly sliding to me. "You really don't remember?"

"Barely," I say flatly, pulling out my pack of smokes from my jeans pocket. "I didn't say anything too embarrassing, I hope?" I mumble around the cigarette between my lips.

"*You* might find it embarrassing. But I think it's adorable."

I groan. "Adorable? Great, there goes my allure," I say only half-jokingly, taking a long drag.

She giggles. "Don't worry, you didn't say anything too incriminating."

"At least give me something, sweetheart, I'm dying over here," I counter back.

Her smile turns smug. "You told me my hair reminded you of cotton candy and that I tasted just as sweet." She chokes on a laugh but continues, "You also told me that you'd rather be cuddling with me in bed than watching Alec try to get laid at the bar."

I smirk, tapping the ash from my cigarette into the grass. "I thought I embarrassed myself, but that was just the truth."

Our gazes lock, and a loaded beat passes between us.

I'm the one who moves first, reaching over to steal a kiss, her giggles melting on my tongue like sugar. She tastes like peaches.

"Anyway," I say, after pulling away, hoping to change the subject. "What are you painting?"

"Just some flowers," she says, looking down at her sketchbook. "Something about them calms me."

I hum in understanding. "Cooking is like that for me,

sometimes." I stub my cigarette in the dirt, pinching the smoldering tobacco out of the stub and putting it back in the pack. "Did you always want to be a painter?"

I lay on my back, my hands clasped over my stomach. James lays next to me, staring at the puffy clouds, before she answers my question.

"I've romanticized that lifestyle for as long as I remember."

"What lifestyle?" I ask, taking her arm and placing it over my chest, my fingers drawing circles on the skin of her forearm.

She stays silent for a beat. "You know that famous hotel in New York City that was really popular back in the 60s and 70s? It had all these starving artists staying there."

I breathe out a small chuckle. "Hotel Chelsea? Yeah of course I've heard of it."

She takes back her arm and rolls over onto her stomach to look at me, both hands cradling her chin. "Okay well, I used to daydream about what it would have been like to live during that time. You know? Where nothing mattered but your art. Imagine being able to pay your rent with your paintings if you were too broke that week?" she says wistfully, her eyes glimmering. "I don't know … people's creativity felt more pure back then. There were no brands or social media. No need for marketing. No influencer bull-shit. The goal wasn't to get famous. Art wasn't a way to make money. Life was art, art was life and that was good enough for them." I study her with a grin. "Look," she adds, "I've heard all of it before, 'rich girl cosplaying at being poor'," she says while air-quoting her last few words. "I know how it sounds." She shrugs. "Doesn't change the fact that they somehow seemed happier." She pauses.

"Maybe because they were living authentically … I don't know."

I can't help but stare, my body reacting conflictingly—a painful pinch to the heart clashing with a surge of adoration. Getting to know James on a deeper level is turning me into an addict. I could spend my whole life here in this park, rain or shine, listening to her talk.

I reach over and drag my thumb across her glossy bottom lip. It's tacky under my touch, pulling at her lip. My thoughts turn filthy, but I just sit with the feeling staring into her starry blue eyes.

"I like how your brain works, Jimbo."

Her cheeks pinken, her expression turning coy. After another loaded silence, she asks, "And what about you?"

"What about me?" I repeat.

She sits up, sliding herself closer to me. Placing her palm on my chest, she slowly moves it down my stomach. "What did you spend your time daydreaming about when you were a teenager?"

Distracted, my eyes track her hand, now toying with the bottom of my shirt. When I don't immediately answer she gives my stomach a small tap. My gaze jumps to her face, and she gives me an impatient look as if waiting for an answer.

What did I daydream about as a teenager?

I spent most of my time locked in my room, blasting music and wishing my parents weren't my parents. But there's no way I'm telling James that. So, I choose a more light-hearted answer.

"Touring the world with my band."

"Your band? I didn't know you were a musician."

"Hardly. You don't need much talent when you're in a punk band playing for a crowd of three."

My phone vibrates in my pocket but I ignore it.

"I wonder if we would have liked each other back then," she muses.

I bark a laugh. "Considering you were fifteen when I was eighteen, that's a hard pass."

She chuckles, face seeking the sun. "Right."

My phone vibrates in my pocket again. That's two calls in less than a minute.

I groan, reluctantly releasing James' hand from my grasp. Hers falls on the blanket next to me as I fish out my phone from my front pocket.

It's Huxley.

I can't remember the last time he called me. I sit up straight, my heart immediately sinking to my stomach.

"Is everything okay?" I ask instead of a hello.

His tone is flat. "Dad's in the hospital."

"What?" I say in alarm.

I stand up, ignoring James' concerned look.

"Where's everyone?"

"Sophia has Charlie with her at Mercy General. I'm heading over there now."

"Why didn't she call me?"

"She did. Said you didn't pick up."

I curse under my breath, the guilt so intense I feel like I might choke on it.

"Okay. I'm on my way."

I hang up, not bothering to wait for a reply. I look down at James, remorse chewing at my insides at having to leave her like this.

"What's wrong?" she asks, worry marring her face.

Whatever is happening with my dad categorically falls into the shit we agreed we wouldn't bring into our arrangement. So I avoid the subject.

"Something came up. I've got to go." I lean down to kiss her. "I'm so sorry." Standing back up, my phone is still gripped in my hand. "I'll call you later, okay?"

She nods, her eyebrows still pinched together, and whispers a soft, "Okay."

I linger for half a second, watching her.

I feel split in half.

But I turn around and leave.

27

OZZY

The distinct antiseptic smell permeating the hospital corridors reminds me of the time I broke my arm when I was thirteen. I tried to land a trick on a halfpipe in the skate park near school. My left arm broke the fall—the bone snapped clean in half—and I was stuck in a cast for five weeks.

It's also the last memory I have of my mother taking care of me.

I'm ashamed to admit … when she ultimately disappeared again, I yearned for another injury to land me in the hospital, just so she would come back and act like a mother again.

Bitterness smarts my throat and I swallow hard.

At the nurse's station, I ask what room I can find Richard McKenna in. The charge nurse directs me to the fourth door on the left. My feet feel like lead, while the glare of the fluorescent lights gives me a headache.

The muted beeps of hospital machines and the intermittent coughs of sick patients become the background noise to my slow walk up to the room, my heart pumping anxiety straight into my blood.

I see Huxley first. I notice he's shaved his hair into a green mohawk. His new haircut paired with the combat boots and leather jacket, makes his already serious features look even more severe.

My eyes then land on Sophia and Charlie. They haven't noticed me yet, staring down at the first bed to my right. It's a shared room, the faded yellow curtains drawn shut between the stainless steel beds for some semblance of privacy. Huxley's a few steps away from the other two. The divide in our family can be felt—and seen—even here.

My attention swings to my dad sleeping, or uncon-scious, I still have no clue. But by the look of him, it might be the latter. His face is black and blue, his right eye swollen shut with a butterfly stitch closing a gash near his brow.

Jesus fucking Christ.

I can't imagine what he did to look as beat up as he does.

But I have a few ideas.

Charlie notices me first. "Oz!" he exclaims, running into my arms.

Sophia immediately shushes him.

"Hey buddy," I whisper, ruffling his short curls, his head still only reaching up to the middle of my chest. "Are you okay?"

"Dad got beat up," he deadpans, looking up at me with big blue eyes.

"Did he now?" I mutter, looking over to Hux. He confirms with a nod.

I can't seem to muster any sympathy for my dad. All I feel is disappointment in his actions, and rage for the kids having to deal with his bullshit.

Charlie releases me from his hug and I walk over to Sophia, dragging her into me. Her arms wrap tightly around my waist and she sniffles into my chest. My heart cracks. With my chin resting on the crown of her head, I make large circles with my palm on her back.

"What happened this time," I ask Huxley from over Sophia's head.

"Same shit, different day," he responds with an eye roll. "He was found unconscious behind O'Toole's in the early hours of the morning. He got dropped off at the hospital by EMTs." He scratches his head, then drops his hand in exhausted defeat. "It took them a while to figure out who he was. It was only at shift change that one of the nurses— Betty's niece actually—realized it was Dad."

Betty was my mother's friend, once upon a time. It ended badly. Betty found out that Carol—our mom—had been fucking her husband. It didn't take long for the whole neighborhood to find out. Dad never mentioned it.

"Was it Matty?" I ask. The loser loan shark working out of O'Toole's. My dad has been digging a bigger and bigger hole with him for as long as I can remember. With his connection to the Irish mob, I'm surprised Richard hasn't gotten himself killed by now.

Huxley shrugs. "Probably. He hasn't woken up to tell us himself."

Gently pushing Sophia out of my arms, I walk closer to the bed and peer down.

Shit. This is the worst I've ever seen him. My hand moves to touch him like it has a mind of its own. Managing to stop it before reaching his arm, I grip the bed railing instead. "Is he sleeping or …"

"Sleeping," Sophia murmurs.

"He's on a lot of painkillers," Huxley adds. "He's got a few broken ribs and a punctured lung."

I nod but say nothing.

We all fall silent for a while. Then finally, I ask, "Are you guys hungry?" The youngest two nod emphatically, and I give them a small motion of the head toward the door. "Let's go find something to eat then."

Sophia and Charlie head out, but I stay back, noticing that Huxley hasn't moved. Fists shoved in his pockets, shoulders tense and brows creased, he's still staring down at the hospital bed.

"You coming?"

He doesn't look up. "In a bit."

I pat him on the shoulder and he tenses even more, his body jerking slightly away from my touch. Not bothering to say anything, I leave the room. Regret trails behind me like a melancholic ghost, wishing things could be different between Huxley and I.

FEELING like my soul has just slammed back into my body, I jerk awake, nearly toppling out of the chair I've been sleeping in. My head swivels around the room trying to orientate myself, but my foggy brain lags until finally I remember I'm still in my dad's hospital room.

When it was clear Richard wasn't going to wake up for a while, I told Huxley to take the kids back home and I stayed behind. I'm not even sure why I stayed overnight.

For Sophia and Charlie's sake maybe.

Definitely not mine.

I groan softly, dragging my hand over my face. My gaze lands on the hospital bed and I swallow a yelp when I find swollen eyes, color so similar to mine, staring back at me.

"*Jesus Christ,*" I curse slowly, my heart slamming hard against my chest. "You scared me."

My dad doesn't say a word, his face half-cloaked in darkness. The beep of machines and the patter of rain against the window are the only sounds in the room. He doesn't even move, just continues to stare. I'd think he was dead if not for his intermittent slow blinks.

Sick of the silence, I fill it with a half-hearted question. "How are you feeling?"

Still he doesn't respond. Irritation percolates behind my chest, growing more and more frustrated the longer he doesn't speak.

Slowly he licks his busted lip. "Your mother was my first love, did you know that? And I was hers." His voice is hoarse like someone sucker punched him in the vocal cords.

They probably did.

I blink a few times, letting his words slowly drift in my head like snowflakes laced with poison. What the hell is he on about?

I nod, hands clasped, elbows resting on my thighs. "Yeah, I knew that."

He turns his head forward, now staring at the ceiling. "We were high school sweethearts. And oh … she had such a bright future ahead of her when we first met. She was going to become a lawyer." His head falls back toward me, his one good eye shiny and wet. "Did you know that? She was going to make a difference, your mother. She was going too—" He chokes on a cough, it crackles in his throat. It looks painful by the way he keeps hacking and wincing.

I lack the empathy to care. I just sit silently and watch.

He wheezes and slumps back into his pillow as if his coughing fit took everything out of him.

My nape prickles as if I'm sensing an invisible danger. I get the sudden urge to leave.

"But then she got pregnant at seventeen." His eyes back on the ceiling. "I convinced her to keep it." *It* … He means me. "Convinced her to marry me. She dropped out of school after that …" His gaze finds me in the dark. "Never was the same after having you. Started looking at me like I ruined her life. Like I took something precious from her, when all I did was love her. Then she got hooked on meth after Huxley was born. She would've never cheated on me if she was right in the head."

"Why are you telling me all this?" I say through a clenched jaw.

His lungs whistle when he breathes. "Because us McKennas ruin everything we touch." Weakly, he raises his hand. The IV cords tangle loosely as he points a crooked finger at me. "You think you're different because you left young and got out of Pecket?" He smiles, it's malicious, and it tears at my skin the more I look at it. "Stop being a fucking fool, boy. Deep down you and I? We're exactly the same. You have the same blood running through your veins. Don't be surprised if one day, you end up just like your old man."

I'm shaking with rage. I stand up, fists tight against my sides.

"Fuck you," I spit. "At least I take care of this family, you worthless piece of shit."

I leave the hospital before I surrender to the overwhelming urge to wrap my hands around his scrawny neck and strangle him half to death.

28

OZZY

The rain soaks my shirt while I walk through the hospital parking lot. It's cold against my skin, but it does nothing to extinguish the anger burning inside of me. It feels like my chest is about to crack open and if I'm not careful, I'll bleed out before I get to my car.

My vision is blurring, my breaths shortening, and I'm shaking by the time I unlock my car. Slamming the door closed, I let my head fall back on the headrest, squeezing my eyes shut, struggling to get air into my lungs. My hearing is dimming, the thrum of my own heartbeat overtaking the sounds in my ears.

You're having a panic attack.

I squeeze my eyes shut even harder, hitting the headrest with the back of my head again and again.

Breathe Ozzy. Fucking breathe.

My mind feels like it's about to get ripped out of my brain. It's like an outside force is trying to throw me out of my own body, while simultaneously trapping me in.

So fucking trapped.

Stuck. As if this state of being is now my forever.

My palms start to sweat and I clench them around my thighs to stave off the shaking.

Although it feels like the hardest thing I've ever tried to do, I start to breathe in from my nose, and out from my mouth. I need to slow my heart rate down. I peel my eyes open and start to name things I can see. Name things I can touch.

I listen to the sound of the rain.

I listen to my own breathing.

I'm not sure how long I sit there, staring out into the dark night but eventually, I calm down. I'm still on edge, my jaw painfully clenched, but at least I'm no longer in a downward spiral.

I pull out a cigarette from my damp pack and with still shaky hands I light it—hoping the nicotine will help.

It does. But only a little.

Starting the car, I put on a death metal playlist and let the music wash over me. The melody reverberates in a similar tune as my frantic thoughts and it settles me somehow.

It gives voice to how I'm feeling inside.

Still, my dad's voice rings loudly in my head as I pull out of the parking lot.

Us McKennas ruin everything we touch.

I cling to his words.

Chewing on them.

Tasting them.

Swallowing them.

I cling to them until they're so deeply entrenched inside me that I can no longer remember who said it first. Only that it sounds like the truth. It echoes in my ears as if my ancestors were brought back to life, just for them to remind me of my legacy.

Us McKennas ruin everything we touch.

Ruin everything.

Ruin everything.

Ruin.

Everything.

I can't tell how long I've been driving, only that I thought I was driving aimlessly.

Until I'm two blocks away from James' apartment complex.

I slow down.

Now that her face is at the forefront of my mind.

Now that her name is on the tip of my tongue.

I can see the entrance of her building.

I need to see her.

I park.

I look at the time. It's two in the morning ... I chew on my lip, deliberating. And then call her anyway. She picks up on the second ring.

"Hey you," she says. Her voice sounds alert as if she was still awake at this hour, and I'm immediately soothed by the cadence of it.

"I thought you'd be sleeping."

"Couldn't sleep."

My fingers drum the steering wheel, the rain loud against the car roof.

"A lot on your mind?" I ask.

She chuckles. "Always."

"When was the last time you played in the rain?"

Her giggle is filled with delight and I ache to have her under my touch. "Are you serious?" she says playfully.

"Deadly." There's a grin slowly forming on my lips and I let it happen.

The line goes silent for a beat. "Where are you?"

"Downstairs."

"Downstairs?" she repeats, slight surprise in her voice. Then another pause. "Okay, I'll come down."

I chuckle. "That's my girl. Oh, and Jimbo?

"Yeah?"

"Put on something white."

I end the call, throwing my phone in the passenger seat. I don't know if she'll actually listen to my last request, but I hope she will. The thought of wet fabric clinging to her soft tits makes me chew on my thumb, leg bouncing as I wait.

I'm suddenly starving for her.

A few minutes later, I see the building door open and I climb out of the car so she can spot me since I'm parked in a vacant spot, away from most other vehicles.

And fuck, she has on a white tank top, pink gym shorts and slides. I lick my lips, barely feeling the rain now that James is in my line of vision. I start making my way toward her, and everything else begins to melt away.

Under the awning, she peers upwards as if gauging how hard it's raining. Then looks around, eventually spotting me. When she does, she walks straight into the rain. Laughing, she raises her shoulders and hands as if trying to offset the shock of getting wet.

Her top is see-through in seconds. I groan out loud when I realize she's not wearing a bra underneath that flimsy top of hers, her nipples visible through the fabric. I speed up, and she does too until she sprints the last few feet and jumps into my arms giggling. I spin her around, her feet swinging, and if I could turn her laugh into a drug, I'd be addicted to it for the rest of my worthless fucking life.

Her gaze turns serious, her blue eyes sparkling like the stars above us as I gently place her feet back on the ground. Her wet hair sticks to her face and I suddenly crave to taste the rain falling over her lips.

I kiss her like we have a lifetime in front of us.

I kiss her like I won't ruin this eventually.

Pulling away, I lead her back to my car. I have her sit on the hood, her legs falling open as I step into the open space. I lack the words to tell her how much I want her. How much I need her. So I stare at her some more, my thumb stroking her cheek while the other rests on her hip.

She grabs my soaking shirt into her fists. Her voice pierces the sound of the rain around us. "Kiss me."

My lips crash into hers, my tongue sweeping into her mouth. She tastes like life itself. Like the life I wish for myself, but know I'll never attain. Quickly, our kiss turns urgent. My hands find her hard nipples against her wet top, tugging and twisting them as I push my hips into hers. She gasps eagerly, wrapping her legs around my waist, leaning back as I grind my erection into her center.

"Ozzy," she moans against my ear, her hands desperate, fighting against the button of my jeans. "Fuck me." Her tongue is hot on my earlobe, and I shiver. "Here. Now. *Please*."

I don't even have time to form a real coherent thought before I've spun James around and shoved her shorts down her round ass. Her hands land flat on the hood as I snake my arm around her chest, my palm collaring her throat.

"James, James, James," I taunt, my other hand finding her pussy soaking and *so delectably* ready for me. "Look at you." I slide two fingers inside her exquisite cunt. "Dripping wet and begging to be fucked." I don't waste any time, springing my cock out and pushing her down against the hood. "I can't *fucking* wait to feel you bare against my cock."

Her long moan is answer enough, I'm practically reverberating with my need for her. Notching myself against her entrance, I fist her tank top in my hand and manage to thrust my cock halfway inside. Her pussy flutters around me and I lean down, caressing her wet hair off her face. "Let me in, baby. Let me fuck you as hard as you're craving."

She whimpers at the words, and I feel her body relax. Taking the opportunity, I slam to the hilt, both of us gasping in unison. I've fucked without a condom before, but this feels closer to a spiritual experience than just the sensation of skin on skin. I want it to last forever. I want her pussy wrapped around my cock till death do us part.

Pulling her up, her back leans into my chest. One of my hands finds her neck again while the other travels down to her clit. "You feel ..." she sounds breathless. "Fucking amazing."

My hips slap hard against her ass, the rain still pouring down in sheets, cloaking us inside our own little bubble. I can tell I won't last much longer. Not when her cunt keeps gripping me like a vice, her quick, short moans fraying my concentration with the perfect sexual melody.

Taking my hand away from her clit, I push her back down and slide my thumb beside my cock inside her tight cunt. Her little mewl at the intrusion has my balls tightening. Sliding it in and out, I gather some of her arousal and then take my thumb and gently push it into her ass. Holding her in place with my fingers splayed over her backbone, I make circles with my thumb while fucking her even harder than before.

"Oh my god ..." she moans, her hands reach back,

trying to grasp at me as if needing to touch me. "Don't stop, don't stop," she repeats, "Please don't stop."

I wouldn't stop with a gun pointed to my head.

Not if it means I can come inside her. Not if it means I can stay buried deep.

Her body seizes and I fight against her squeezing my cock as she comes. I pound into her, my vision turning black as I chase my orgasm, pumping my cum deep into her well-fucked pussy.

I can almost hear the angels sing.

I don't believe there's a word for what I just experienced.

Letting us drop onto the hood, I bracket her with my arms, both of us catching our breaths.

After what feels like an eternity, but is most likely only a few seconds, I push myself up and slide out of her. I watch as a trickle of cum drips out of her cunt and before tugging her shorts back up, I gather it with two fingers and push it back inside, a small moan drifting from her lips as I do so.

While the rain still pelts our skin, I shove myself back into my jeans and pull her up away from the hood. Turning her around, I wrap my arms around her. She hums in delight as I kiss her one last time.

"Come on, let's go get dried off."

29

JAMES

W e're both shivering by the time we get upstairs. Ozzy leaves his soggy Converse and wet socks by the door. Leading him down the hallway, I hold a finger to my lips telling him to stay quiet, a silent reminder not to wake up my roommate.

In my bedroom, I start to pull my top off but Ozzy crowds me, wrapping his hands around mine as a way to stop my movement.

"Let me," he murmurs.

I feel shy, unsure why this moment feels a lot more intimate than what we just did downstairs. Slowly, I raise my arms as I study his face.

Now out of the pouring rain, I notice the hints of exhaustion in the dark circles under his eyes. There's something I can't quite place in his gaze.

All I know is that it hurts when his eyes reflect it back to me.

Delicately, he peels my wet shirt off my waist, my

breasts, and then over my head. While still holding my top in his hand, he wraps his arms around me and pulls me into a kiss, my hands snaking into his wet curls. I hear my shirt fall with a splat on the floor behind me as Ozzy deepens the kiss, flattening his hands near my shoulder blades, his body curling around me.

Before we get caught up in the feeling again, I gently push him away.

"My turn," I whisper.

He quirks a smile, raising his arms. There's melancholy in the curve of his lip. It's on the tip of my tongue to ask what's wrong. But I convince myself not to say anything, feeling like I'm probing a much too personal subject. But seeing him like this … I'm now regretting that I told him we should keep our problems to ourselves. Deep down, I meant mine. Not his.

While his arms are still up, I reach up and press a kiss to his cheek, then the other, then his nose, and by the time I kiss his chin we're both giggling. Finally, I slip his shirt up and over his head. When it hits the floor, he hooks his thumbs into my shorts and pulls them down along with my panties. While I step out of them, I unbuckle his belt and jeans, pushing them down his thighs with his boxers.

Then we're naked.

Standing in front of each other.

We both stare as if we've never seen each other like this.

As if our vulnerability was stripped away with the wet clothes.

The way he looks at me feels like being seen for the first time.

I hope he sees the same thing in my eyes.

When he offers his hand, I take it.

"Let's get you warmed up," he rasps.

I turn off the light and climb under the covers beside him.

Our bodies are clammy, the cold still seeped deep. Taking the duvet, he wraps it tight around me, while his arms do the same. I melt into his chest, my arms curled up tight between us. He puts one leg over mine, tugging me even closer. Our hips lock into place against one another and I let out a satisfied sigh. "This is nice," I murmur, the cold tip of my nose burrowing itself into the warmth of his neck. Ozzy stays silent. I don't expect much of an answer. Especially when my eyes are already falling closed, the rise of his chest like a hypnotic lullaby.

I'm barely conscious, halfway asleep when I hear him whisper in my hair.

"It's where you belong."

It's early morning when I wake up and find Ozzy sitting on the edge of the bed. He's naked, his back facing me, holding one of my latest paintings in his hands that I had left on my desk. It's small, the size of a notebook. Simple too: Three oysters on a plate of ice with a slice of lemon.

Hearing the rustle of the sheets, he turns around.

A few messy curls fall on his forehead, his smile subdued as if still lost in thought.

"Morning, baby."

"Morning," I reply with a smile of my own.

"When did you make this?" he asks, referring to the painting in his hand.

"A few days ago." My voice is still deep with sleep. And then, a little timidly. "Do you like it?"

"Like it?" His eyebrows raise in surprise. "I love it."

I don't linger on the feeling of how good hearing him say that makes me feel, instead I say, "You can have it if you want."

His eyes light up with a spark I haven't seen since he met me at the park. "Really?"

I nod my answer, a bashful smile on my lips.

He looks down at the painting, and then back up, grinning. "Thank you." Then he falls serious, dropping his smile. "I've got to go."

"It's not even eight a.m. yet," I say in a half-hearted protest, checking the time.

"I know." Leaning over, he grabs my chin between his thumb and finger, kissing me softly as if in apology. Standing up, he walks to his jeans still crumpled on the floor. "I just …" He stops himself, looking like he's weighing his words. It's clear this is a personal issue, and if I had to guess why he's not opening up to me, it's because I'm the one who asked to keep things casual. I stew in my poor decisions and wait for him to finish his sentence. "There's just a few things I've got to do before work."

I decide to drop the subject and wince watching him put on his jeans. "Those must still be wet," I say with an appalled expression.

He chuckles, jumping a few times to get them on. "Yeah, they are. We had fun though didn't we," he drawls with a wink.

My cheeks heat, remembering our little public romp last night. "Never thought I was such an exhibitionist," I reply with a laugh.

With his shirt, also still wet, back on, he jogs back to the bed and leans down, smiling. "Never change, princess," he says, stroking my cheek before kissing me. "You're perfect just the way you are."

My words catch in my throat. He waves goodbye while grabbing the painting on his way out, and I give him a small wave back.

His last words echo in my ears for the rest of the day.

30

JAMES

Waiting by the curb, outside my building complex, I fix my dress for the fifteenth time while I wait for Ozzy to pick me up.

I'm a ball of nerves

It's late Sunday morning, and we're heading to the Fine Arts Museum.

He'd asked me if I wanted to go yesterday before I left Orso. There was a slight blush on his face while he waited for my answer, seemingly nervous about my response as if I wouldn't jump at the chance to hang out with him. Because the answer is always yes.

Aside from work, I've barely seen Ozzy since he showed up in the middle of the night last Tuesday. Even during service, he's looked distracted, subdued, and less buoyant than usual.

We're still pretending nothing is going on between us in front of the Orso staff, and the secret is starting to itch like a bad rash. Especially when I catch him with a thousand-yard stare mid-shift, and I can't do anything about it.

When we manage to find hidden corners of the restaurant to paw at each other, he reassures me in between kisses that take my breath away that he's fine, just busy.

I don't pry.

But when I'm alone, I overthink.

What's he doing …

Who's he with …

It's left me on edge, and now I'm smoothing my dress, fixing my hair and reapplying my peach lip gloss as if we've never spent time alone together—like I'm trying to impress him.

Who am I kidding? Of course, I'm trying to impress him.

When I see his car appear down the street, my stomach flips and I press my lips together in anticipation. Parking in front of me, he leans down closer to the steering wheel to look at me through the open passenger window, white t-shirt rolled up his biceps like a 50s greaser. His grin is cocky and my stomach does another flip. "Hey cutie, what are you doing standing alone on the curb like that? Need a ride somewhere?"

I snort a laugh and roll my eyes. "Maybe," I say, playing along while leaning into the window, arms crossed. "This boy promised to bring me to the museum. But I guess he's running late."

He hums in concern. "That *boy* doesn't sound like a keeper if he leaves a pretty thing like you waiting."

"I don't know," I say, looking at him with a coy smile. "I kind of like him."

He raises an eyebrow, his voice dropping an octave. "Oh, do you now?"

I nod while I get in, now a little more serious as I watch Ozzy's eyes darken.

"Come here," he rasps.

Reaching over, he pulls me toward him by the back of my neck, and shivers snake down my spine at his touch. His lips are warm. They taste like unabashed pleasure. I tug on the bottom one and he groans into my mouth, his grip tightening on my nape.

"I've missed you so fucking much," he says heatedly against my lips before deepening the kiss. His tone is so serious that I almost ruin the moment. I almost tell him that he shouldn't be missing me. That we saw each other last night at work. Something to tamper the gravity I hear in his words, because something about it scares me.

Instead, I lean even closer and give in to the same feeling, my lips as hungry as his. "I've missed you too." My voice sounds desperate, needy, but I don't care, not when Ozzy's kissing me like this. Not when his breath is hot against my lips, and his hand is sliding up my thigh. Not when time has slowed down, wrapping us in a stasis bubble full of this … this addictive *need* we have for one another.

Eventually, we pull away, keeping our faces close to one another, catching our breath, our gazes magnetized. Ozzy quirks a smile, settling back into the driver's seat.

"Now let's go see some paintings," he says with an upbeat tone, pulling into the street and putting on some music, acting as if he didn't shift my entire world on its axis with just that one kiss. He keeps his hand on my thigh, and I place mine over his, giving it a little squeeze.

The music is loud enough that we don't need to carry a conversation, so I fall silent, chewing on my lip, losing myself in thought while I look out the window.

Because suddenly there's only one thought bouncing around in my head …

I don't think *just friends* is supposed to make me feel like this.

———————

On our way into the museum, Ozzy takes my hand in his. My gaze falls on his nails, painted a light purple. "Nice nails," I say offhandedly.

He raises his free hand up as if studying them. "Thanks," he says with a laugh, dropping his hand back down. "Soph painted them."

My stomach drops and my eyes narrow, but I don't respond.

Soph?

My mind travels quickly back to the times when Sophia has called him.

The sting of jealousy is sharp.

I thought we agreed not to see anyone else.

Why would he be so open about it?

Maybe it's not what I think it is.

Once again, I feel like it's not my place to ask so I just let the comment linger and burrow itself under my skin. My mood sours as we head inside, but I try to hide it as best I can.

Especially since I had been looking forward to today. No one, other than some of my classmates, has shown any interest in going to the Fine Arts Museum with me. Luckily, I was able to purchase a membership before money was tight, and I come here whenever I need my mind to pause.

I know the museum layout by heart now.

But it's different bringing someone else with me, getting to experience it through their eyes.

Or more specifically: Experiencing it through Ozzy's thoughtful aquamarine ones.

The bit of jealousy sticks with me, following me through the halls and exhibits, but I try to ignore it.

I study Ozzy while he's, in turn, busy studying the Baroque and Rococo paintings in one of my favorite rooms. The walls of the room are a deep red, a rich contrast to the softer tones of the paintings themselves. The lights are low, and there's a projector somewhere in the room, displaying images of trees and leaves swaying softly in the breeze higher up near the ceiling. It makes it feel like we're in a private garden. I could spend hours in this one room alone.

I could spend hours watching Ozzy in this room too.

Especially when there's not a hint of boredom on his face—something I feared would eventually happen.

His brows are furrowed in concentration, his hair curling around his ears as he leans closer to the painting in front of us. He reads the small plaque beside it and steps back to study the painting again.

I didn't know I could find such a simple act so damn attractive.

Then jealousy gives me a little jab to remind me it's still there.

I imagine Ozzy experiencing this with someone else.

I imagine this person watching him like I am now.

The thought rewires something inside of me. Challenges me to act on these feelings I have for Ozzy. He might not be mine to claim, but surely I can claim him for the day, the week … maybe the month. If there's any game to be won—I'm the one who's going to win.

Linking our hands together, I gently tug him toward the next painting.

"What do you see?" I ask him.

"A girl on a swing."

He's not wrong, but I can tell he's being glib on purpose and I swat his arm. He chuckles in response.

The painting is of a smiling young woman on a cushioned seat swing, surrounded by lush gardens, her pink gown billowing around her while she swings in mid-air. Her leg is raised up, causing her to lose her pink slipper.

It's an innocent painting at first glance.

I lean into Ozzy's body, my arm snaking around his waist, hooking my thumb in one of his belt loops, my mouth near his ear.

"The girl," I say in a near whisper, "was a courtier's mistress." I point to the man in the painting. He's lying in the gardens just below the swing, one arm outstretched toward her. "That's him." My hand climbs up Ozzy's back, now on his nape, slowly raking my nails over his scalp. "Secretly admiring her from below." I feel him shiver under my touch. "But," I say, my mouth still close to his ear, nipping his earlobe. "You see how her leg is raised?" His Adam's apple bobs on a hard swallow as he nods. My other hand flattens low on his stomach, my pinky finger caressing the skin just beneath his shirt. "Women back then didn't wear anything under their gowns." I pause, chuckling darkly. "A little bit like me today."

"James," Ozzy says slowly. It sounds like a warning and my pussy throbs at the implication.

But I continue, "So from the courtier's vantage point, he's seeing *a lot more* than just her leg." Leaning even closer, I feel Ozzy's body wound tight under my touch. I grin with satisfaction. "Don't you wish that was you?" My whisper is taunting, full of unspoken desires. "Don't you wish you could see what's underneath my dress?" I pause, slowly licking my lips, my heart racing with the risk I'm about to take. "You pathetic little slut."

Ozzy groans deep in his chest but stays silent for a beat, dragging his tongue over his teeth and I feel intoxicatingly victorious.

His voice is low and gravelly when he finally speaks. "I'm about to bend you over in front of all these people and fuck the tease right out of you if you don't stop this shit right now."

The heady thrill I feel from hearing him say those words leaves me lightheaded.

I take his hand. "Follow me."

Leaving the exhibition, I drag him along the museum halls until I find a private bathroom down a vacant corridor. I push him inside and I barely manage to lock the door before I'm on my knees, reaching for his belt. He leans his weight on the sink behind him, his movements as frantic as mine while he helps me unbutton his jeans.

His erection strains against the zipper, the bulge thick and impressive. I salivate at the mere sight of it. When he tugs his jeans down his thighs, his cock springs out and I don't know if I've ever craved something so much in my life.

I want to stop and stare. To study his cock with awe and reverence like one of the priceless works of art hanging on the walls. But I'm much too eager. Much too impatient to feel the thick head of his cock stretch my mouth wide open.

I want to suffocate around it.

I want to feel tears prick my eyes when he hits the back of my throat.

I want everything Ozzy has to give me and more.

"Wrap those perfect lips around my cock, *please*," he

says breathlessly. "It's so pathetic how desperate I am to fuck your throat. Would you let a slut like me do that to you, huh baby?" There's a strain in his voice as if he's holding himself back. My gaze flicks up to find his is already trained on me, eyes nearly black with desire, both hands gripping the sides of the sink, knuckles turning white.

Circling my hand at the base, I give his cock a long tug. Then, I lave my tongue up his shaft before swallowing as much as I can fit of him down my throat. He's so fucking big that the corners of my mouth strain, the skin pulled taut. Struggling to take him makes it feel even more salacious somehow and I moan shamelessly around him.

He curses under his breath, one hand finding the back of my head. At first, he lets me set the pace, his soft groans and whimpers turning the flames inside of me into a burning inferno. When he hears me gag, the lewd throaty sounds filling the space around us, his grip tightens around my hair.

I can feel his self-restraint fray under the tremble of his palm.

Sliding his cock out of my mouth, I look up and into his blazing gaze, a trail of saliva still connecting us together. "Make me take it."

His jaw tenses, his cock twitching in my grip. "*Fuck*, James …" He grabs my face with one hand, squeezing my cheeks together, a slow and depraved grin curling up his lips. "I'm going to shove my cock so far down your throat, you'll be tasting me for days."

Then, he does just that. I choke on the mere width of him, moaning feverishly around his shaft, my air slowly depleting. But I don't care, I invite the lack of oxygen. With his two hands on the back of my head, he holds me there for a few seconds, my nails digging into his thighs, then he releases me. I pull back a little, his cock still all-consuming but now allowing me to breathe.

Saliva dribbles down my chin as Ozzy mercilessly fucks my mouth, my knees digging into the hard tiles under me and I'm euphoric.

I am one breath away from sobbing from this raptured feeling.

My senses are so heightened I can almost feel the molecules hanging in the air between us.

I feel transported. Timeless.

My clit is throbbing, aching to be touched. Hastily, I lift my dress up, now so fucking grateful that I didn't wear any panties today.

I'm so wet that my fingers glide into my pussy effortlessly, I pump in and out and then pull them up, circling my clit with my slippery arousal. But it's not enough. Nothing is enough when Ozzy's breathy grunts are making me dizzy with need. I plunge three fingers into my pussy and start to rock my hips, grinding my palm against my clit.

"Look at me," Ozzy rasps through clenched teeth.

I strain my gaze up to his. My eyelids flutter, straining to keep them open when everything about this moment feels almost *too* much.

His head falls backward, his groan a beautiful confirmation of how I'm making him feel. Then his eyes snap back to me. "I'd gladly go blind if it meant that the last thing I saw was you, fucking yourself while my cock is buried deep down your throat."

My eyes roll backward, and I thrust my fingers even deeper into my throbbing pussy. My orgasm is a slow, perfect build of unadulterated bliss. My muscles turn to jelly, my throat relaxing even more and Ozzy takes full advantage, pitching his hips forward while his hands keep me steady. His cock swells against my tongue, and the taste of his cum shooting down my throat only brightens the effects of my lingering orgasm. I swallow greedily and mindlessly.

I don't even have time to take a full breath before Ozzy pulls me up on my feet.

Balling my dress in his fists, he drags me into his body, his mouth as hungry as I still feel, even after all of *this*. My desire for Ozzy is insatiable and by the way he kisses me, he must feel the same.

Minutes later, we leave the bathroom, both our cheeks flushed and faces beaming.

And while we return to examining paintings, his hand squeezing mine any time something piques his interest, I realize quite unexpectedly ... I've never been this happy before.

31

OZZY

By the time I get home after my shift, it's way past midnight. I begrudgingly dropped James off at her place after the museum, when really I wished I could just keep her by my side at all times.

Orso was dead and time dragged on. James wasn't working, which just made my shift feel even longer. My eyes continuously forgot that she wasn't there and kept landing near the server station expecting to see her pink hair and perfect ass.

Closing the apartment door with a soft snick, I notice the light over the oven is on and realize Alec is home, sitting outside on the balcony. Haphazardly dropping my backpack somewhere in the hallway, I make my way to the kitchen and grab a beer out of the fridge before sliding the balcony door open.

"Thought you'd be out," I say, sitting on the rusty metal chair facing him.

He gives me a non-commital grunt and takes a swig of beer before answering, "Felt like staying in for a change."

Grabbing the half-smoked joint from the ashtray on the table between us, I hum in agreement and light up. "Yeah, me too." Exhaling the smoke into the dark sky, I rub my eye. "It's been a long week."

Alec's gaze slides to mine. "Is your dad back home yet?"

I nod, taking another hit of the joint. "Got home on Thursday," I say, my voice straining against the smoke still in my lungs.

He shoots me an expression that's a mix of pity and apprehension. "How's that been?"

I laugh dryly, smoke curling around my lips. "Still kicking." My grip on the beer can tightens. "I thought maybe this time he'd take it as a reality check." I shake my head. "But he's just meaner than ever. You'd think with my mom in jail, he would have hit rock bottom by now—but he just keeps digging himself deeper and deeper."

Alec snorts and takes another sip of his beer, obviously agreeing with me. He falls silent, taking the joint out of my hand. "How long does she still have?"

I roll my eyes. "Two years. Maybe one, depending on 'good behavior'," I say, air-quoting the last two words.

Alec doesn't answer immediately. Instead, he looks into the distance, tapping his finger on the table, joint still in hand. "Shit's heavy, dude," he finally says.

I answer with another disingenuous laugh. "Tell me about it." I drink down a large gulp of beer, growing agitated with our current topic of conversation.

Alec seems to pick up on my irritation. Passing the joint back to me, he changes the subject, his tone a lot more jovial. "So?" he says. He smiles wide, mustache quirking and tonguing his cheek. His body hits the back of his chair, one foot over his thigh, and crosses his arms as if he's getting ready for a hell of a story. "Are you ever going to tell me about you and the new girl?"

I bark out of a laugh. "When have you ever been interested in who I'm fucking?"

"Please," he chuckles, "you must think I'm an idiot."

I act dumb, taking a sip of beer to hide my squirrelly expression. "What do you mean?"

He gives me a look and holds out his finger as if he's about to list off his speaking points, and I groan internally. "You've never had any of them sleep over before, for one. You dated Liam for months and Isabelle for even longer and I never bumped into them in the mornings. Frankie was basically in love with you and they barely saw the interior of your bedroom."

Rubbing the back of my neck, I grumble. "Okay, I get your fucking point. I guess James is different."

But Alec isn't finished, unfurling another long finger and leaning forward in his chair.

"*Secondly*, I've never seen you date anyone exclusively before either." He waves a bored hand in the air. "Unless you're still fucking random servers behind the dumpster."

"I'm not fucking anyone else," I bite out. Then add quickly, "And we're not dating."

He scoffs. "Okay," he says laughing into his beer can. "All I'm saying is that when you're not with Charlie and Soph, you're spending most of your time with James. I've barely seen you in three weeks, don't you fucking lie to me," he says casually, followed by a cocky grin.

This time I groan out loud, my head falling into my hands, dragging them slowly over my face before looking back up at my best friend. I don't know why I'm even attempting to lie to him.

"I'm down bad," I finally admit.

I try not to get offended by the belly laugh that follows.

"Yeah, no shit, dude. I'm surprised no one at work has caught on with those fucking moon eyes you guys keep throwing at one another."

"We're not that obvious," I shoot back.

"Oh yeah?" He leans his elbows on his knees and stares at me for a beat.

I start sweating.

"Had fun in the dry storage last week?"

Choking on the sip of beer I just took, I start coughing. "What?" I croak.

"Please," he says, his toothy smile a little too satisfied. "Why do you think you guys didn't get caught?" He points a thumb to his chest, then directs his index finger my way. "I'm the one who covered for your ass, you fucking horndog."

I can't do anything but laugh, raking my fingers through my hair.

"Oh come on, don't be acting coy now, Oz," he says, kicking his foot against mine. "Spill. How is she?"

I straighten up. "What? In bed?"

He shrugs. "What else, dummy."

Grabbing his pack of smokes from the table, he pulls one out for himself, then leans over for me to fish one out too. I take my time lighting up my cigarette, carefully gathering up the words forming in my head as I rub my chin with the back of my thumb, the barely there twinkle of the stars above catching my eye.

I chew my inner lip, lost in thought, then finally speak.

"You know when you finally get something so good that your mind tricks you into believing you don't deserve it?" Alec's eyebrow perks up, but stays silent, knowing that it's a rhetorical question. "But you hold on to it despite the feeling … despite knowing you're being selfish. Despite knowing this bright light is not meant to be yours. So you hold on to it with everything you have for the time being and soak up all the fucking goodness you can manage because you don't want to let go of a singular piece of that feeling? Well," I say, tapping the ash into the ashtray. "If I don't deserve to have it for even a fucking *second*, you, you fucking dipshit, *definitely* don't deserve to hear about it."

Alec stays serious for a few seconds, then bursts out laughing.

"Jesus fucking Christ dude," he says, stubbing his cigarette. "You really are down bad." Standing up, he pats me on the shoulder. "I'm heading to bed. See you tomorrow."

I grunt a goodnight and listen to him leave as he slides the door closed.

I sit outside for another hour, chain-smoking and reflecting on what I just told Alec, not knowing what the hell I'm going to do about all these feelings.

32

JAMES

I flop into a seat at the bar with a sigh next to Michelle. The Wednesday shift was slow, she got cut before me but stayed for a drink to keep Quinn company.

"Drink?" Quinn asks.

"Please," I answer with a tired smile. "Malbec."

They nod, turning toward our red wine selection.

As soon as we're alone, Michelle turns to me, her chin perched on her palm, and stares.

"You know ..." She narrows her brown eyes. "Something is different about you lately."

Quinn comes back with my wine, but leaves right after, busy with another customer.

"I don't know what you mean," I say coyly, taking a sip of wine, looking away with a smile.

"And I don't just mean the breakup. You're practically glow—oh my god!" she declares with a swat of my arm, mouth opened in mock shock. Her voice drops, her tone conspiratorial, finger pointed at me in a circular motion. "You *are* fucking someone, aren't you?"

I guffaw into my wine glass, taking another long sip. "Maybe."

Her face lights up, eyebrows high up her forehead as she squeezes my arm in glee.

"Is it …" She doesn't finish her sentence but points her head to the kitchen and my stomach squeezes in nerves, knowing exactly who she's referring to and how *very* right she is.

Laughing, I shake my head. "No, it's not Ozzy. I *told* you nothing is happening between us."

The lie doesn't roll off my tongue as easily and smoothly as last time.

"Okay, sure," she replies pompously, taking a sip of her dirty martini. "Maybe not now but you two are circling the same drain, bound to collide."

"Poetic," I say dismissively.

"*Anyway*," she says, looking at me with a pointed look. "I will excuse you from keeping this from me if you tell me every single little detail right this second," she urges, her chin falling back onto her open palm. "Who is he? What's he like? And most importantly what's the *sex* like? Actually, let's start with the last question, I'm much too invested."

"It's been, um …" My cheeks heat, not knowing how much I want to divulge. "New."

She grins, looking at me squirm in my seat. "New?" she repeats with a small chuckle.

I shrug a shoulder, having a hard time holding her gaze. "Well, new to me at least. And um … eye-opening?"

Her jaw drops, her eyes twinkling with delight. She lowers her voice. "How kinky are we talking?" I choke on my sip of wine as she presses on, "Ropes? Paddles? A little bit of somno maybe?"

I blink. By her tone, I can't tell if she's joking.

I'm about to deny everything when I hear a familiar voice behind me.

"Looks serious, what am I interrupting?"

I startle, my shoulders jumping. Swiveling around, my gaze lands on Ozzy behind the bar, filling up a plastic container with ice and water from the soda gun. He's still in his chef's jacket, a few Sharpies sticking out of his breast pocket, blue bandana around his forehead.

I'm struck by his casual beauty and my throat dries.

"Cute nails," Michelle points out. "Was your sister practicing on you again?"

Ozzy chuckles. "Yeah, getting real good at it too."

My mind flashes back to the museum parking lot.

Soph painted them.

Sophia is his *sister*?

I begin to churn in embarrassment, recalling the unfounded jealousy I felt that day. But it's cut short when Ozzy asks, "So? What were you two talking about before I walked up?"

"James is dating someone," Michelle says with a conspiratorial laugh.

"Michelle!" I say, turning around in my seat, slapping her arm.

"Sorry," she says unbothered by my outburst, holding her martini glass loosely in one hand. "Not dating. *Fucking.*"

"Oh my god," I groan, dropping my face in my hands. The thought of Ozzy knowing I've been gossiping about us makes my cheeks burn with embarrassment.

"Oh, are you now?" Ozzy says, one eyebrow raised and a mischievous grin on his lips.

I pop my head back up as he walks closer to us, leaning his open palm on the bar. His gaze slides smoothly to meet mine. The faint dimple on his cheek, paired with the shine in his blue-green eyes settles my nerves, but I can still feel myself blushing.

"Says the sex is *wild*," Michelle pipes up beside me.

I turn to her with wide eyes. "Do you ever shut up?"

She laughs, tongue pushing against her cheek but says nothing.

My attention pulls back to Ozzy when I hear him say, "Wild huh, Jimbo? I have a hard time believing that. How wild are we talking about?"

His tone is playful, but my eyes narrow, slightly irked by the implication that I can't have fun.

"I don't kiss and tell," I shoot back, straightening my shoulders.

"Please," he says with a smirk, taking a sip of water, his eyes burning right through me. "We're all *friends* here, aren't we?" He pauses, his tongue smoothing over the scar on his lip, and I swallow hard. "Come on, how wild are we talking?" I hide behind my wine glass while he continues to stare. "Are we talking like, oh I don't know, getting fingered in public at a party? I did that once, hot as fuck." The air around us soars to a boiling point as his mouth tugs into an arrogant grin. "You wouldn't let someone do that to you, right James? You're not a bad girl like that."

Michelle nearly chokes on the sip she just took. I can't look away from Ozzy. He's monopolizing all my attention, his eyes darkening the more we stare at each other. My heart slams in my chest, wondering if we're being too obvious, but I can't back down now, not when Ozzy is clearly expecting me not to push back.

"Well," I say, picking up my wine glass. Taking a prim sip, I settle it back down and clasp my hands in front of me, giving him a smug tight-lipped smile. "He fucked me on the hood of his car in an open parking lot last week, so maybe I'm not as goody-goody as you think, *salad boy.*"

"Excuse me?" Michelle says in surprise, elongating every syllable but both Ozzy and I ignore her.

Ozzy hums, drumming his fingers on the bar. "Naughty." He leans a little closer, his eyes playful while he lowers his voice. "You should try giving him head in a museum bathroom. I'm talking from experience, it will blow his mind."

On that note, he takes his drink and walks back into the kitchen, leaving both Michelle and I dumbfounded but for wildly different reasons.

"Good god, James," Michelle finally says. "If you don't fuck him soon, I'll fuck him for you, and I'm not even *into* guys."

I LEAVE Orso after my staff drink, knowing Ozzy has to stay late to help clean up. I'm also trying to inconspicuously dodge Michelle's questions, which only grew more probing when Ozzy left the bar.

I drop my tote bag on the back of my desk chair, change into a comfy lounge set before falling backwards into bed, my body tired from a long shift but my mind still buzzing.

Mostly stuck on Michelle's earlier comment ...

Somno?

What the hell is that?

I sit upright, eyeing my laptop sitting on my desk. I chew on the inside of my cheek deliberating, but eventually, my curiosity takes over and I slink over. Turning on the screen, I click on my browser, then immediately switch to a private window, convinced someone will track my indecent google searches.

After a few failed hits, I land on a kink website and discover somno is short for somnophilia.

A person who derives sexual pleasure from someone who is sleeping or unconscious.

My breath hitches, my fingers flying off the keyboard as if burned.

That sounds a lot like …

I don't finish my train of thought.

I lick my lips, unsure how to navigate the warring feelings toying with my insides.

My cursor hovers over a link, which I know will undoubtedly lead to a porn video.

The thought of watching a recreation of something so similar to my own negative experiences.

It should repulse me.

Instead a heady, but shameful, arousal pulses through my core and I squeeze my thighs tightly together.

Taking a deep breath, I click the link. When I realize I have my volume on, I scurry to slam the mute button. Steve isn't even home, but my paranoia doesn't care. I jump up to lock the door for safe measure and sit back down, my attention now trained on the video on screen. The camera doesn't show the man recording, only the woman lying face down on the bed in front of him, seemingly asleep.

He approaches the bed, his hand coming into view.

He slowly begins to grope her ass.

My heart rate skyrockets.

He tugs her shorts, pulling her panties to the side.

I can't look away.

I'm so turned on that I can barely think.

Especially heightened by the act of watching something that feels so ... *wrong*.

My eyes never leave the screen.

His fingers slide against her pussy. She barely stirs.

My own fingers twitch, aching with desire to touch myself.

My breathing turns heavy as my mind begins to drift—now imagining Ozzy hovering over me while I sleep. His soft coos in the dark while he fucks me with his fingers. Imagining his thick cock stretching my pussy as he uses me as he pleases.

Giving into the overwhelming urge, I place my heels on the chair on either side of me. With the video still playing, paired with my own wretched imagination, my hand slips into my shorts. I practically sob with relief when I finally begin to stroke my clit, my panties soaked with obvious arousal while my mind still tries to fight the feeling.

I grip the chair with my free hand, my head dropping back with a moan.

"Fuck ... " I say breathlessly. *I can't believe I'm doing this.*

It doesn't take long. Not when just the mere *thought* of Ozzy fucking me while I'm half-asleep has me biting my lip so hard, I think I taste blood. My orgasm slams into me and it's anything but gentle. No, it ravages, razing every single thing it touches to the ground.

I let out a shocked cry, my muscles seizing almost painfully.

I'm left wide-eyed, sucking back big gulps of air into my lungs.

Holy shit.

What the hell was that?

Now thinking rationally, I scramble to close the browser

as if hiding a dirty secret, suddenly very much uninterested in finishing the video.

I jump up from the chair, turn off the bedroom light, and slip under the covers, pretending that the last fifteen minutes never happened.

33

OZZY

J ames answers the front door of her apartment looking like an ethereal vision in a rose gold silk set. Momentarily stunned, I stare at her from the doorway.

"Hey," she whispers. It's late, her roommate must be sleeping. "Thanks for coming over." Taking my hand in hers, she pulls me inside.

"Of course I was coming over, Jimbo," I say with a crooked smile, gripping a handful of her ample hips while dragging her into me. "Did you miss me?" I growl low against her lips.

She chuckles softly. "It's only been a day."

"Answer the question," I reply with a gentle smack on her ass.

She startles with the impact and dissolves into another giggle.

I want to bathe in the sound.

"Yes," she says, her tone hinting at some lingering shyness. "Of course, I missed you."

She gives me a tender kiss and my heart squeezes with unbridled affection.

Pulling away, she grabs my hand and I dutifully follow her into her bedroom. As soon as her door is closed and locked, I pin her to the wall, my hips grinding against hers, both hands on her face as if I'm always starving for any small morsel she can give me. A small sigh of satisfaction leaves her lips, her body melting into mine as both her arms wrap around my neck.

But after a few more heated seconds, it's as if she remembers herself and gently pushes me off her. Inside, I feel like a snarling dog with a bone, but I relent and step back.

"There was actually a specific reason why I wanted you to come by," she says.

As soon as the words are suspended in the air between us, she distances herself, walking toward her desk, and sits down.

Her body language has turned nervous, her movements slightly choppy as she waves for me to sit in front of her at the foot of her bed.

My mind immediately latches onto the obvious.

She's about to end this.

My hands turn clammy, my heart beating faster.

I swallow hard.

"What's up?" I say, in the most laid-back tone I can manage.

She chews on her thumb, her eyebrows dipped low. She opens her mouth to speak, then changes her mind, shooting me a nervous look. "I don't know how to say it, so I'm just going to come out with it," she finally blurts out.

I keep my mouth shut and brace myself for the worst.

"I want you to fuck me when I'm sleeping."

My eyes go wide. "You want me to do what now?"

Her laugh is full of nerves. "Please don't make me repeat it."

I swipe a hand through my hair, trying to wrap my head around what James just said, especially when my assumption was so far off.

I pin her with a stare, eyes narrowing. "You mean like somnophilia?"

She lets out a small scoff and rolls her eyes, crossing her legs. "Was I the only one who didn't know about this?"

I can't help but chuckle. "Oh, princess." Still, a small thrill zips through my chest at the subject matter. Intrigued and tempted.

"Don't mock me," she says in a playful tone, a shy smirk on her lips.

After a brief shared laugh, she falls serious again and begins to worry her bottom lip. "So do you think this is something we could do … together?"

Admittedly, I've never given it much thought until now, but I can't deny that the idea is a turn-on.

"Are you sure that's something you'd want?" My words are carefully chosen, and full of concern. "Given what happened with—"

She holds both her hands up, signaling me to stop. I close my mouth shut.

"That's exactly *why* I want to explore this."

Studying her, I stay silent for a beat, chewing on the implications of what she's asking me.

She trusts me.

My chest swells with pride, and I try to tamper my reaction when I realize how important this moment is. James wouldn't be asking me this if she still saw us as *just* a hookup. Maybe she's still hiding under the safety of our friends with benefits label, but I can see beyond it.

And if this is what she wants? And it's something I can easily give her?

"I've never done that before, but I'm willing to try just about anything if it means doing it with you, baby," I finally say, hoping my smile is a reassuring one.

The way she beams in response to my answer feels like a gut punch. It leaves me yearning for more. More of her, more of this. More and more and fucking more.

"Thank you," she gushes, but then her smile drops. "One more thing though."

I laugh, resting my forearms on my thighs. "Lay it on me."

"I want you to—" She clears her throat, her fingers fidgeting with the hem of her silk shorts. "I want you to do whatever you … want with me, even if I say no." Her voice dips lower with every word she says until it's almost a whisper. I know what she's implying, I've used safe words before. As if reading my mind she says, "I'll just say red, if I actually want you to stop."

I let the words settle between us. A different kind of pride than before blooms inside of me. This time it's for her, and how self-assured she's becoming lately—like right now, brazenly asking for what she wants.

I crave to give her everything she's ever wanted.

My gaze turns slightly predatory. "Jimbo's done her research I see?"

Her cheeks pinken and my cock twitches. "So that's a yes?" she presses.

"Yes, princess." I extend my hand toward her. "We can definitely try that together."

She stands up, a small victorious grin pulling at the

corners of her perfect lips. When she places her hand in mine, I curl my fingers and give it a quick reassuring squeeze.

"So when are we doing this?" she asks, excitement twinkling in her eyes.

"Let me decide when. I'll need a key."

Her eyebrows jump in surprise, but she nods animatedly as if electrified by the thought.

"Okay," she says a little breathlessly. "Deal."

Tugging her arm toward me, she falls on the bed with a shrieking giggle. I bury my face into her neck and pepper her with kisses, her bright laughter tickling my eardrums.

Popping my head up, I take a moment to stare, immersing myself in her glittering blue eyes.

"Are you hungry?" I ask, followed by a quick kiss on her lips. "I brought some gnocchi with that rosé sauce from work."

Her expression turns pensive but she keeps her thoughts to herself, simply smiling and nodding.

"Great," I say, giving her a final kiss on the forehead before helping us off the bed, and into the kitchen.

THREE DAYS LATER, I'm slowly creeping up the stairs to James' apartment at two in the morning. The key she gave me is burning a hole in my pocket. It's as if I can somehow feel the outline of it against my thigh. I idly trace it with my fingers as my heartbeat accelerates with every step I take.

I needed a few days to think through how I'd initiate her little plan. To let my mind drift to the most indecent parts of my brain. Allow myself to wonder what role I'd play, and *what* exactly I'd do with her when she actually was at my willing disposal.

It's now Sunday, and I'm ready, practically buzzing with anticipation. In a roundabout way, I made sure she was alone tonight when she texted me goodnight a few hours ago. She confirmed that she was home alone and that her roommate was staying over at his girlfriend's. The few hours I had left at Orso were painfully slow, now that I knew what was waiting for me.

Finally arriving at her front door, I stand still for a few seconds, frozen in the anticipation of what will follow when I let myself in. I carefully pull the key out of my pocket. Holding it in front of me, I feel like a plebian version of King Arthur holding up the fucking Excalibur.

My movements are slow and calculated, trying to make as little noise as possible while unlocking her door.

I step inside.

Close and lock the door behind me.

One step.

Two steps.

Three steps down the hallway.

Her door is ajar.

I try to keep my breathing steady, but my hand shakes with nerves when I slowly push the door open the rest of the way. A small sliver of moonlight illuminates the side of her bed, most of her body cloaked in darkness, an upright fan droning in the corner.

On light feet, I approach the bed as cautiously as possible. She's on her stomach, her face turned away from me. In this end-of-summer heat, she's only wearing a small white cami with just a thin sheet to cover her, pushed down to her waist. I can see the curve of her ass just underneath it. I peel the sheet off her body with the same steady concentration as an EOD defusing a bomb.

When I realize she's only wearing panties on her bottom half, her leg bent toward her chest making her ass jut upwards, my dick throbs against my zipper, growing harder by the fucking second.

I take a second to stare at her.

She's so fucking perfect.

I gently rest my knee on the mattress so I can better reach her. My fingers graze the cotton covering her pussy, softly rubbing her clit.

I suddenly feel high on drugs, my head swimming.

I push her panties to the side, slowly spreading her pussy open with two fingers.

Fuck.

This feels so delectably wrong, but my brain is on fucking fire, my cock throbbing, aching to sink into her pretty little heat. Especially when I remember her instructions.

I want you to do whatever you want with me, even if I say no.

I palm my dick over my jeans with my free hand, trying to control my breathing; thankfully the fan in the corner of her room cloaks most of the incriminating sounds I'm making. Circling a finger around her entrance, my body pulses with my most primal needs. I bring two fingers to my lips and swirl them over my tongue, covering them in spit. With those same two fingers, I slowly push my way into her pussy until I'm knuckle deep.

James squirms, a small mumble drifting out of her lips.

I pause, my heart slamming in my chest like I'm being caught. But with this overwhelming, heightening desire I can barely control myself. I can't be sure if she's already awake and pretending to sleep, but I'm too far gone to care.

I hush her softly, a feather-light trail down her back. "Go back to sleep, princess," I whisper as I start to fuck her with my fingers. A slow glide in, and then out. "You're just dreaming."

She settles and I close my eyes on a deep exhale, my muscles shaking with barely controlled restraint. Sliding out of her, I slowly crawl fully onto the mattress and pinch her panties with my fingers. Delicately sliding them down her ass, I keep them around her upper thighs.

I stroke her pussy with two fingers again and this time she's considerably more wet than before. Biting down on a groan, I smooth my tongue over my teeth.

She's getting off on this.

I turn feverish at the thought of fucking her when she's so pliable.

So fucking *mine* to do as I please.

Bending down, I squeeze her ass with as little force as possible, spreading her open for me. When my tongue finally tastes her hot cunt, I shift into another reality entirely. One where I spend my days adoring her like this. One where I sustain solely on the flavors of her arousal.

I can't help but moan into her soft skin, my fingers pressing deeper into her supple ass.

I feel her squirm again, this time her hand finds my head, weakly trying to push me away.

"What are you doing?" she mutters, as if half-unconscious, her hand limp but reaching. "Stop."

I freeze for only a second but then grin to myself, knowing that our little game has just begun. My hand travels up her back, my mouth now licking her clit, petting her as if trying to calm her back into a deep slumber. "Be quiet for me, princess," I coo softly, "I promise you'll like it."

Licking from her cunt up to her ass, I slip two fingers back into her. Her pussy squeezes around my fingers, her arousal squelching around them and my self-control begins to fray.

Pulling away, still on my knees, I swallow hard and unzip my jeans as silently as possible, pulling my cock out. I fist it hard, smoothing the pre-cum over the head, my balls tightening with debauched desire.

I notch my cock to her entrance, placing my open palm on the small of her back to soothe and steady her. James mumbles a protest again and it takes everything in me not to sink down to the hilt in one single thrust. Her hand tries to reach me, but her position on her stomach makes the angle difficult. It's a half-hearted effort to push me away.

"Don't," she mutters again.

I make comforting sounds, my hand smoothing up her thigh. My voice is shaking as I slowly stretch her open with the wide head of my cock. I hush her again. "I'm not going to stop now, you feel too fucking good."

Her protests turn louder, her nails manage to find my leg, digging into my skin.

"You can fight this all you want baby, but there's no one in this house but me to hear you." With small thrusts, I begin to fuck her, my cock sinking deeper and deeper with every rock of my hips. Soon, my thrusts turn more urgent, fucking her harder.

"Fucking tease, look at what you made me do," I whisper harshly. My eyes are locked on the place where my cock disappears into her. "Look how desperate I am for you."

I'm just playing a role to fulfill her fantasy, but there's a soul-deep truth to my filthy words—I find myself more and more desperate for her every day. Pulling out, I take her leg and turn her over onto her back. With her face revealed, her eyes are closed, eyebrows furrowed, still pretending she's barely conscious, but there's a hint of a smile on her lips. When I try to sink back into her, her eyes fly open and she starts to fight me.

"Please." Her voice is laced with panic. "Don't do this to me."

I study her face, finding nothing but bliss in the curve of her expression. The trust she has in me urges me on, wanting nothing more than to give her everything she wants, including space for her to explore her darkest fantasies.

Reinforcing the roles we're playing, I swat her hands easily, ignoring her pleas as I plunge my cock back into her perfect wet cunt. Still on my knees, I lean over her and curl my hand over her half-opened mouth, my other hand cradling her neck, fingers digging into her nape.

"Shut up princess, not a single sound," I growl through clenched teeth, my hips pistoning into her. "If you really wanted me to stop, you wouldn't be so wet now would you?"

She tries to swallow down her moan, still protesting, still fighting but she's grinning against the hand covering her mouth.

My mind empties at the sight of her.

34

JAMES

I don't think I've ever felt so overcome by desire before.
There's a catharsis clawing its way through my psyche. A release I'm desperate for. One I've been craving for so long. Every thrust, squeeze, groan only heightens the effect.

And I could cry.

I could fucking cry.

Ozzy's eyes are nearly black as he fucks me, curls plastered on his forehead, watching me from above, his hand still wrapped around my mouth. I can't stop grinning. I feel euphoric, but something inside me wants to push this even further. To allow myself to truly let go. To allow myself the space to aimlessly follow the urges asking to be let out.

Especially when I have the aching comfort of knowing that I can stop this whenever I want.

I hold all the power between us.

It only makes me want to play harder. *Feel* him harder.

"Let me go!" I shout through his fingers.

The sound of my voice this loud startles Ozzy for half a

second and I take the opportunity to fight my way out of his hold, his cock slipping out of me. I twist my torso around and grab the side of the bed trying to pull myself away, my hands blindly trying to grasp at anything to help me escape.

Ozzy's goading laugh sends a dark thrill zipping through me. And it takes him little effort to slam me back down on the mattress, pulling my wrists above my head and gripping them with one hand.

"Naughty girl," he tsks, "do you really think you can get away from me?" He presses his hard cock between my thighs, licking up my chest with indecent strokes of his tongue until his hot mouth grazes my ear. "Not until I've had my fill of you, princess. You're mine now."

I let out a needy whimper, my heart beating wildly.

His teasing laugh makes me press myself against him, while I simultaneously struggle in his grasp, desperate to know what he will do next.

The rough material of his jeans drags over my sensitive skin and I break out into near feverish shivers. I hold the image of him fully clothed on top of me while I'm mostly naked in my mind, making our little game that much more illicit.

Pinning me down with his weight he leans over, and with his free hand opens the small drawer beside the bed. "Let's see if you have anything good hiding in here," he rasps as he rifles through it, eventually pulling out a small bottle of lube.

The moonlight cuts across his face, his triumphant smile etched deep and illuminated with the white light. His tongue swipes over his lip, his dark grin growing wide, and my arousal spikes.

"Now what would you need this for?" he says slowly

and tauntingly. While opening the cap with his teeth, he uses his knees to push my legs apart with a hard shove and lets the lube trickle over my pussy and down my ass. "You want me to fuck your tight hole, don't you?" Throwing the bottle on the bed beside us, he gathers the lube and glides it down to my asshole. "Admit it," he says, probing my tight entrance with his fingers. "That's all you're good for." His administration almost feels clinical, his voice monotone and my pussy clenches at his seeming indifference, while one of his fingers breaches the muscles.

I arch my back but start to struggle again.

"Get off me," I growl, bearing my teeth.

But deep down, I've never needed to feel his touch more than at this very moment.

I've never needed Ozzy quite like this.

"Look at you," he says, looking me up and down, his grip tightening around my wrists, the heat back in his hooded gaze. "So responsive, even when you pretend you don't want it."

He circles his thumb over my swollen clit. I whimper, arching my back. "See how you're easily opening up for me?" he growls as he slides a second finger next to the first. A sharp gasp escapes my lips, the sensation coiling deep at the base of my stomach. "You can't deny how much your body wants this." He slowly stretches me open, pushing a third finger inside, readying me for what I can only imagine will soon be his cock.

While he fucks my ass with his fingers, he suddenly leans over me, catching my lips with his. I push my body against him, whimpering into his mouth as he leaves me breathless with need. It's over as fast as it began, but before he pulls away he whispers near my ear, "You're so fucking pretty like this." His voice is gentle and full of awe and sounds exactly like the Ozzy I've come to know—as if he couldn't control himself and needed to break out of character just to tell me that.

My reaction is immediate. Tears spring to my eyes, and a slew of warring emotions overflows up my throat. Elation, anguish, euphoria, grief—all just as overpowering as the next.

By the time he's straightened himself up, his hard expression is back, but he stops moving while he tracks the tear falling down my temple and into my hair.

His gaze snaps to mine.

The last thing I want him to do is stop.

Not now. Not ever.

He studies my face and I give him the smallest of nods, fighting another euphoric grin while I struggle against his firm grip, more tears now freely falling.

When his dark chuckle returns, I feel untethered.

Sliding his fingers out, he reaches for the lube, pouring some more over his fingers and then on his cock, stroking himself greedily after throwing the bottle back down.

He grips the base of his length and pushes the head of his cock against my ass. "Cry as much as you want, princess," he says while he slowly pushes against the muscles. "It'll only make me fuck you harder."

The sensation of his cock slowly stretching my asshole is almost too much, tethering close to pain, but I invite the discomfort. The blurred lines of pleasure and pain closely mirror the conflicting emotions that seem to always exist inside of me. The same ones I'm communing with now while Ozzy gradually pushes himself inside of me.

"Stop. *Please, please, please,*" I chant. "You're hurting me." The words don't hold the weight they're meant to carry, instead, I sound breathless, my voice verging on a moan.

Ozzy shushes me, his free hand traveling up to my throat. "Stop your whining, princess." His fingers don't curl around my throat like I expect, instead, he places his palm wide over my chest just below my collarbone. The weight of him pushes me down, pinning me to the bed. His eyes are black and greedy. "You're practically *begging* me to fuck your ass."

And with those words, he pitches his hips forward, thrusting himself deep inside of me.

My back arches as I gasp loudly, my eyes fixed on his.

He doesn't wait for me to adjust, pulling out up to the tip and slamming back inside, falling into a steady and punishing rhythm.

My mind scrambles to stay coherent but I'm failing so miserably that I begin to babble. I forget the game we're playing, forget to pretend because all I want to do is beg him not to stop.

"Harder," I nearly sob. "*Please*, harder."

I beg him for more when he's already giving me so much.

His grasp loosens on my wrists, and I pull out of his hold, my hands immediately tugging at his shirt. "Take it off."

I need to feel him, touch him.

I need to feel the heat of his skin under my fingernails.

With one hand over his shoulder, he pulls his shirt over his head and throws it across the room. Harshly tugging my top down, he fists it around his hand as if giving himself traction to fuck me even harder. While my breasts spill out, his eyes rove voraciously over my bare chest. Shoving his other hand between my legs, he thrusts two fingers inside my pussy.

"Oh my god," I moan out, suddenly feeling so perfectly filled.

His hand follows the rhythm he's already set. Every delirious glide of his fingers, paired with the throbbing stretch of his cock in my ass has my muscles growing taut, ready to snap.

"That's it, baby," he growls, "scream for me."

"I'm going to——" My words get lost somewhere between my throat and lips as my body throbs in indescribable pleasure, a warm, pulsing tingle flowing into every little crook of myself.

My chest cracks open, and I burst into a sob, feeling shaken but *so fucking good*.

"*Fuck, James,*" he bites out through clenched teeth, fucking me through my orgasm until he falls over me, moaning into my neck as he comes deep inside me.

Both out of breath, we stay motionless for a few seconds until Ozzy pushes himself up on one elbow, cradling my face with his free hand, gently stroking my hair out of my face.

"Shit, baby," he says before kissing me softly but still full of need. "That was …"

I find his gaze, my eyes watery but my smile wide and beaming. "Amazing."

35

JAMES

It's early afternoon when we wake up the next day. Luckily, it's Monday, and Orso is closed, so neither of us needs to rush to work.

Still half-snoozing in bed, Ozzy burrows his nose into my hair from behind and sighs deeply, his arm banded around my waist. My mind drifts to last night, the emotions attached to the memory still raw and vivid, but this morning I feel ... lighter.

Logically, I know that whatever happened last night doesn't magically fix the lingering wounds that have just begun to heal. But maybe, at least, it helped me connect with feelings that were too amorphous to process. Feelings that were maybe buried too deep, or locked away too tightly, that speaking about them wouldn't even have helped.

And feeling Ozzy's weight around me, the sense of security I feel when around him. I can't help but think that maybe Ozzy is also helping me heal parts of myself that I wasn't even aware needed healing. I take his arm, loose around my waist, and hug myself tighter with it. After a few more minutes of soft, lazy cuddling, we finally crawl out of bed.

"Coffee?" Ozzy asks, followed by a yawn and a full-body stretch.

"I'll make some, I just need a shower first."

"Great idea, I'll join you."

I give him a pointed look. "Small, shitty shower, remember?"

He harrumphs my reply. "I don't give a shit, sweetheart. Not falling for that excuse again."

I roll my eyes and fight off a smile. "Fine, I'll grab you a towel."

After a cramped shower full of giggles and chaste wet kisses, I slip into a floral summer dress, Ozzy putting back on yesterday's jeans and red t-shirt.

I make a pot of coffee and walk to the living room with two steaming mugs, where Ozzy is waiting for me. I sit on the opposite side of the couch from him, silently watching him type on his phone while I sip my coffee. His damp hair curls around his ear, full lips slightly pressed together in concentration, his cheeks beginning to show some scruff.

There's such effortless beauty to his appearance, that I can't stop staring.

It dawns on me that I've never taken a picture of him before.

Placing my mug on the coffee table, I spring to my feet and head for my room.

"Where are you going?" Ozzy says from behind me.

"I'll be right back!" I yell from down the hallway.

Snatching my phone from the desk, I return to the living room and lean it against the mug on the table.

"What's going on?" Ozzy says slowly.

I laugh. "So full of questions," I say looking back at him while I switch my camera to selfie mode. "I want to take a picture of us."

His eyebrows shoot up in surprise, but his expression quickly morphs into a cocky smile as he leans back into the couch, one arm over the back. Setting up the timer, I curl into his side, one arm around his waist while I tuck my legs under me, my head tilted toward him.

"So, what's this all about? Is this going to be our soft launch to all of your friends or something?" Ozzy says jokingly after the photo is taken.

I laugh. "It's not called a soft launch if your face is in it," I reply, busy studying the picture we just took. *We look so good together.* "Besides, you only soft launch someone you're actually dating."

I can feel the air suddenly shift around us, and I know I've said something wrong before I even look up.

"Right," Ozzy says with a dry laugh, scratching his head.

Shit.

"I just meant—"

He gives me a reassuring smile and stands up. "It's fine, Jimbo. I know what we are." Holding out his hand for me to take, he asks, "You hungry? I know just the place."

My anxiety spikes, my gaze lifting up to his while my phone is still clutched in my hand. I don't know what to say, and by the look he's giving me, I don't think Ozzy wants me to add anything to the conversation.

Letting out the smallest of sighs, I take his proffered hand. "Food sounds great."

"How DID I not know about this place?" I ask in amazement while Ozzy holds the door open and waves me into Bella's Café.

Walking in, I take in the decor, an awestruck smile on my face, the back wall filled with rows and rows of raw ceramics ready to be picked out and painted.

"Had a feeling you'd like it," Ozzy says with a smirk.

"Like?" I say, "I *love*."

He slides his hands into his back pockets, rocking on his heels, a pleased look painted over his features. My heart flutters with appreciation.

I don't think I was aware someone could be so considerate.

So attentive.

After being shown to a table, we head over to pick out something to paint together.

"How did you find out about this café?" I ask while perusing the mugs and bowls.

"I've been here a few times with Soph," he replies, picking up a mug and turning it around to better study it.

Now that I know who Sophia is, I don't miss a beat. "Are you close with your sister?"

"Aside from Alec, she's my best friend."

I stop in my tracks and look at him, but he doesn't notice my reaction, busy crouching down to look at the lower shelves. I force myself not to fawn over how adorable that statement was and press on.

"How old is she?"

"Fourteen—how 'bout this one?" he says, standing back up, showing me a serving bowl with a wide lip.

I trail my finger over the bowl, my eyes meeting his. "Sure," I say with a smile.

Back at our table, we both sit on the same side of the

booth. After ordering a plate of nachos to share, we gather our paints and supplies.

"So what are we painting?" I ask.

Ozzy nudges me with his knee. "Since you're the talented painter, I thought I'd let you take the helm on this one."

A small giggle slips out. "That's not fair, this is supposed to be a group effort." I hand him a paintbrush. "You can paint the base color, deal?"

His lips lift up ever so slightly, dimpling his cheek. "Deal."

Mixing some purple paint with some white, he begins to paint the bowl a light lavender color, matching his chipped nail polish.

I tap his fingertips. "Is purple your favorite color?"

His eyes snap to mine, crystalline aqua twinkling with amusement. "It is now."

"What do you mean?"

He barks a laugh. "You don't remember?"

My eyes narrow, looking at him quizzically.

Tonguing his cheek, he answers, "That video you sent me?" His eyes dip down to my chest, then back up. "You were wearing lavender lingerie."

"Oh." I feel my cheeks heat, slightly horrified that I'm still blushing after everything we've done together.

Holding in a laugh, he pulls me into a kiss before turning back to painting the bowl.

After we've eaten our fill of nachos and waited for the first layer of paint to dry, I try to think of what I could paint as decoration.

"What's your favorite vegetable?" I ask.

He presses his lips together as if genuinely thinking about it. "Avocado," he finally answers.

"Favorite fruit?"

"Pineapple."

"What about pasta shapes?"

"Definitely farfalle."

I continue asking him questions, and he continues to answer them with all the seriousness in the world. Keeping track of his answers, I start on the bowl, planning to fill the bottom and sides with all his favorite foods, making sure to add a Snickers bar somewhere in there.

"Fall semester starts next week," I say out of the blue after a small lull in the conversation. My gaze is on the pineapple I'm painting but I feel Ozzy shift beside me.

"You excited?" His tone feels casual but forced and I pretend not to notice.

"I guess … except a lot has changed since last year. I'm not sure how I feel about it to be honest," I say, a little lost in thought. "Plus, that also means I won't be working at Orso as much, probably just once or twice a week."

I keep my eyes down, avoiding Ozzy's gaze because I don't know how to tell him what I'm feeling inside. That just because summer is ending, it doesn't mean that what-ever is going on between us needs to end too. That I want to find time for him, that Orso isn't the glue that holds us together.

I'm not even sure why I'm having trouble telling him this, but I lack the words to explain my feelings and end up keeping it all to myself.

Before we leave the café hours later, I sneakily take a picture of our finished bowl, his tattooed hand and arm clearly in the background of the image, and post it online, my heart beating hard in my chest at the subtle implication.

36

OZZY

There's a knock at the door and my heart skips a beat. James and I have been seeing each other for over a month now, and it still seems like I haven't gotten over the nervous jitters of being around her.

When I realized earlier this week that she only had a week left before college started again, I suggested a nice dinner at my place to celebrate the end of summer. I didn't call it a date.

But to me it is. It always is.

I pat myself down and tug on my clothes as if my frayed jeans and t-shirt actually need any kind of straightening up.

Idiot. Just open the door.

When I do, James greets me with a wide smile, wearing a white lace top and a flowy skirt belted at the waist. She holds up a bottle of red and a small bouquet of flowers as she walks in.

"Are those for me?" I ask, surprised.

Her cheeks pinken as she stutters over her response. "Yeah, I just thought, that maybe—it's silly really."

"What's silly about flowers?" Taking them from her grasp, I kiss her softly on the lips. "Thank you."

She gives me a sheepish smile and follows me into the kitchen.

Humming in delight, she asks, "What's that smell?"

"It's the tomato sauce, been simmering for the past hour," I reply while finding a random jar, filling it with water, and placing the flowers in the middle of the table.

"I can't believe we both managed to get Saturday off," she says with glee, setting down the bottle of wine. "Do you want some?"

"Sure. Glasses are in the cupboard on your left."

I had to bribe Itzel for me to get the night off, but it was worth it.

Any time spent with James is worth the prep shifts I had to agree to.

Especially after seeing the picture she posted online after we left Bella's Café—my arm clearly in the background. Was it an oversight? Did she not notice? I studied it for far too long, wondering if I was reading into it, while her words from earlier that morning rang in my head.

Besides, you only soft launch someone you're actually dating.

I've been so careful not to push James too far, too fast. My actions have been cautious, giving her the space she needs to process the trauma her past relationship left her with, biding my time—but *fuck.*

I'd be down at the town hall right now, locking her down forever if it was up to me.

She's the one.

There's not a single doubt in my mind.

"Before I forget," I mutter, taking her key out of my pocket. "I should give this back to you."

She sneaks a peek from over her shoulder while reaching into the cupboard to see what I'm holding up. "Oh," she says, turning back to look at the cabinet. "You can keep it if you want. It's a spare."

I can't see her expression, but her tone sounds a little nervous.

She wants me to keep it?

"Really? You sure?" I ask, the surprised pleasure clear in my voice.

"Yeah," James says, handing me a glass of wine. "It's no big—I mean, yes I want you to keep it."

This feels much bigger than how casual she's trying to make it sound, but I say nothing more. I nod and smile, keeping eye contact while I ceremoniously unclip my cara-biner and slide the key onto one of my metal rings. Sipping on my wine, I take my time soaking her in as we lean on opposite counters, smiling into our glasses.

"Want to sous-chef me?"

Her face lights up, and my stomach warms in contentment.

"Of course," she says, looking around the kitchen.

Taking out my pasta maker, I make space on the counter. "Want to learn how to make pasta?"

"Sounds hard," she says with a soft giggle.

"It's really not." I shoot her a smirk. "Just follow my lead."

She eyes the pasta maker as if facing down a foe but nods in determination. "Let's do this."

I take flour, salt, and an egg out and tell her to mix the flour and salt in a bowl first. After she's done, I crowd her against the counter, her back leaning into my chest.

Taking her hands in mine, I show her how to make a well in the middle of the flour and have her crack the egg. I try not to laugh at her extreme concentration, but I don't think I've ever seen anything cuter. I trail my nose up her neck while she finishes.

"You're distracting me," she says with a breathy giggle.

I give her a small tut, my hands on her hips. "Concentrate."

I instruct her to dust the counter with flour, and she shoots me an amused side glance but does as I say. When she's done, I take her hands in mine again and teach her how to knead the dough with the heel of her palm.

"You're doing so well," I whisper in her ear, my hands moving up her arm.

"Ozzy," she warns, leaning into me.

I snicker, finally pulling away. Letting her continue, I check on the sauce, tasting it, adding more salt, and then tasting it again, all the while observing James.

"I like seeing you in my kitchen," I say, maybe a little too thoughtfully, charmed by the domesticity of it all. Putting my hand over hers to have her stop kneading, I turn her around to face me. I tuck a loose strand of hair behind her ear before kissing her, my thumb smoothing over her cheek as I do.

"Am I the first person you've taught how to make pasta?" she says in a near whisper, her eyes hooded and looking deeply sated.

"Romantically? Yes." My fingers tighten around her nape, and I trail my lips over hers, giving her another slow kiss. "You're the first person for a lot of things, baby."

"I like that," she says a little breathlessly, her eyes half closed from the kiss.

In that very instant, I want to tell her to give in to this

feeling. To stop pretending we're only friends with benefits when I don't think we've ever been *just* friends.

But I don't want to ruin the moment, knowing that the decision needs to come from her. I'm not the one wanting to keep things fun and casual. I've been ready for something serious ever since I first saw her.

She'll want the same eventually, I don't doubt that.

She just needs a bit more time.

And I can give that to her.

Because I'm not going anywhere.

———

AFTER A MEAL OF HOMEMADE PASTA, a shared bottle of wine, and a few shots from an old Jameson bottle I had lying around, we decide to go out for a nightcap. We head to Darling, a new cocktail bar that opened earlier this summer.

It's after midnight and the place is packed, but we manage to find a high top near the back. Tipsy James is more handsy in public than usual, and I take full advantage. I drag her chair close to mine, and she tugs on my collar so that I need to lean even closer. I revel in our intimacy, my chest swelling in pride at being with her like this. I don't know if there was ever a better time to describe a kiss as horny, but this is it, my hand slipping over her thigh as I taste her tongue on mine.

"Oh my fucking god."

It takes a second for me to place the voice but by the time I do, James has already pulled away with a small gasp.

"Michelle! What are you doing here?" she chirps.

Michelle's eyes narrow as she points her finger from

James' face to mine. "I *knew* it. I knew something was going on with you two."

"It's nothing—well it's not nothing, I mean, uh …" James babbles.

I'm somehow struck dumb and sit there not able to say a single word as I listen to James fail to successfully finish a single sentence.

Michelle's attention zeroes in on my hand still on James' thigh and she snatches it quickly, seemingly staring at my finger tattoos. "I thought I recognized those!" Her face lights up, dropping my hand back on my lap and turning to James. "That was *Ozzy* in the background of your picture." Pointing her finger to my face yet again, I swat it away. "So, what?" she presses. "Are you two dating?"

My gaze slides to James. Her eyes are wide like she's been caught in a lie. "Yeah Jimbo, answer Michelle's question—are we dating?" I flash her a cocksure grin and tilt my head to the side as I wait for her to answer. Inside, my heart is pounding a mile a minute.

James matches my gaze, giving me a challenging look, and presses her lips together, but then a smile slowly forms. She addresses Michelle, but her eyes never leave mine. "Yes, as a matter of fact, we are."

I assume this is how it feels to win the lottery.

I try to save face, holding back the urge to tackle her to the ground and smother her with kisses.

We're fucking dating.

"You little sneaks," Michelle says, giving James a playful shove. "How long has this been going on?"

Finding my ability to speak again, I answer for us. "A while."

"Wait …" Michelle says, her smile dropping, eyes snapping to James. "Is *Ozzy* the one who's been giving you all kinds of sexual enlightenment?" She holds up her hand, and cringes. "Actually, please don't answer that, I really don't want to know."

"Enlightenment, huh?" I tell James, not even bothering to acknowledge Michelle's reaction.

James laughs into her hand while I grin from ear to ear.

"Anyway," Michelle adds, "I was just leaving, I'm here with—doesn't matter. I'll see you both at work!"

Then she's off, making it feel like she was just one big fever dream.

My gaze slowly finds James', both of us silent.

We burst out laughing, James burying her face in the crook of my neck, her giggles tickling my ear. Taking her hand in mine, I give it a kiss, then cover it with my own.

"So we're dating," I say as if I need another confirmation now that we're alone.

James' smile is coy while she slowly nods.

I squeeze her hand in response.

I really *did* win the lottery.

37

OZZY

My phone rings while I'm getting ready to leave James' apartment. We came back to hers after Darling, giddy and on cloud nine. We stayed in bed this morning cuddling for as long as we could. But now I have to swing by my place before my Sunday shift.

"It's Soph," I say absentmindedly to James who's still lounging in bed.

I answer and stick my phone between my head and shoulder as I side-step into my jeans.

"Hey Soph, what's up."

There's a pause, followed by a gravelly, wheezing cough that somehow is so *fucking* distinguishable that I immediately know who's on the other end of the line before he even speaks. "It's Richard."

"Dad?" My stomach sinks. "Why are you calling me on Sophia's phone? Is she okay?"

"She's fine, she's fine," he mumbles, "she's in the living room. My phone got disconnected, that's all."

Relief washes over me hearing that Sophia is safe, still, I

roll my eyes. He probably didn't pay his phone bill again. Luckily, I'm the one in charge of Sophia's. I notice James straighten up in bed from the corner of my eye, and I'm suddenly hyper-aware of her witnessing this conversation.

Turning around, I face the door and lower my voice. "What do you want, Dad?" I impatiently wait for his answer as I chew on the skin of my thumb.

In a defeated tone, he answers, "Huxley's been arrested."

At first, I'm not sure if I've heard him right, the words ringing louder and louder in my ear.

"Hux was—" I stop short of saying the word out loud, I shoot James a quick look over my shoulder, worried she'll hear. Anxious adrenaline rushes through my veins, my mind already ten steps ahead knowing the responsibility of bailing Hux out will fall square on my shoulders. "I'll be right there."

I hang up and pocket my phone. Turning back around, I grab my shirt from the chair and pull it over my head before finally looking at James.

I keep my face blank, even though I'm having a hard time managing these chaotic feelings. One thing I'm sure of is that I don't want to rope James into this. Especially not now, when we finally started dating.

The last thing I want to do is ruin it with my family bullshit.

I can manage this alone. I always have before.

James looks up from the bed as I walk up to her. "Everything okay?" The hint of worry in her voice pinches at my heart, but I dismiss it.

"Everything's fine, baby," I tell her, kissing her quickly on the forehead. "Just something I need to handle at home. I'll call you later, okay?"

I barely wait for her response before turning around and running out the door.

Fifteen minutes later, I park my car in the driveway. Anxiety mixed with debilitating rage burns a hole in my stomach as I march up the half-rotten stairs to the porch. The front door leads directly into the living room, and I swing the screen door open, walking in to find Charlie, Sophia and my dad sitting on the couch watching a football game.

"Ozzy!" Charlie scrambles over the top of the couch, jumping down to come to greet me, barefoot and still wearing his Spider-Man PJs.

"Hey, buddy," I say, giving him a hug, trying to keep my voice light. "Excited for the first day of school tomorrow?"

I catch Sophia's morose expression from across the living room, her arms tucked tightly over her chest, she doesn't even let Charlie respond before saying, "Huxley's in jail, just like Mom."

My veins turn to ice, my eyes swinging to my dad. "You fucking told them?"

Richard's mouth opens, shuts, then opens again like a dying fish out of water. "Why wouldn't I?" he finally says.

My first instinct is to verbally eviscerate him. Of course, he told the kids. He never did understand how parenting works. Never understood that children should be shielded from situations like these. They don't need to be privy to every bad thing that happens. At least, not until we have the answers to the questions they'll inevitably have.

Charlie struts back to the couch, flopping back beside

Sophia, looking unfazed by what's going on. He clearly doesn't understand the severity of the situation.

Or maybe having family members end up in jail is all he fucking knows.

After swallowing the venom-filled words down into the swirling pit in my stomach, I motion to my dad with my head to follow me out back.

The yard is a desolate-looking thing. Overgrown weeds and yellow grass cover most of it. The white-painted fence is crooked and chipped, while piles of old bikes rust near the back shed, kept for their parts but never actually serving any real purpose.

The yard is just another embarrassing facet of this fucking dump.

Pulling a cigarette out of my pack, I pop it between my lips.

"Can I have one?" my dad asks before the flame even hits the tip.

I let out another long, annoyed sigh and hand him one. He grunts in what I assume is a thank you because it's impossible for him to say the actual words. After lighting both our cigarettes, I take a long drag, closing my eyes while I do so, desperately needing to calm down a few notches.

Not feeling even remotely settled, I blow the smoke out and turn to Richard. "So what the hell happened?

"Huxley didn't say much," he answers, eyes squinting, looking at the sky. "Something about robbing a liquor store."

I blink, trying to process what he just told me.

"Something about robbing a liquor store?" I repeat back incredulously. "That's all you know about your son being in jail?"

He shrugs, scuffing the tip of his shoe against a small

mound of dirt as he takes another drag. He's been out of the hospital for two weeks but still moves as if his entire body hurts. "You know Hux, I couldn't get a word out of him. Figured you'd have a talk with him tomorrow when you pick him up."

Hearing confirmation that my dad has no intention of getting involved still stings, as if this was the first time he's ever let me down.

"You're fucking useless," I spit, my breathing hard and shallow.

"Hey," my dad says half-heartedly, "don't talk to me like that. I'm still your father."

"Yeah?" I say, crushing my cigarette into the ground, my eyes burning him with all the hatred I have in me. "Couldn't tell."

———

It's early Monday morning and I'm sitting on a hard plastic chair in the reception area of our local precinct. I slept at the house last night after my shift at Orso, wanting to drive the kids to school on their first day. Huxley's arrest couldn't have happened at a worse time.

Shit. I guess there's never a good time for Huxley to get arrested.

Sophia was still awake when I got home. Instead of telling her to go to bed, we stayed up playing video games and talking about everything but our brother being in jail.

Huxley's bail was set to twenty-thousand, and even ten percent of that amount nearly wiped out the entirety of my savings.

I shoot to my feet when I see my brother turn the corner, bleary-eyed, gray t-shirt wrinkled and looking like he didn't sleep a wink last night. I have a feeling I'm sporting a similar look.

His hand tightens around the plastic bag holding his personal effects when he spots me. My throat tightens along with it, a suffocating wave of guilt washing over me when the sudden reality of how dire this is finally hits me.

I failed him.

I fucking failed him.

Huxley doesn't smile when he sees me. Why would he? He barely acknowledges me as he passes by me, heading for the exit. I wordlessly follow him to my car, unlocking the passenger door from inside.

It takes leaving the parking lot for me to finally say something. I try to keep my tone patient.

"What the hell happened, Hux?"

He scoffs, readjusting himself in his seat. "Don't pretend to care now."

Frustration travels up my spine like the hot flash of a flame.

"Look, this isn't the time to play *poor fucking me*, Huxley. We've all had a hard fucking life. All four of us had the same shitty parents growing up. But you're the only one who seems dead set on following in their footsteps."

The car falls silent, and I immediately regret comparing him to our parents. But I chew on my lip refusing to voice my remorse.

Huxley takes a long deep breath before he begins to speak.

"I was with the Finnegans."

I groan internally. The Finnegan brothers. Their family has an even worse reputation than ours. I fight against the urge to ask him why the hell he was with those two since they're well into their twenties and Hux is a month shy of turning eighteen. Instead, I wait for him to continue to speak.

"It was just supposed to be a quick and easy break-in. We chose an easy target and everything—the liquor store Patrick used to work at. He knew the code for the back door. I was supposed to be the getaway driver … hotwired an old Buick in the neighborhood. But then …" Huxley squirms in his seat, dragging his hand over his mouth.

"*Fucking hell,*" I curse under my breath. This is worse than I thought. "What happened next?"

He swallows hard. Clears his throat. "Turns out the owner was still in the back office. They tried to fight him off and ended up knocking him out with a fire extinguisher, then ran."

"Oh my god," I choke out, barely able to breathe. Stopping at a red light, I rest my head over my hands gripping the steering wheel before looking back at my younger brother.

"This is fucking serious, Huxley. Do you understand that?"

"I know," he mutters, crossing his arms and staring straight ahead.

My voice is rising and I can't do anything to stop it. "That's grand theft auto! Not to mention assault on top of breaking and entering!"

"I. Know," he says slowly in between clenched teeth.

"Do you?" I press, "They'll most likely try you as an adult, do you realize that?—this is bad, this is so fucking bad," I repeat the few last words more to myself as the light turns green.

I should have tried harder to protect him. I should have *fucking* tried harder.

"I fucked up."

I turn on Blume Boulevard, leading into our neighborhood.

"You fucked up?" I repeat, laughing dryly. "This isn't just a slap on the wrist, Hux. This is *real fucking life*. I don't think you understand the severity of what you just fucking did."

Huxley slams his fist into the dash. "I do, okay?" he says, his voice cracking. "*I do.*"

There's something in the tone of his voice that gives me pause.

Still not home, I park by the curb anyway, needing to invest my full attention to finish this conversation. I turn around in my seat to face him, my left arm leaning against the wheel.

Huxley is still staring straight ahead, his chest heaving, jaw clenched.

"Hux …" I coax, a lot more gentle now. "Look at me, man."

It takes me saying it a second time for him to finally do what I say. And when he does, the effect is the same as a knife slowly gutting me from the inside.

There's a crack in his hard exterior, and behind it is just a scared child.

He may look like an adult, but deep down he's still my teenage brother.

His eyes are large, full of repressed, watery emotions. His bottom lip trembles but he presses them together to make it stop. "I don't want to end up like Mom."

He says it so quietly that I almost miss it.

The crushing guilt returns, along with some of the most excruciating pain I've yet to ever experience.

How did I let this happen?

I pull him into me, circling my arms around his shoulders.

He doesn't resist. Doesn't even fight it.

His head falls into the crook of my shoulder as he chokes on a sob and I don't know if I'm going to survive seeing my brother like this.

"It's okay." I pat his hair as if he was Charlie, desperate to soothe him. Desperate to have him understand that I'll always be there for him. "We'll figure it out together. It's going to be okay. We'll be okay."

I don't even know if my words hold any truth, but they're the only thing keeping me together right now. I repeat them over and over like a prayer into Huxley's hair, wishing I knew what his future holds.

38

JAMES

I stop in front of a window, a block away from Mignon, to reapply my nude lipstick and fuss over my hair. This place is a high-end restaurant that I can no longer afford— but my mother certainly can. Dodging her calls for over a month clearly hasn't removed the effect she has on me. The need to look perfect for her is pathological.

I hate it, but I can't stop myself from doing it.

For the occasion, I wore my black Saint Laurent cock-tail dress that I haven't had the heart to sell yet. I hope my mother won't mention how *declassé* it is to still be wearing last season's fashion, not to mention how I paired it with the pumps I bought on sale last week.

Dropping my lipstick in the baguette bag I borrowed from Michelle, I check my phone.

No text.

Even if I pretend not to care, disappointment swoops heavily in the pit of my stomach. Ozzy and I have barely talked since he left my place on Sunday. I've been busy enough with my first week of school that I've pushed the lack of communication to the side. But it's now Saturday, and he's only called me twice since, sounding distracted both times.

I can tell something is wrong.

I could tell something was wrong before he even left that day, but I'm not sure how to approach it. Maybe I'm reading too much into it ... but I really don't think I am this time. I wish he would just talk to me. All I want is to be there for him, but I don't know how much I can push him for information when our *real* relationship has only just begun.

Luckily, I'm working tonight, so at least I know I'll be seeing him later.

Letting out a long exhale, I try to shake off the nerves from seeing my mother and square my shoulders, walking up to Mignon. Inside, the maître d' escorts me to a table near the window. Since I arrived early on purpose, my mother is thankfully not waiting for me. The maître d' pulls out the chair and I thank him as I sit down.

Hands wringing together on my lap, I wait.

Five minutes later, at one p.m. sharp, she arrives.

Even in the late summer weather, she has her Burberry coat delicately placed over her shoulders, a white satin top tucked into a tweed skirt, and black Chanel sunglasses daintily dangling from her French-tip nails.

She looks like the million bucks she's *actually* worth.

I scurry to my feet before she gets to the table.

"Mom," I say when she's finally close enough for a hug. "You look great as always."

She leans in for one of those no-contact air kisses, squeezing my arms with both hands before pulling away. "James, darling, you look——" she pauses to give me a condescending once-over while handing her coat to the server. "Different."

"Different?" My laugh is apprehensive as we both sit down. "Nothing about my appearance has changed since you last saw me."

She presses her lips together, a half-mocking smirk on her lips. "Just call it motherly instincts."

The strength it takes for me not to retort back with a snarky quip about her failings as a mother is superhuman. Whatever she meant by her remark is left unanswered. It swirls between us with the already growing tension as we stay silent while the server pours sparkling water into crystal glasses.

The first half-hour of our meal is spent exchanging platitudes. However, I'm on high alert the whole time, waiting for the moment when she'll strike.

"I heard from the Garrets that Zachary Benjamin is back home," my mother says innocently while she picks at her salad. "Poor boy, what a *dreadful* accident. You should go visit him, I'm sure he'd love that."

And there it is.

My anxiety spikes with just the mention of his name, worsened by the knowledge that I'm partly to blame for the real reason his hand is mangled.

"We broke up, Mom," I say with a puff of frustration. "It's been over a month. Besides, he was a piece of shit."

She lets out a small haughty inhale, her eyes darting around the room as if to check that no one heard me. She gently places her fork down, her gaze slowly dragging over to meet mine. Her movements are deliberate and I can tell that we've finally moved away from the boring small talk segment of this lunch.

"And how would I know that, James? *You* certainly

didn't bother to tell me." She lowers her voice in a near hiss. "I had to learn it from his mother, do you know how *humiliating* that was?"

I smile coldly. "And that's all you care about, right? The family image. Your place in that charade of a friend group?"

"Please." She scoffs, looking away, her blonde hair swishing with the movement. "Don't act as if this is all beneath you now that you're slumming it with the working class." Her cold stare returns, pinning me in my seat. "Your father and I know that this is just a phase. A simple teenage rebellion, a spoiled tantrum," she says with a dismissive wave of her hand. I grip my fork, my heart pounding against my eardrums. "Eventually, you'll come to your senses. You'll come back home, and marry that sweet boy Zachary Benjamin."

That sweet boy Zachary Benjamin.

My mind immediately goes to Ozzy.

And how astronomical the differences in their character are.

Maybe money isn't the core issue of why Zachary turned out so horribly. Maybe he was already rotten to begin with, but I'm sure it didn't help. I stay silent, turning her words over in my head, feeling nothing but cold contempt as she resumes eating her salad. I take a sip of my sparkling water, the bubbles dancing on my tongue and *strike*.

"You know, Elizabeth, I pity you. When I look at you all I see is a bored housewife. Insecure and spiteful, needing to put others down just to feel better about your own miserable life. I feel bad for you, I really do. So much wasted potential spent on redecorating the pool house, and planning DAR luncheons." I pause, my mother's eyes grow wide, and I barely feel any type of satisfaction. "I wonder who you'd be if you hadn't married rich—if you weren't stuck in such a loveless marriage." I stand up, sliding my purse up my shoulder. "I won't turn out like you."

My mother's eyes narrow, lips pursed into a thin line.

"James, sit back down," she spits between clenched teeth.

"*No.*"

Turning around, I march out of Mignon, shaking with adrenaline, not once looking back.

***

A FEW HOURS LATER, I'm still on a high from standing up to my mother as I stroll into the Orso kitchen.

"Is Ozzy around?" I ask one of the bussers.

"Smoking."

I give him a thanks from over my shoulder and open the back door.

As expected, Ozzy is near the dumpsters, wearing his unbuttoned chef's jacket, a cigarette tucked between two fingers.

His face lights up when he sees me but quickly a dark shadow passes over his expression and his smile drops.

"Hey, Jimbo." His voice is a little too neutral. "Forgot you were working tonight."

Feels like you forgot about me altogether this week.

I don't give voice to my anxiety but feel rattled none-theless.

Something is definitely up.

Stepping closer, I smile. I have the reflex to go for a kiss but something stops me.

"Happy to see me?" I say hesitantly.

Blowing the smoke into the air, his eyes soften, but his overall demeanor stays distant. A foreboding chill skitters down my spine.

"Of course, I'm happy to see you," he says. Taking my hand, his thumb strokes the top but he keeps distance between us. "I've just been … busy." After only a few seconds he drops it. Flicking his half-smoked cigarette onto the ground, he says, "Anyway, I got to get back to it."

He goes back inside with barely a glance my way.

What the hell?

Feeling unnerved and dismissed, I stay outside while I try to regulate my unwanted emotions.

When has Ozzy ever acted this way?

And why now? When we finally admitted that we're dating.

A malignant thought slips in unannounced.

What if he's been playing me all along?

Maybe the chase was more exciting than the real commitment.

I huff a long sigh, rolling my eyes at the sky. No way. I'm not about to entertain such a paranoid train of thought —not after weeks of nothing but kindness.

Something *must* be going on.

Deciding to table this until after the shift, I head back in to start on my side duties.

———

"WHAT THE HELL is going on with Ozzy?" Michelle asks as she sits beside me so she can give me a hand rolling cutlery.

"Why?"

I don't know why I'm asking.

I think everyone here knows why Michelle would be asking me that question.

"The guy has been in a foul mood all night, all week actually," she exclaims, pulling out her ponytail while she speaks. "More than foul—*rotten*. Nearly tore me a new one when I forgot to punch in that niçoise for table 12."

I sigh, not really knowing what to say. Even I wasn't impervious to Ozzy's barks and snarls, albeit a lot more subdued. I chalked it up to the kitchen being slammed but it still left a bad taste in my mouth. "I'll talk to him. Something *must* be up with him."

"Too late."

"What do you mean too late?" I say finishing another rolled-up cutlery.

"I saw him get in his car about five minutes ago."

"Are you shitting me?" I say a little too loudly, suddenly at my wits end with him.

What is he thinking? That he can just avoid me and I'll sit there and take it?

Absolutely not.

I give Michelle a sheepish look. "Do you mind finishing up alone?"

"Of course not," she says, shooing me away. "Go."

"Thanks, you're the best." I give her a quick hug and run to get changed.

I BANG on Ozzy's door, not caring how late it is. I know he's in there, I saw his car parked on the street when the taxi dropped me off. I didn't bother texting or calling, convinced he would have left my messages unanswered.

I hear his muffled voice from inside. "Who the fuck is banging on—"

The door swings open and Ozzy stops in his tracks. "James?"

"Remember me?" I say haughtily, my hip cocked and arms crossed.

Clipping my shoulder with his, I push him to the side and walk in.

"You shouldn't have come here," he says, his tone laced with bitter defeat.

"And why is that?" I say, swinging back around to face him, my arms up in exasperation. "Care to explain why you've been ignoring me for the past week?"

"I haven't been ignor—"

I cut him off. "Please, Ozzy. I'm not stupid."

"Fine," he says, the muscles of his jaw pulsing. He holds up his hand toward his room, and I hold his gaze for a long beat before turning on my heels, walking into his bedroom.

I face him as soon as he follows me in.

"Did I do something wrong? What is it?" I press harder.

"Not everything is about you, James," Ozzy snaps.

I fall silent, an uncomfortable but painfully familiar feeling settling in my gut.

"I'm sorry," he quickly adds. "I didn't mean it like that."

"So what *do* you mean?" I say, impatience pushing me on.

"I mean …" Ozzy trails off, both hands swiping over his curls, then cradling his palms on the back of his head as he looks up at the ceiling.

"What?" I urge. "Spit it out."

I can feel Ozzy's thread snap as he drops his arms back down, his gaze slamming into mine.

"We're a mistake, James. Don't you get it?" he says with a cold laugh. "Don't you see?"

My stomach sinks. Somehow, for some unexplainable and ludicrous reason, I didn't expect Ozzy to say that. Inexplicably, I hoped that his distance was all in my head. I try not to let my past insecurities convince me he doesn't care, but his words hurt nonetheless.

He circles around me and starts to pace while I turn slowly with him, the silence deafening.

"A mistake?" I say weakly.

"You should leave." It's forceful but desperate.

My mouth opens with a heated reply, but my gaze catches on something by the side of his bed, and I go silent.

It's the painting I gave him.

And it's … hanging on his wall.

He does care.

The realization is sudden: Whatever is happening is not about me.

Knowing that gives me the strength to stay and not turn around and leave. To not feel victimized by his stinging words. Tears form in my eyes but I blink them quickly back, my gaze back on him.

"No," I say forcefully.

Ozzy takes a second before replying. "No?" he repeats with a shocked chuckle.

"I'm not going anywhere."

"James," Ozzy says slowly as a warning.

Boiling tension rises as I simply stare at him, not budging.

His voice rises. "I told you to fucking *go!*"

He walks past me, heading for the door, seemingly trying to end this conversation.

My frustration boils over, tears springing back into my eyes.

I point a menacing finger toward him even with his back to me. "I know this isn't about us, stop being such a *coward* and talk to me!"

He stops in his tracks, tilting his head over his shoulder, tension crackling almost audibly between us.

"What did you say?" he asks slowly.

There's no hesitation in my voice. "I said stop being so weak, it's pathetic!"

His back is still to me, the silence slowly settling around us, loud and menacing. I track his movements intensively. Taking a careful step forward, he quietly closes the bedroom door and locks it.

My heart begins to beat even faster. I'm somehow *feeling* that something new is brewing between us. I just don't know what it is yet.

Finally, he turns to face me.

"Say it again," he drawls, his voice low and gravelly.

My eyebrows raise up in surprise, an almost impercep-tible *what?* leaving my lips.

Ozzy takes a step closer toward me, his gaze turning dark and hooded as it trails up and down my body.

"Tell me more about how pathetic I am." The curve of the letters sounds tauntingly delicious, my breathing turning shallow as I take in what he's asking of me.

I find my answer in the way he looks at me. It's desperate and needy and suddenly I understand exactly what he is asking.

What he needs from me right now.

The mischievous smile forming on his lips is the only intoxicating confirmation I need before I decide to make my move.

39

OZZY

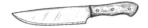

My mind is a haze.

I feel locked in a cage, slamming on the iron bars, pleading with whatever is controlling me right now to *please* stop.

Stop pushing away the only good thing to ever happen to me. Stop trying to hurt James, so I can harm myself in return.

I can barely recognize myself. My body feels like one of a stranger's.

As we both stare at each other, the silence pulsing between us, I take my time to drink her in. Her perfect, heavy tits pushed into a white top, chest heaving, cheeks rosy.

Three quick steps and she's in front of me. She hesitates as if trying to gather the courage, then finally grabs my throat.

"Pathetic little boy," she snides, "you can't even use your words, is that it?" Her fingers squeeze around my neck. "Tragic."

"Harder," I rasp.

As soon as I speak her hand leaves my throat, and tugs my hair hard at the base of my neck. My head jerks backward and I can't help but smile like an idiot, my mind gradually going quiet.

She tsks. "Did I say you could speak?" She gives me another sharp tug. "That's not what your slutty mouth is meant for."

Releasing me, her hand trails down my stomach, groping my quickly hardening cock through my jeans. Her laugh is mocking, and my eyes nearly roll into the back of my head. "Look at you, you're so hard it's embarrassing," she whispers near my ear. "You can't even help yourself." She smooths her palm up and down over my shaft. "Just a desperate little boy hoping I might let him fuck me."

I let out a low groan, it rumbles in my chest as I bite my lip.

I am desperate. So *fucking* desperate.

James finds my gaze, it's seeking, a small pause in her actions.

I give her a small nod and grin to urge her forward.

She returns the nod and takes a step back, giving her chin a quick flick downward. "On your knees."

I follow her order with zero hesitation, my cock throbbing, balls tightening. From my position on the ground, I look up at her obediently. My mind slowly quiets, like a rippleless pond, the burning ire living behind my chest turning to embers.

God, she's so beautiful like this. Control fucking suits her.

"Take off my panties," she orders. She stops my lunge forward with a simple open hand in the air. "Touch me *anywhere* else, and you'll be punished."

Her cold stare shouldn't have such a powerful effect on me, but I'm humming with arousal nonetheless. I watch her hike up her skirt. Slow. Deliberate. All the way up to her hips.

I feel like I'm reaching for a forbidden fruit, my movements choppy but focused.

Hooking both index fingers around the thin fabric of her thong, I stop myself for a single breath, devouring the sight of her from my vantage point. My thumb drags over her pussy before I even realize I'm doing it.

James swats the back of my head, my hands flying back onto my lap, undeserving.

Taking a handful of my hair, she pulls my head up so I have no choice but to look at her.

"Pitiful, stupid boy," she spits. "Can't even follow orders right. Is there anything you *can* do?"

Releasing my hair, she slowly smooths her palm down my face, cradling my chin. Her thumb pushes into my mouth, my tongue flattening as if waiting to receive sacramental bread.

"I think someone needs to be taught a lesson."

My lips wrap around her thumb, sucking on it greedily while I nod.

She laughs coldly, her thumb spreading my own spit on my lips, then gives me a small slap on the cheek. "So eager to please." She sneers. "It's pitiful, salad boy."

Pulling her skirt back up over her hips, she says, "Use your teeth this time."

Maybe I should be embarrassed by the wide dopey smile I flash at her, but my mind is blank, lost in my subservience to her.

Slowly, I lean over, my hands gripping my thighs while my teeth clasp her panties. Tugging them over her ass and hips, I let them fall to her feet and look up like a dog waiting for a treat.

As if reading my facial expressions, James coos, "Aw, see? I knew you could do it." She pats my head. "Such a good boy."

My fingers tremble, aching to palm my cock which is now pushing painfully against my jeans.

Turning around, James goes to sit on the edge of my bed. She points to the spot in front of her, an arrogant smirk pulling at her lips. "Crawl."

I'm on all fours in an instant. But I take my time to crawl to her. A slow relish of how good it feels to not be in control. The way the hardwood floor feels digging into my knees, how my palm flattens on the ground on my way to her.

Her.

James.

My world.

"Sit," she commands.

I listen faithfully, sitting back on my heels, my breath hitching as I wait for her next command. She spreads her legs, my gaze slamming down to her parting thighs, watching James bare her glistening pussy to me.

"Hands behind your back," she says when she notices my hands twitch. I mindlessly growl at the order, but still follow it, leashed and starving. "Time to put that slutty mouth of yours to good use," she purrs.

I dive forward, but she stops me with another handful of my hair. My eyes lock on hers, breathing heavy, my lips parted on a small whimper. She slides a finger into my mouth and I suck on it, the taste of her skin on my tongue lighting a fire in me.

"Mouth only, show me you can follow directions," she reminds me.

Releasing me, she falls back and leans on her elbows, widening her legs. I'm trembling with need, my gaze ping-ponging from her face to her cunt. Both equally seductive.

"Don't keep me waiting," she coaxes.

Half-expecting for her to stop me again, I let out a long groan when my tongue finally laps her from hole to clit.

She tastes even sweeter like this, when she's in control.

I alternate between broad licks to sucking her clit, and her soft, hushed moans are the only reward I need. She drapes one of her legs over my shoulder and pushes me even closer. I smile against her cunt like a fucking fool. Laving against her slit, I then push my tongue into her pussy, crazed with lust, feeling how she's equally affected.

I'm free-falling, head first and mindless, into my animalistic desires when she pulls me away from her. I'm practically snarling as I fall back on my heels.

She pushes herself up, cheeks and chest flushed but her cold, calculating look is back. She tilts her head to the side as if assessing me.

"Silly boy," she says as she stands up. "Thinking he could ever deserve more." With a flick of two fingers, she adds, "Up. Take your clothes off."

The relief I feel hearing those words is fucking otherwordly.

"On your back," she says, snapping toward the bed. "Hands over your head."

Her tone is bored, dismissive even, and I can't get enough.

I do as she says, ripping my clothes off and settling into position. Her gaze slides over my body, a small look of mocking disgust flickering in her expression when she lands on my hard cock laying heavy on my stomach.

This shouldn't turn me on, but *oh*, does it ever.

"Poor little fucktoy, practically begging to be sucked and used."

I moan at her words, on the verge of actually begging for real, wondering if I can physically die from her lack of touch. Her words are stitching me back up, her voice a calming pause for the storm raging inside of me.

James keeps her clothes on, crawling up the mattress.

Slow. Predatory.

She pulls her skirt up, and straddles me, the fabric fluttering back down, tragically obstructing the view. By the smirk on her face, she's doing it on purpose. I feel her hot, wet cunt slide against my cock and I think I might come on the spot. She grinds herself on me, one teasing finger trailing down my torso.

Reaching back and under her skirt, she curls her fist around my shaft. Holding herself steady with one hand on my stomach, she hovers over my cock, the head barely stretching open her entrance.

She hums. "See this is what you're good for. You like being used like this?" she asks innocently.

I haven't spoken since she told me to shut up, so I nod eagerly again.

Her cunt swallows another inch of my cock.

My fingers grip the mattress above me, my self-control fraying.

She spits in my face, landing on my cheek. "Fucking slut," she says snidely, and slams down, sheathing my cock down to the hilt. The combination of shock and arousal flooding my system is damn near euphoric.

James begins to fucks herself on my cock, riding me hard and fast and I'm losing all sense of fucking reason.

"Hit me," I growl.

Her blue eyes jump to mine questioningly.

"Hit me, *please*, baby," I repeat, with a dark, coaxing grin, my hands still up over my head.

It doesn't take much convincing, which only makes it that much hotter. On her next thrust down, she slaps me across the face, and my skin tingles beautifully with the sting.

She laughs. Cold and delectable. "So desperate for me to touch you that you'll even beg me to hit you." Squeezing my cheeks with one hand, she leans over and kisses me forcefully.

I take what I can, sucking on her bottom lip before she ultimately pulls away.

When she does, she slams both palms on my chest and grinds herself in a slow circle against my hips. "*Fuck*," she breathes, "I'm coming." Her nails dig into my heated skin and her pussy pulses around me.

"Please, let me touch you," I whisper desperately.

"Yes," she whimpers and my hands fly to her lush ass, gripping two beautiful, fucking handfuls.

I pitch my hips upwards and fuck her hard through her orgasm, her head thrown blissfully back, my own orgasm following close behind. I come hard, unloading deep in her quivering pussy, biting my lip until I taste blood.

James falls into my arms, my cock still inside her, as she nestles into my neck, pressing a soft kiss on my wild pulse. My head is empty, weightless like a cloud, focused only on the comforting weight of James' body on mine.

"How are you feeling?" she whispers against my warm skin, it tickles like a small fluttering butterfly.

I breathe in deeply before answering her. "I feel … peaceful."

I can feel her smile, and she gently squeezes my arm. "Peaceful is good," she replies with a pleased sigh.

We both fall silent and continue to lay in each other's arms for what feels like forever, breathless and sated.

40

OZZY

The apartment is quiet while I pad across the living room and into the kitchen, turning on the light. I left James sleeping in bed, but even with her comforting presence beside me, I couldn't fall asleep.

So I decided to do what comes naturally—cooking.

It didn't take long for my mind to start racing again. Sex was just a balm. I knew that. But *fuck* was it amazing while it lasted.

But now I can't help but replay our argument. So much is still left unsaid. And as much as I would rather pretend nothing is bothering me—pretend I didn't ignore James for the past week—I know we need to talk.

Maybe sharing a grilled cheese while having this difficult conversation can ease some of the ache.

Careful not to make any loud noises, I gather the ingredients I need.

Sourdough bread, butter, one green apple, and brie.

I put a pan on a burner, and prepare everything while it heats. Reaching for the cutting board, I focus my thoughts on the sound of the cracking crust while I cut through the bread. Then on the gritty crunch of the sliced apple.

Slowly, the kitchen becomes a liminal space existing outside of time and space.

My thoughts fizzle out, and the trained focus of my movements allows my mind some much-needed respite.

There's a love/hate relationship to cooking. After a while, working in kitchens sucks the joy out of it. But then there are moments like these when making a grilled cheese in the middle of the night for the person I … *love*, saves me from spiraling into another panic attack.

Because, of course, I love James.

Falling in love with her was the easiest thing I've ever done.

But *saying* it out loud to her?

I don't think I should. Not yet.

I don't want to scare her away. Or come off too strong.

I'm perfectly fine loving her quietly—for now.

It definitely doesn't explain why I pushed her away this week.

Which is why this talk is so needed.

The butter sizzles, and I gently place the bread slices into the pan, layering the brie and apple on top. I flip a dry rag over my shoulder and keep an eye on the pan while I prepare a dipping sauce, whipping whole-grain mustard, mayonnaise, and honey together.

When the brie turns gooey and the bread is nice and toasted, I cut the grilled cheese in half and plate them with one half leaning over top the other one. I smooth some of the dipping sauce on the plate with the back of a spoon and put the rest in a ramekin.

On soft feet, I return to the bedroom with our food. The lamp on my bedside table is still on from before, not seeming to bother James one bit. Setting the plates down on the bedside table, I crouch on the bed with one knee, and kiss James' cheek to gently rouse her.

Her eyes blink open, brows pinched together with an adorable pout on her lips.

"What time is it?" she rasps.

"Just after two," I say, my tone hushed. "Here, sit up. I made you some food."

Suddenly wide awake, James' eyes sparkle with gleeful excitement when I hand her a plate, after she's scooted herself against the headboard.

"You made this for me?" she says in awe, placing the plate on her lap and looking down at it as if I gave her a bowl full of diamonds. "What's in it?" she asks as she picks up the grilled cheese and examines it.

I stifle a laugh, and answer honestly, having learned that James prefers to know what she's eating before taking the first bite. "It's grilled cheese, with brie and apples."

"Yum!" she says, squeezing her shoulders up to her chin, in the purest and most wholesome reaction I've ever seen. She hums in delight after the first bite, my heart glowing with warmth in response.

Sitting near her, on the edge of the bed, my plate on my lap, I wait until she's eaten half of her sandwich before addressing the elephant in the room.

"We—" My voice cracks. I clear my throat and start again. "We should talk."

James' gaze softens when her eyes flit to mine. But I don't miss the flash of pain she tries to conceal when she looks down at her plate, then back up.

"You first," she responds, with an assertive nod of her head.

It might not be the right moment, but I feel pride nonetheless. Of the confidence she now carries. It's how she doesn't second-guess her actions anymore and the self-assured tone she uses when she speaks. It's been gradual, but so powerful to notice. And I'm so happy I've been there through her metamorphosis.

I take a bite full of brie and apples and slowly chew my food as well as my words.

"I'm sorry," I finally say, although quite tentatively. "It wasn't fair for me to push you away like I did. You didn't deserve that."

She studies me with an open expression, licking her lips and swallowing hard. "So why did you?" The hurt returns, now living somewhere in her voice, and I try, quite unsuccessfully, not to hate myself.

My throat closes at the thought of telling her about my home life. It would be so simple to evade the subject—blame my aloofness on something else, and use humor to deflect.

But she deserves my truth.

And I'm more than willing to give it to her. Even if it hurts like hell to vocalize it.

I let out a defeated sigh and place my half-eaten plate on the bedside table, turning my body so I'm facing James directly.

"I just didn't know how to …" I look up at the ceiling, grasping at my words, and eventually land on something vague. "Handle everything." My heart squeezes in my chest, a hard ball forming in my throat.

"Handle what?" James asks gently as she hands me her empty plate.

I drag a hand down my face, delaying the inevitable.

"I told you I was the oldest of four, but that wasn't really the full picture."

James cocks her head to the side, signaling me to continue.

After a long exhale, I tell her everything. From my dad being a gambler and a drunk, my mother going to prison when I was twenty-one, to finally, me being the main provider for my younger siblings.

Sometime during all this mess, James reaches over and grabs my hand in hers, staying silent and letting me talk, but squeezing my palm in hers now and again in support.

"And then last week." My voice cracks again. I clear my throat. "My brother got arrested for trying to rob a liquor store ..." I feel empty and miserably vulnerable when it's finally all out, finding it harder and harder to maintain eye contact with James. "We still don't know if he'll be convicted. But shit ..." I try to swallow down the hard knot in my throat. "He's only seventeen. I should've been there for him."

"I'm so sorry," she rushes out. "I–I can't imagine how hard this has all been for you."

"Don't be," I tell her, already trying to evade the weight of the pain. Still, I allow her words to soothe some of the ache. It helps to finally feel ... heard.

"But," she says, looking like she's trying to solve a puzzle. "What did that have to do with us?" she asks gently, placing her other hand on top of our joined ones. "I could have been there for you this week, instead of ... just ... not?" she finishes with a sad smile.

My first reflex is to dismiss her question entirely. Tell her she just wouldn't get it.

I bite the inside of my cheek instead, trying to formulate a better, and more mature, response.

"I guess I just got scared," I finally say, looking down at the bed.

"Of what?" Her tone is agonizingly gentle and I'm not sure how to navigate the care I hear in her voice.

I lift my gaze back to hers. She waits patiently for my answer.

"Of ruining the best thing that's ever happened to me."

Tears spring in James' eyes and I want to look away.

But I can't.

"Why would you think that?" she says softly.

"Because …" My voice suddenly sounds too young as if the past is reaching out from inside my throat, but I manage to choke out the rest of the words. "Us McKennas ruin everything we touch."

Echoing my dad's words tastes foul, but somehow it still sounds like the truth.

I try to take my hand away, but James resists, instead getting on her knees and shifting herself closer to me. She lets go only to cradle my face with both hands.

"Ozzy," she whispers, her mouth against mine, her lips soft and warm. "If anything, being with you has felt like quite the opposite of you ruining things."

My eyes find hers, seeking more of an explanation for what she just said.

She sits back on her heels, hands falling onto her lap, gaze to the ceiling in thought.

Then she looks down, pinning me with her stare, she says, "When I'm with you, I feel like you see the person I am behind all the cracks … behind all the versions of myself I've created to please others. It's like you've always seen *me*, from the very first day we met."

My heart wants to burst into a million little pieces.

I stroke her cheek with my thumb and smirk, hoping to alleviate some of the tension.

"Is that right, Jimbo?"

She nods. "Yeah, it is, salad boy." Her smile so full of genuine sincerity.

And somewhere deep inside of me, a small part of me begins to heal, knowing I could be that person for James.

That I *am* that person for her.

41

JAMES

"Yeah she's a total bitch," one of the suits says.

I pretend not to listen while I replenish the half-empty wine glass, bottle in hand, a white cloth draped over my wrist, with my other arm tucked behind me. Men like him always act as if the waitstaff is invisible. It does make for juicy gossip when swapping stories back at the server station.

"A nag too, always calling to see when I'll be home. Or whining about me spending more time with the kids. Next, she'll be asking me to throw on an apron and help with dinner!" He barks a laugh and the three other men at the table mirror his energy.

I internally groan when I realize he's talking about his girlfriend. My eyes dip down to his left hand, finding a wedding band on his finger—worse, his *wife*.

One of the men chimes in with a similar story, bemoaning about his girlfriend and calling her crazy.

I leave the table quietly, feeling slightly rattled.

While I punch in an order of agnolotti, I can't stop

thinking about what they just said—what they just revealed, seemingly unbothered that a complete stranger was standing within earshot. How vicious those remarks sounded, said with zero culpability, about the women they claim to love.

My stomach sinks, my past crashing into me, swallowing me like a tidal wave and reminding me of how I used to be treated. That could very well have been me they were talking about. Thinking of the kind of vitriol Zachary could spew directly to my face, I can't imagine the shit he said about me behind my back.

My head swivels unconsciously to the kitchen pass, my gaze finding Ozzy effortlessly. I watch him exchange some words and a laugh with Itzel, and relief washes away whatever shit feeling I was experiencing only moments ago.

It's an intricate kind of relief.

One that soothes hidden cracks within me that I still don't know how to reach on my own. It tells me, with unequivocal certainty, that Ozzy would never speak about me like that.

It's a staggering kind of relief.

And I let myself sink deeper and deeper into it while I continue to stare at him.

As if sensing me, he turns and catches my gaze. His face lights up when he sees me watching as if surprised to find me standing there. He blows me a quick kiss, followed by a warm smile before returning to his conversation and I don't think I've ever loved such a quiet show of affection quite like this.

After our conversation last night, a lot between us feels … transformed. I've never felt this stable in any of my relationships, romantic or otherwise. Like I could count on Ozzy for anything. And I hope he feels the same about me.

Because like I told him last night, I'm not going anywhere.

But I also know the power of actions. Words are often too intangible. Instead, I make a quiet promise to myself, to make sure he knows that I choose him every day, even if it takes time for him to believe that he deserves me.

Even Orso feels different somehow.

When I walked into work today, I felt like my perspective had shifted. The familiar smells of the kitchen, the sound of clinking racks of glasses getting carried to the bar, the hushed laughter of my coworkers—turned friends— busy setting up the dining room.

It all somehow reminds me of the day I walked in and asked Elle for a job.

How different I was back then, insecure and impressionable.

Funny how three months can feel like a lifetime.

I owe a lot to Orso.

It gave me a life, outside of the crippling weight of my parent's influence.

Most importantly, it gave me Ozzy.

Two hours later, I'm trying to make the table of suits pay up so I can close out. They're visibly drunk and annoyingly loud. I walk back to their table, hoping they'll finally hand me a credit card to charge. The married one seems to finally notice my presence and hands me the check presenter with a leering grin.

But when I reach for it, he quickly pulls it back into his chest, followed by a dark chuckle. His friends laugh like hyenas beside him. I let out a dry laugh, smiling politely, but secretly I'm cursing the entire table of fucking idiots.

"What kind of tip would it take for you to open those pretty legs of yours."

I feel sick, but I act unbothered, smiling smugly.

"I have a boyfriend," I respond flatly, holding out my hand for the check presenter.

"Your boyfriend doesn't need to know. It'll be our little secret."

The table snickers and my patience frays, ready to snap.

Already facing the kitchen, I point to the pass. "Careful, he's probably watching you flirt with his girlfriend as we speak."

The asshole's smile drops, his head turning to whoever I'm pointing at. I can't even see Ozzy from my vantage point, but seeing this guy squirm is satisfying enough.

While he's distracted, I rip the check presenter from his grip. "*Gentlemen*," I say before walking away from the table with a haughty step.

On my way back to the bar, I try to tamper the triumphant grin on my lips when I see Ozzy's head pop out of the swiveling doors. He strolls out into the dining room, one hand in his pocket as he takes a bite of a Snickers bar.

My stomach flips seeing his cocky smile, his ocean eyes blazing. "Boyfriend, huh?" he says, oh so casually, the muscles of his jaw working as he slowly chews and then swallows.

A small burst of laughter escapes me. "How did you even hear that?"

He shrugs, a mischievous expression on his face, as he looks away smugly. His gaze returns, answering my question. "Jules was behind you bussing a table."

He steps closer to me, touching my elbow as he lowers his voice. "Did you mean it?"

I giggle. "Of course, I meant it."

Beaming, he shoves the half-eaten chocolate bar into his pocket and takes my hand, tugging me toward him, while his free hand opens one of the kitchen doors.

"Guys," he yells loudly, "Jimbo's my girlfriend!" He holds our hands up over our heads as if we've won some kind of prize, while the kitchen bursts into a series of hoots and howlers and *yes, chef!*

Somewhere in the back, I hear Alec say, "We already knew, you clowns, now get back to work!"

My cheeks hurt from smiling, slapping Ozzy's chest playfully. He pushes us through the doors, swiveling us around to hide from the dining room, just to kiss me. It's quick but possessive, his fingers digging into my nape.

Releasing me just as quickly, he gives me a small tap on the ass and winks.

"I'll see you later, *girlfriend*."

42

OZZY

"What kind of eggs do you want?" I ask James, kissing her before jumping out of bed.

She gives me a sleepy smile. "Whatever you're having."

"You sure? I can make them special for you," I say while throwing some boxers and a t-shirt on.

She shakes her head, her satisfied smile still on her lips. "I *want* what you're having."

"Sunny side up it is then," I tell her with a side grin before walking out of the bedroom.

I convinced James to stay over last night after our Sunday shift. She said she had class early this morning, so I promised her that I'd make her breakfast and drive her to campus as a compromise. She accepted with a slow nod, studying me like I had promised her the world.

When she agreed, I kissed her like she had already given me the world.

The sun is barely peeking out from the horizon as I make my way to the kitchen. I put on some coffee while the eggs cook, butter some toast, and slice half an avocado.

I feel jubilant while setting up our plates as if I can't wait to get back to James, even if she's just in the other room waiting for me.

I bring her breakfast first with a steaming cup of coffee. Circling to her side I put on a show just to make her laugh, acting as if this is the fanciest thing I've ever cooked for her.

Her giggles are infectious, my chest tingling with happiness.

I place the mug on the bedside table, handing her the plate and cutlery. I notice her gaze turn thoughtful before I lean down to steal another kiss.

"I love you," she says against my lips.

The declaration is rushed, sounding like she said it quickly before she lost the courage.

She catches me off guard, my head popping up to better look at her, my arm shooting out as if it has a mind of its own, nearly knocking the coffee all over the floor.

"Wait, did you just—" I say, still clearly frazzled.

She nods, her eyes wide with unwavering emotions.

"I *love* you, Ozzy," she repeats.

My stomach explodes in a flurry of butterflies, and I suddenly feel light-headed. I swallow hard, eyes wide, a dumbstruck grin on my face.

I've never heard lovelier words come out of that perfect mouth.

"Oh, baby," I say with a dark chuckle, taking her plate of food out of her hands. "Fuck these eggs."

She laughs in surprise, watching me crawl up on the bed, bracketing her body with my knees. I catch her lips, kissing her feverishly before finally taking her face into my hands, and staring deeply into her eyes.

"James, this was never *just* friends for me. As soon as I

first saw you, I knew you were about to change my fucking *world*, baby. I love you doesn't even come close to describing what I feel for you," I profess, kissing her lips, her nose, her cheeks. "But I'll tell you every minute of every fucking day that I love you if it means I can keep you forever."

James stays silent for a few breaths, her face serious as she studies me.

But then she smiles, and it feels like witnessing my very own sunrise.

"Yes, chef," she says, her eyes sparkling like the brightest stars.

Her laugh is a weightless and effervescent thing as she wraps her arms around my neck and pulls me into her.

Breakfast eventually turns cold, discarded, and forgotten.

Because nothing compares to the taste of James on my tongue.

EPILOGUE

OZZY

Three months later

"Charlie, if you break that coffee table, all you're getting for Christmas is coal!" I yell from the hallway while I make my way back to the kitchen. "And Alec you're no better than him!"

My brother shrieks while jumping off the table as Alec continues to chase him around the living and dining room, weaving around bodies. I shoot them a glare, but the teasing tone in my voice is an obvious giveaway: I'm just happy to have everyone here for a friend's Christmas dinner, siblings included.

My gaze lands on James standing near the window, Sophia standing next to her. Ever since I introduced them they've been attached to the hip, my sister taking to James like she was the best thing to ever happen to us.

She's not wrong.

Everyone deserves to have a little bit of James in their life.

James is off on a tangent about her latest painting to Soph and Connie, who's visiting from LA. The piece is of me and Alec in the busy Orso kitchen, now proudly hanging above the couch.

I must have lingered a little too long because James's eyes skate to mine while she's still talking. Her smile brightens as she sends me a quick wink, before returning her attention to Connie and Sophia.

My heart flutters and I can feel my cheeks flush. I still act like a schoolboy with a crush when I'm around her. But I don't think that feeling will ever wane, not when her love and attention have become the best part of my days.

I clear my throat, and turn on my heels, walking into the kitchen where I find Itzel peering over the stove.

"You can't help yourself, can you," I say, followed by a playful laugh.

She snickers, rubbing her neck. "I feel weird not doing anything."

"Don't we all." I know how hard it is to stay out of the kitchen when cooking is all you know. "Everything is almost ready anyway. Hux and I've got this, right?" I ask while slapping my brother on the shoulder.

He lets out a small grunt, head down, busy cutting onions while trying to pretend his eyes aren't watering.

Itzel throws up her hands. "Fine, fine, fine," she says as she returns to the living room with a fresh beer from the fridge.

Huxley and I have gotten a lot closer since he got arrested. Ironic. And admittedly a little sad, but something changed between us the day I picked him up from jail, and I've been building on that change.

After turning eighteen back in October, he's been talking about moving out which I wholeheartedly support.

He's been crashing on my couch most days anyway. Our father hasn't noticed his absence. Too drunk to care, I'm sure.

We're still awaiting Huxley's sentencing. It's the dark cloud we try to ignore on most days, but whatever happens, at least now he knows that I'll be there for him no matter what.

I step closer to him. "Curl your fingers, remember like I showed you?" I say gently, reminding him how to properly position his hand to avoid cutting a finger while chopping.

His eyebrows crease in concentration, giving me a quick assured nod as he fixes his hand holding the onion and I resist the urge to ruffle his green hair.

Half an hour later, after managing to herd everyone to the dining room table, I set the glazed ham down amongst the plethora of mismatched plates and bowls. An array of them filled with roasted vegetables, salads, and bread, with the lavender ceramic bowl James and I painted together as the centerpiece.

I settle into my chair with a pleased sigh, my heart full as I look around the table. Michelle shares a joke with Quinn. Connie passes a bowl of mashed potatoes to Gustavo. Itzel and Alec cut into the ham. Sophia chides Charlie about not sitting upright, while Huxley punches him in the arm, clearly not helping the situation.

A hand squeezes my wrist, and I look at James, sitting to my left.

We share a look—unconditional love and comfort wrapped into a thousand words, a small moment of quiet gratitude.

"This is beautiful," she says, referring to the spread of food.

"Not nearly as beautiful as you, Jimbo," I say leaning into her.

"Oh stop," she says, giggling into a kiss.

"Never," I answer as I lean back into my chair, a stupid grin slapped on my face. "You're stuck with me, remember?"

"Happily," she says, taking a sip of wine, her blue eyes sparkling.

AFTER DINNER, the whole gang gathers in the living room, having promised the kids, Charlie especially, that we could open a few presents.

Charlie sits on the floor, beside the Christmas tree, legs criss-crossed, looking up at everyone expectantly as if awaiting some kind of coronation.

He's damn near vibrating when James hands him a present.

"You didn't have to," I tell her under my breath. "They're just happy to have you around."

She shoots me a bewildered look like I'm being ridiculous, and I press my lips together trying not to burst out laughing.

"Spider-Man PJs!" Charlie squeals, throwing himself in James' arms as a thank you.

"I thought it was time for a new set," she says amused, while Charlie runs out of the room, PJs in hand, unable to wait to try them on.

My body trickles with warmth as if I'm the one who was just given a gift. Seeing James not only take notice of my siblings' needs but also act on them, touches me in ways that leave me nearly speechless.

I catch Alec's gaze from across the room, there's a small knowing smile on his lips as he smooths his mustache with the palm of his hand, a wordless conversation exchanged as more gifts are opened. I know he notices it too, how James has integrated herself seamlessly into my life—into my family's life.

I never thought I could deserve this kind of happiness.

I never believed *family* could feel this healing either.

But that's what James has become.

Looking around the room at everyone here, I realize that's what they all are. Not just friends, but a chosen family. And what's more meaningful than to *choose* to love someone, while they do the same in return? I would do anything for my siblings, but family is so much more than the lazy expectation of loyalty because of a family name.

It's showing up every day no matter what.

It's love under no conditions.

Alec gives me a small knowing nod, smiling as he takes a swig of his beer.

I return his nod, suddenly filled with so much pride and bubbling hope, knowing I have the rest of my life to bask in this new feeling of completeness.

With James by my side.

RECIPES FOR JIMBO

LOVE, OZZY

Oysters with Mignonette

Ingredients:
1 dozen raw oysters, shucked
1/2 cup red wine vinegar
4 tbsp shallot minced
½ tsp freshly cracked black pepper
pinch of salt

Directions:
Set shucked oysters on a bed of crushed ice.
In a small bowl, mix the rest of the ingredients.
Whisk to combine.
Place a tsp on top of each oyster, and enjoy.

Serving suggestion: Best eaten from the hand of a horny line cook.

Breakfast Burrit♡s

Ingredients:
4 eggs
2-3 green onions, finely chopped
1 tomato, diced
1 tsp smoked paprika
1 tbsp olive oil
1 cup and half of shredded cheese
4 12-inch tortillas
1 tsp butter

Directions:
Crack eggs in a medium bowl, whisk until mixed. Add chopped green onions, diced tomatoes, and paprika. Mix well.
In a medium nonstick pan, over medium heat, add olive oil. Add egg mixture. With a spoon or spatula, very gently stir the mixture, letting small soft curds form. Add cheese.
Continue lightly cooking over low heat until the eggs are scrambled and cheese is melted. Season to taste with salt and pepper.
To assemble, place a heaping spoonful of egg mixture onto the middle of a tortilla. Tuck in the sides and roll the tortilla until closed.
Melt a tsp of butter in a medium nonstick pan over medium-low heat, place burrito folded-side down, cook until crispy then flip. Same to the other side.

Serving suggestion: Best served as the eldest child to your younger siblings to cheer them up.

FR♡ƷEN SNICKERS

Ingredients:
Snickers bar, unwrapped

Directions:
Still in the wrapper, place Snickers bar in walk-in freezer until frozen.
Wait until you feel out of control and the rage has begun to bubble over.
Unwrap and insert in *redacted*.

Serving suggestion: Best served after losing a bet with the flirty line cook while feeling the need to get back at your soon-to-be shitty ex-boyfriend.

Note: Author is not liable for any UTI's and/or yeast infections.

Cheese Quesadilla

Ingredients:
Two 12-inch flour tortillas
1/2 cup grated cheddar
1/4 cup grated mozzarella
1/2 cup grated queso fresco
1 tbsp butter

Directions:
In a medium nonstick pan, melt butter at medium heat. When butter is melted, sprinkle a handful of cheese mix directly onto the pan.
Lay one tortilla flat on the pan on top of the cheese, then sprinkle more of the cheese mix onto the tortilla. Top with remaining tortilla and press to seal. When the cheese at the bottom turns crunchy, flip to the other side and cook until golden brown. Repeat with the other quesadilla.
Let cool for 5 minutes. Slice into 4 or 6 pieces. Serve with salsa or guacamole.

Serving suggestion: Best eaten after finally breaking up with your shitty boyfriend.

Agnolotti with White Wine & Pecorino Sauce

Ingredients:
1 cup white wine
4-5 tbsp butter
½ cup veggie stock
1 shallot, thinly sliced
1 garlic clove, thinly sliced
1/2 red chili pepper, thinly sliced
1 1/2 cup pecorino
1 tbsp olive oil
Salt & pepper
Fresh basil leaves
2 cups agnolotti

Directions:
Bring a large pot of salted water to a boil.
In a large saucepan over medium heat add olive oil, shallot, chili, garlic and sauté until cooked.
Deglaze pan with white wine. Cook until alcohol has evaporated (you should not be able to smell it).
Add veggie stock, butter, salt & pepper to the pan and stir until butter is melted. Sauce will thicken a little. Add 1 cup of pecorino cheese and then turn off heat. Stir well until sauce thickens to your preference. (If the sauce is too thick, add stock.) Add the agnolotti pasta to the boiling water and cook according to label instructions. Drain and transfer to the sauce. Over medium heat, cook pasta in sauce for 3-4 minutes, then turn off heat. Add the rest of pecorino, and mix well. Served with fresh basil on top.

Serving suggestion: Best served after a drunken night out after finally bringing your crush back to your place.

Fresh Sem♡lina & Egg Pasta

Ingredients:
2 cups semolina flour
2 cups all-purpose flour, plus extra for dusting
Pinch of salt
6 large eggs, at room temperature
2 tbsp extra-virgin olive oil

Directions:
Sift all-purpose flour, semolina flour, and a pinch of salt together in a large bowl. Make a mountain out of flour mixture on a clean surface; create a deep well in the center.
Break eggs into the well and add olive oil. Whisk eggs very gently with a fork, gradually incorporating flour from the sides of the well. When mixture becomes too thick to mix with a fork, begin kneading with your hands.
Knead dough until it is smooth and supple, 8 to 12 minutes. Dust dough and work surface with semolina as needed to keep dough from becoming sticky. Wrap dough tightly in plastic wrap; allow it to rest at room temperature for 30 minutes. Sexy pro tip: Help her knead the dough while standing closely behind your date. Caution: May cause butterflies and/or poorly concealed boners.
Roll out dough with a pasta machine or a rolling pin to desired thickness. Cut into your favorite style of noodle or stuff with your favorite filling to make ravioli.Bring a large pot of lightly salted water to a boil. Cook pasta in the boiling water until tender yet firm to the bite, 1 to 3 minutes (or longer depending on thickness). Drain immediately and toss with your favorite sauce.

Serving suggestion: Best prepared while trying to impress your situationship and seduce her into becoming your girlfriend.

Brie & Green Apple Grilled Cheese

Ingredients:
3 tbsp salted butter, at room temperature
2 thick slices of hearty multi-grain bread
3 ounces sliced brie
1/2 Granny Smith apple, thinly sliced

Directions:
Build the grilled cheese by placing half of the slices of brie on the bread, followed by the apples. Then add the rest of the cheese. Spread the outside of the top slice with butter.

Transfer the sandwich to the skillet over medium-low heat, buttered side down. Spread butter on the top slice. Toast each side of the sandwich until golden on the outside and the cheese is melted, 3 to 4 minutes per side. Cut in half and serve.

Serving suggestion: Best served as a midnight snack, in a post-orgasmic-new-kink-unlocked high.

Christmas Ham

Ingredients:
1 (14 to 16-pound) fully cooked, spiral-cut smoked ham
on the bone
6 garlic cloves
8 1/2 ounces orange marmalade
1/2 cup dijon mustard
1 cup light brown sugar, packed
1 orange, zested
1/4 cup freshly squeezed orange juice

Directions:
Preheat the oven to 350F. Place the ham in a heavy
roasting pan.
Mince the garlic in a food processor fitted with the
steel blade. Add the marmalade, mustard, brown sugar,
orange zest, and orange juice and process until smooth.
Pour the glaze over the ham and bake for 1 hour, until
the ham is fully heated and the glaze is well browned.
Serve hot or at room temperature.

Serving suggestion: Best served after your happily
ever after.

MORE FROM NAOMI LOUD

Don't miss out on the bestselling dark romance series "Was I Ever".

Sunny and Byzantine	Was I Ever Here
Lenix and Connor	Was I Ever Real
Lucy and Bastian	Was I Ever Free

If you don't want to miss out on any future book announcements make sure to follow me on instagram and tiktok at naomi.loud or subscribe to my newsletter! You can find the link on my website: www.naomiloud.com

You can also join my Patreon to receive exclusive behind the scenes updates, teasers, character art, giveaways and bonus scenes!

And if you loved On the Line, I'd be forever grateful if you could leave a positive review on Amazon. Your support is why indie authors can continue doing what we love.
Thank you!

ACKNOWLEDGMENTS

First, I'd like to thank Caitlin. Without your casual bullying online, I don't think I would have ever taken this idea seriously. I genuinely can't remember how this line cook romance came about but I will always give you due for never letting the idea die! So from the bottom of my heart, thank you sweet bb angel.

Thank you to my muse for On the Line, my husband Aldo. Of course, all the best parts of Ozzy are based on you. You taught me what unconditional love was supposed to feel like after a lifetime of conditional love. You never gave up on me, just like Ozzy never gave up on James. You are my forever person in this life and the next.

Thank you to my alpha team: Meghan, Bella, Shani, Caitlin, Lotte, Summer, Marissa, and Angie. Without your daily help, my creativity could never bloom to its full potential, and I truly believe that. Thank you for being my rock-solid foundation and allowing me the grace to spiral and be dramatic, IT JUST HELPS OKAY??

Thank you to my beta team: Janine, Jessy, Dani, and Casadi aka the clean-up crew lmao, thank you for your dedication and willingness to lend your valuable time to read my silly little manuscripts.

Thank you to my editor Louise, a pleasure as usual, and my proofreader Salma. Thank you to Rae and Mary for sensitivity reading a particularly delicate scene for me. And Val for all the behind-the-scenes side quests I made you go on while writing this book.

And lastly, thank you to my graphic designer, Cat!! Not only did I find a friend in you, but also found someone whose work ethic is out of this world and your creativity is a magical little fairy that managed to come up with the most perfect cover for my book baby. Forever grateful!!!

ABOUT THE AUTHOR

Naomi Loud is an author of angsty dark romance. While her first love are words; spirituality and magic are the lenses through which she experiences the world and this heavily influences her writing. She lives in Montreal, Canada with her husband and three cats but secretly wishes she could live underwater.

Made in the USA
Middletown, DE
24 February 2024